A Town Called Immaculate

PETER ANTHONY

A Town Called Immaculate

MACMILLAN NEW WRITING

First published 2007 by Macmillan New Writing
an imprint of Pan Macmillan Ltd
Pan Macmillan, 20 New Wharf Road, London N1 9RR
Basingstoke and Oxford
Associated companies throughout the world
www.panmacmillan.com

ISBN 978-0-230-53206-9

Copyright © Peter Anthony 2007

3 5 7 9 8 6 4 2

A CIP catalogue record for this book is available
from the British Library.

Typeset by Intype Libra Ltd
Printed and bound in Great Britain by
MPG Books Ltd, Bodmin, Cornwall

This is a work of fiction and is the product of the
author's imagination. Any relationship with real events,
places or people is entirely coincidental.

I

With a bigger hole in the ice, Jacob imagined that the fish would be easier to catch. He could drop the five-gallon pail directly into the water, put the dog kibbles in the bottom and then sit back and wait.

Before picking up the ice-drill again, he looked at his ten-year-old brother, Ethan, who sat on the other side of the pond staring down at his conventional-sized hole. Satisfied that Ethan would not ruin the experiment by acting like a parent, Jacob laid the ice-drill flat on the surface and used it like an architect's compass, scribing a circle in the snow. He lifted the drill up to his chest, dropped the point on the ice, and started turning the handcrank. At a rate of one per minute he twisted holes through the ice along the outer edge of the circle. After completing six holes, he dropped to his knees and peered into one of them, shielding his eyes with his mitten in case a fish tried to jump out and bite him.

Jacob spoke into the dark water: 'When I was a seed this was much easier.' He looked across the pond and saw Ethan shaking his head with disdain.

Jacob turned his neck up towards the grey sky and closed his eyes. On his knees, he rocked his head back and forth, wiggled his toes in his moon boots and crossed and uncrossed and scrunched his fingers to keep the blood flowing. The day's high temperature of 20° had already been reached. The warm spell ended just in time for a true Minnesota Christmas.

The pond sat in the bottom of the pasture valley, tucked away out of the wind, but when Jacob tipped his head back and looked at the clouds passing over the sun, he saw the wind swaying the tops of naked trees, and when he looked straight up, the tallest maple tree leaned into a slow fall. The illusion exhilarated Jacob. He flinched and nearly jumped to his feet. To reproduce the effect he looked down at the ice to reset his eyes. When he looked up, the tree started to tip again. He watched the world fall over and over until he became dizzy.

With his tongue clamped between his teeth, he jumped to his feet and resumed work on the ice. He huffed and puffed until he'd drilled the last hole and the ice looked like a rotary telephone dial. But the ice did not open up as expected. Jacob stood on the ice-round bewildered, until he noticed the joints between the holes. He drilled at them but the ice would not budge. In a scene that would have made his mother scream, he jumped up and down on the middle of the ice-round, hoping to jar it loose so that he could shove it underwater. He leaped with fury but his sixty pounds had no effect. He chipped at the joints for another three minutes but finally tossed the drill on the ice again and resumed the simpler method of violent leaping until his feet tingled with a dull pain. The ice joints still held.

Sweat had formed under his stocking cap and his feet were no longer cold. He plopped down on the ice to cool off and to reconsider the whole affair. His father used wire to fix all kinds of problems. Jacob got up and dragged a sheaf of barbed wire on to the ice, wincing as the barbs poked through his mittens. But he soon arrived at the conclusion that the wire was useless. Finally, he picked up his fishing pole to resume the traditional method of squatting over a single hole in the ice. He sighed often, projecting his disappointment towards the unseen fish.

Ethan, the patient fisherman, shook his head at the mess. The scene reminded him of the mess left behind when Jacob played with every toy in the house at once and Ethan ended up being janitor. He felt like scolding his brother, but before he could think of the right thing to say, his fishing pole began to bounce: up, down, to the left, to the right. Ethan stood to lever the pole against his body.

Seeing the action, Jacob sped across the pond, dropping his fishing pole halfway. Sliding on his knees, he tried to peer down the hole to see the fish but Ethan kicked him in the stomach and shouted, 'Get away from it, moron!'

The pole went limp. The fish was gone.

'What happened?' Jacob asked.

'I don't know. He's not tugging any more.'

'Maybe he went over to my hook now that he's eaten your kibble,' Jacob taunted. 'He probably wants a new kibble.'

Ethan ignored the remark.

'I bet he ate the kibble,' Jacob snickered, 'and cleaned his teeth with your hook, like it was a toothpick.'

With pursed lips, Ethan stared at the hole.

'Might as well reel it in,' Jacob needled. 'Yep, that fish is gone.'

Ethan opened his mouth to rebut, but saw Jacob's pole jerk. Thirty feet away, still lying on the ice where Jacob had dropped it, the pole pulsed like an electric fence. The boys froze and watched to see what the unmanned pole would do next.

'It moved,' Jacob whispered.

'No shit.'

'You swore. Wiggled again!'

'Don't say a thing! Shh!'

The pole stopped pulsing and the boys exhaled. Then the pole burst to life and skittered across the ice towards Jacob's ice-round. They took off in a sprint, each trying to reach it before the fish got away or pulled the pole underwater.

Ethan outran Jacob as they neared the edge and jumped towards the hole, reaching out for the pole. His knees came down on the centre of the ice-round, cracking the remaining ice-joints, but his momentum carried him across. He stood up and faced the woods, holding the pole in his triumphant hands over his head like a hockey stick.

Following his older brother's lead, Jacob leaped into the air, landing slightly right of the centre of the ice-round. The disc dipped into the water just long enough for Jacob to slip through the hole and the ice-round fell neatly back into place, with the boy underneath it.

When Ethan turned around he was alone on the ice. He turned around three times, wondering if Jacob had run over the nearby edge of the pond and was hiding behind one of the oaks. If so, the game did not interest Ethan. He would claim the catch for himself. Finders keepers, losers weepers.

But the pole went limp. Ethan whined, 'Now what happened?' He reeled in the line until the hook snagged on something. Tugging on the pole, he continued to look around for Jacob.

'Jake?'

A wet mitten poked out of one of the holes in the ice and startled Ethan. At first he thought it was a muskrat. He stepped forward to get a closer look and when he put weight on the ice-round his foot sank into the water. He lunged backward and the nerves in his shoulders became rigid with fear, but he did not hesitate: picking up the ice-drill, he squatted at the edge of the ice-round. He placed one foot on the floating ice and applied weight until his boot sank into the freezing water. As the opposite edge of the ice-round rose, he jammed the drill underneath to keep it from falling back into place. Then he pulled his wet foot out of the water and shuffled to the other side of the circle. Using the drill as a lever, he lifted the ice and propped it up, exposing the dark water beneath.

Seconds later a head bobbed up from the hole and a little mouth gaped for air. Jacob choked and coughed, spitting out cold pond water. Ethan grabbed his coat collar and pulled with all of his ten-year-old strength.

'Are you okay?'

Jacob's eyelids started to close.

'Can you run to the barn?'

Jacob coughed and spluttered, unable to concentrate, but he heard Ethan's question and nodded and they lifted each other to their feet. The fishhook had caught Jacob's flannel overcoat and the line wound around his chest, restricting his movement. The coat, cold and wet, hung on Jacob like saddlebags. Mimicking his favourite hockey goon, Larry

Playfair, Ethan grabbed the back of Jacob's coat and stripped it upwards over his head and then down over his arms.

With his brother in a vulnerable position, Ethan slapped his face, knowing that it would be such an affront to Jacob that freezing to death would become a secondary issue. Appalled, Jacob flared snotty nostrils at Ethan, who stuck out his tongue and put his thumbs in his ears. Ethan turned to run, pulling the coat off of Jacob's forearms. Although Jacob was teeming with insults and slurs, he ran in silence, his mouth frozen. Pacing Jacob, Ethan turned around every few seconds to make sure that he was still following.

'Let's go, slowpoke!' Ethan ran backwards for a few steps. 'Oh my God, you run like a girl!'

Summoned by the noise of the boys, their yellow dog, Tippy, who had been wandering the woods, darted down a hill in the distance, plummeting against the background of snow. The dog dipped out of sight, but in a blink he was dancing circles around the running boys, and with such excitement that he nearly tripped Jacob.

When he ran out of taunts, Ethan resorted to saying the Hail Mary, and, too cold to be angry, Jacob took solace in the words, which his mother said with him every night before he went to sleep:

> 'Holy Mary, Mother of God,
> Pray for us sinners
> Now and at the hour of our death, Amen.'

For the first time, the last line made sense to both boys, and it scared Jacob enough to keep him running. He trudged through the pasture woods as fast as he could in his heavy boots. More than once he stumbled over an icy cowpie or a frozen fold of buried sod. The wind increased as they climbed out of the valley. They cut corners to shorten the distance, and Ethan chanted the prayer, again and again, without pausing, like a Sunday rosary leader. Jacob's blue lips bounced dully with each step. He tried to remove his mittens but he could not pinch the fabric hard enough to pull.

They passed over a short hill and the barn came into view. Ethan quickened the pace as they dashed down the last slope, guiding Jacob towards the tool shed, which meant running around the barn and risking being spotted by an adult. So many times he had wished Jacob would disappear, yet now, when his wish was in danger of coming true, he was terrified. He yelled boldly to disguise his anxiety: 'This way, Jacob – the tool shed!'

With the end so near, Jacob felt the ache of seizing joints, as if his mind had tricked his body long enough to get home before letting the pain be known. Rounding the last corner of the barn, Jacob fell in the snow, forcing Ethan to help him the last thirty yards. When they reached the door, Ethan flung it open and pushed Jacob inside by the neck. Like a thrown sack of feed, Jacob flopped down on to a thick rubber mat. Ethan ignited a cylindrical heater that spat fire from one end, and the flame sounded off as heat poured out. Ethan placed Jacob on a stool in front of the flame and the first thing Jacob did was try to put his numbed face and hands directly into the fire. Ethan yanked him backward and cuffed his head, then began to undress him, removing his boots, socks, shirt, pants and long johns. Soon Jacob was naked.

'Stay here. Don't put yourself in the fire. I'll be right back.'

Jacob squealed, rubbed his arms and finally nodded. 'Okay.'

Before making a dash through the farmyard, Ethan peered out to check for adults. Only Tippy stood outside, tongue all awaggle, happily giving away the boys' location. Tippy waited for Ethan to open the door and rushed inside as the boy ran out to find hot water. On his way to the milkhouse Ethan noticed the cats huddled around a large pan of fresh milk that had just been put out by the hired man. Feeling somewhat guilty, Ethan stole the milk from the herd of cats and carried the pan to the tool shed. The cats cried and crowded his feet, undercutting his legs with every step, in vain trying to regain their daily milk.

'Well, I'm so sorry.' Ethan shut the cats out of the shed. The milk caught Tippy's attention, too, and his tongue grew two sizes and lolled out of his mouth, while his tail busily swept at the dusty floor in anticipation.

'This is not for you, Tippy.'

Ethan forced Jacob to stick his bare feet into the milk. The sound of the wailing cats made Jacob smile. Jacob asked with stiff lips, 'Can't the wuss-pusses come in?'

'Oh, why not?' Ethan laughed. 'I'll let the cats in.'

With chattering teeth, Jacob said, 'Listen to them!'

Like a flood, cats streamed into the tool shed to resume their lapping. They didn't seem the least bit concerned about toes in their breakfast. Ethan ran outside again to get warm water. In the milkhouse, keeping a low profile, he filled three one-gallon pails with warm water and ran back to the tool shed, spilling water all the way. When he re-entered, he saw that Tippy, lacking all manners, had nosed two cats out of the way and was slurping so recklessly that milk slopped on to cat ears.

'Oh, Tippy.'

Tippy looked at Ethan, smiling shamelessly with a wet white beard.

Jacob kept his hands and face six inches from the flame. His blue lips turned red again as his blood started to circulate. Ethan plunged Jacob's hands into a bucket. He poured warm water into the milk, inciting a round of whiny meows from the cats. Tippy, on the other hand, didn't pause to protest.

Ethan picked up a fat tabby cat and set her on Jacob's lap. 'Oh, stop your crying, Orangey.'

Jacob laughed and pulled his hands out of the water to hold the cat. The tabby meowed for her release.

'Look here,' Ethan said, picking up another cat. 'Whitey wants to sit on your lap too!'

Jacob squeezed the cats and their eyeballs bulged with each compression.

Tears wetted Ethan's eyes. 'I'm so glad you got out of the water, Jacob. I was scared.'

Jacob started to cry. 'I'm sorry, Ethan.'

'Don't be sorry. Just don't . . . be so stupid. Why did you have to drill so many holes?'

Jacob shook his head and cried. Then the boys hugged one another, awkwardly, one of them naked, both crying, and Orangey and Whitey getting squished between.

2

Except for two Lutheran families, every yard in the township had a statue of the Virgin Mary, almost invariably dressed in a blue robe, with her arms open wide and her head canted to one side. Renee Marak often looked, past her kitchen sink, out of the window at the statue. At first she hated it because it had been forced into her yard as a neighbour's wedding gift, but over time she became comfortable with it and enjoyed pondering why Mary wore a smirk on her face. Renee found the local religion a little overbearing, but she enjoyed her Mary, and the wildlife attracted by the surrounding birdbaths and flowerbeds. Whenever snow, or moss, or dust from the summer winds sullied the white and blue stone, Renee always made sure to undo what nature had done.

Immaculate was the name of the nearby town, five miles and ten turns up the road from the Marak farm. The township, Catholic Square, reflected the religion of the immigrants who had settled the area. German and Irish brought their piety with them, or perhaps hard times invented it, and the symbols and the names of people and places were carried on by the succeeding generations. Piety was a survival tool, as effective as any wall, keeping the people inside and other things, such as Darwin, out. Marak was the only Czech name in the township, but marks of nationality were long gone, other than a few residual characteristics. Religion governed

Immaculate more than anything else and the people still observed the Sabbath on Sunday, when working was frowned upon, with the exception of milking cows or baling hay that might rot if left another day. But Renee was a farm house-wife, and for her there really wasn't a Sabbath, or any other kind of holiday.

She had lived in Immaculate for all but one of her thirty years. She had grown up on a dairy farm on the other side of the town. She worked at the public library and was known as the most well-read woman in Immaculate. She had the first opportunity to read any new book that came into the library, and she always kept a stack of books in progress on her night-stand.

She was a tireless woman, modest and calm, but wherever she went in Immaculate, eyes followed. Men and women both hated and loved her, simply because she was beautiful. Some women despised Renee for keeping her hair long, while others adored it. She suffered and flaunted her blondeness. Before she married Ray Marak, nearly every man in town had dreams of being with her and many pursued her while Ray was in Vietnam, but they gave up hope when she left town for the University of Minnesota. Once a woman like Renee Masterson left town, she was unlikely to return with the same last name. But her college career didn't last long. Her mother became terminally ill with emphysema during her freshman year, and life changed irreparably. After the funeral, her father's depression kept Renee from returning to college, and by the time Ray came home from the war, she had made the decision to assist in mending the shattered lives of her father and Ray instead of enjoying the clean world of academia. Her older brothers had both moved away from Immaculate. With careers and families in Minneapolis and Chicago, they never looked back, though they were always glad to phone Renee with advice on local family matters.

Although she had not finished her degree, no one in Immaculate could dispute Renee's knowledge of books. She sometimes imagined finding spare time – in the future, of course – perhaps an entire year, to sit down and write a story. With Jacob in the house she had a teeming supply of ideas, but to sit at a typewriter meant ignoring a small tornado. Jacob needed constant supervision. She liked to think that her own imagination resembled Jacob's, but she didn't recall being such a pest as a child. His energy siphoned her creativity. She viewed her family as a living story, sometimes exciting, but often as dull as doing the dishes. Farm life was mostly monotonous, but certain times of the year contained magic: harvest, summer nights and Christmas. During the high points of the season, when the crops ripened and silos were filled, she could see the boys growing as they helped Ray more actively with every passing year.

That morning, while she waited for Ray and the boys, she dried her hands and went into the living room and sat down at the desk where Ray kept bills and invoices. Very carefully, she slid open the rolltop desk and pulled out a small square wooden board with a nail driven through the centre. Pierced by the nail was a stack of receipts from farm and grocery transactions. From the pocket of her bathrobe she pulled out a notebook and made a summation of expenditures, sighing as she wrote, and shaking her head as the total grew. It was

Christmas Eve, and she suspected it would be the last one the family would spend on the farm.

Amid the blaring sound of the pump in the milkhouse, Joachim, the hired man whom everyone called *Joke*, walked into the parlour and said to Ray Marak, 'I'll finish up these last eight cows if you want to go bed the free stalls.'

Nodding reflexively, Ray retreated from his thoughts. He was a huge man, noticeably big from a distance, but his size and strength were much less evident close up. On his right cheek he wore two long scars of raised skin: one, shaped like a sickle, extended from the outer corner of his right eye, down his cheek, to his ear lobe. The other started under the same eye and connected with the corner of his mouth.

Ray ascended a short galvanized-steel staircase towards the rear parlour door. Once inside the quiet, hollow barn, he noticed that Joke had already set out the square straw bales needed for bedding. Joke was a good worker, nineteen years old and a neighbour. Ray had taken him on as an apprentice, since Joke's father, Bill, drank and used his fists, both too heavy and too often. Bill and Ray shared some equipment, but the relationship did not go beyond swapping a combine, a swather and a few chopper-boxes. Farms around Immaculate had a curious privacy to them. Like islands, each had a different culture, and while one might enjoy a reasonable harmony, the next might suffer a ruthless tyrant.

In the corner of the barn, near an old AMC motorcycle covered in dust, was the shredding machine. Ray never allowed Joke or anyone else, least of all his sons, to use the shredder. Whenever Ray used the machine, he made the boys stand far away. What had once taken hours by pitchfork, the machine did in minutes. A Briggs & Stratton engine was connected to a large blade and the machine resembled an elevated lawnmower in a welded metal box, violating a good portion of OSHA safety regulations. Properly used, the machine posed little risk, but Ray saw loose strings catching on the exposed and spinning parts, and in Immaculate everyone knew by heart far too many stories about loose strings and machines. John Delaney, now the babbling church caretaker, had lost his mind, his farm and his wife, all because of a loose string.

Carrying four bales at a time, Ray walked down the barn alley and made drops at preordained locations. Once the bales were in place he returned to the machine and looked around to ensure that no children or cats had made their way into the barn or the shredder itself. He yanked the starter cord. The engine sputtered and died as the cord recoiled. He pulled the cord again and the engine roared into life. When he lifted a straw bale over his head, Ray's T-shirt slipped down to expose triceps that looked like horseshoes. He dumped the bale into the vertical bucket and grabbed the handles of the pushcart on which the machine was fixed. Walking with the machine down the barn alley, he aimed the spout of the shredder towards the stalls where the cows would spend Christmas. The straw flew out of the shredder into neatly minced piles. Ray paused only for a second to drop in the next straw bale, picking it up with one arm. The machine hacked into the second bale and spewed straw and Ray gripped the handles once again and moved forward. The metal box seemed to vibrate more freely than usual, which worried Ray. When he was done, and every stall had a fresh mattress of golden straw, he flipped off the engine switch to examine the shredder and found that a bolt had rattled out of place. Behind a large wooden gate, the cows looked at Ray through the slats, as if eager to reach their golden stalls.

Ray said, 'Sorry, girls. Give me ten minutes. Preventative maintenance.'

While walking to the shed, Ray wondered which son might run the farm when he retired. Given his current finances, he worried that the farm might not be around long enough for anyone to inherit it. Nevertheless, it was a decision he needed to plan for, and clearly Ethan was the sharper one of the two boys. A successful life seemed imprinted on his character, as if he was predisposed to good decisions. Jacob, on the other hand, lacked all the characteristics of a worker. He left in his wake a constant disarray. The boy looped through moods and emotions, going from wild joy to desperate depression from one minute to another. Every night at the dinner table Jacob poured out his daily imaginings while Ethan quietly cleaned his plate. The *seed* talk and assorted nonsense seemed to consume the child. Ray had put his foot down on the seed talk, believing that he could indoctrinate a serious mood into the boy, but nothing of the sort happened. Instead of talking about seeds, Jacob began to chatter with himself and draw pictures of a cartoon seed on a distant planet.

Ray credited Jacob with making family time fun, but the boy's work ethic was atrocious. Ray often noticed how different from one another the boys looked, polar opposites in almost every respect: Jacob had dark hair, Ethan had light;

Jacob had a stout frame, Ethan was wiry. Ray loved his sons differently, and try as he might to prevent it, he did, in fact, love Ethan more than Jacob.

He walked outside through a side door, moving swiftly – not to avoid the cold but because he didn't know how to walk at a casual pace. When he approached the door of the tool shed he heard noises coming from inside. Ray placed his ear against the door to eavesdrop. The heater was on. He listened carefully and heard Jacob prattling at the pets.

'Yes, kitties, we planted each of you one day in the dirt and you grew into cats. Every year Mom gets a bag of cat seeds, and every spring you pop out of the ground. Yes, even you, Miss Calico . . .'

Ray opened the door of the tool shed, but quickly regretted doing so. There, sitting in front of the blazing heater, was Jacob, naked and holding two cats on his lap. Ray slapped his forehead. 'Holy Lord! Jacob, where in the hell are your pants?'

Ray then noticed that all of the cats were in the tool shed and he saw at least two fresh turds on the floor. As if to avoid a scolding, Tippy skulked past Ray and went outside. Ray waited for Jacob's answer.

Looking up at his six-foot-five giant of a father, Jacob emitted a faint reply.

'I was warming up by the heater. And I was . . . talking . . . to the wusses.'

'Naked? Do you have to be naked to do that? Where are your clothes?' Ray put his hands on his sides, blocked the light from the doorway.

Jacob pointed to a neatly folded pile of dry clothes that

Ethan had managed to sneak out of the house avoiding his mother's watchful eye. His brother had left instructions for Jacob to get dressed while he went back to the pond to retrieve the fishing items, but Jacob had been enjoying the warmth of the heater.

'This is not good, kid. Where's Ethan?'

Jacob answered rotely, 'Ethan is still fishing. He had a fish on the line, but it got away. I was cold, so I came back.'

Ray doubted the story. 'Okay, fine. Jacob, let me explain something. We don't get naked anywhere, okay, except for the bathtub, *or* if we are changing our clothes. And both of those places that we undress are *inside* the house. And never, never, never do we play with the cats, under any circumstances, while naked. Do you understand?'

Jacob nodded and blushed. He had been sitting in front of the heat for so long that sweat had beaded on his upper lip. In his shame, Jacob almost broke down and told his father the truth, but he stuck with the lie and withstood his father's disappointed look.

'All right, Jacob. Get dressed, then go in the house and warm up. From now on, don't use this heater unless I'm around. I didn't know you knew how to start this thing.'

'I saw you do it once.'

Ray turned off the heater and continued while Jacob hung his head. 'It's one thing to be cold and want to warm up, but it's a totally different thing to strip down to your bare butt and then make the cats have to see it. You know, cats don't like to be naked. Why do you think they have all that fur?'

Jacob jerked his head up and looked at his father to discern if the tone had shifted from scolding to joking.

'Honestly, have you ever seen a cat without his fur on?'

'Yes.' Jacob nodded. 'Mr Feathers. When he got caught in the haybine.'

'Exactly!' Ray threw up his hands. 'Cats never take off their fur if they don't have to.'

'Unless they get caught in the haybine . . .'

'Unless they caught in the haybine, yes. Now, get dressed, then go ask Mom to make you some hot cocoa. How about that, huh? Sound good?'

'Okay.'

Jacob scrambled to get dressed. Orangey and Miss Calico whined as he stood up from the stool. He pulled on his dry clothing, which felt very good against his skin now that he was warm. Ethan had managed to get Jacob home in time to avoid a cold injury. He put on his wet boots and ran out of the tool shed towards the house.

Ray shook his head and laughed. 'Just so long as he doesn't grow up to be a pervert. I can stand a fool.' Ray watched out the window, and saw Jacob stop running. He held his breath in anticipation of something bizarre.

Jacob stopped near the oak stump. It looked like a chef's hat, piled up with a layered stack of leaning snow. He reached out his hand and took a large handful of snow from the stump. First he licked at it, and then he took a large bite. After a few mouthfuls, he dropped the snow to the ground, but before moving on towards the house, he took a second handful and scrubbed his face with it.

'What in the name of . . . *Jee-sus*.' Ray shook his head again. His decision about passing on the farm would be simple. As he chased the cats out of the shed, he muttered, 'I swear he's the milkman's kid.'

The distraction had made Ray forget what he came into the tool shed for, so instead he fished out his pack of cigarettes from a drawer and enjoyed his daily smoke.

Before the front door slammed, Renee heard the footsteps in the mudroom. As Jacob rounded the corner to the kitchen she shook a potato peeler at him and said, 'Stop right where you are and turn around, young man!' But Jacob kept running and wound himself on to her leg like a vine. He looked up at her face and smiled, trying to sweeten her.

She was well aware of his tactics. 'Jacob, go back and take off your boots. You know better than that. Why is your face so red?'

'I caught a walleye!'

'Did you now? No stalling!'

She glared at him until he uncoiled from her leg and plodded back to the entryway where the boots and shoes of the family were neatly arranged. Jacob tossed his boots and his clean jacket in three different directions.

'Hang that up,' she said from the kitchen. 'Put those boots in a row. Don't be a slob.' She was smiling but kept up a stern tone.

Jacob scowled at her powerful hearing. He wondered how Ethan possibly could have entered the house and smuggled out the dry clothes when his mother heard *everything*. He had a feeling that she already knew about the pond. The secret would be a hard one to keep.

Renee went back to peeling potatoes for breakfast

hash-browns, looking out the window over the sink. Having made so many meals, her hands operated automatically. A bickering couple on *The Phil Donahue Show* gave her work some background noise. She listened to the show but considered it smut and never sat down to watch. She did, however, occasionally rush out of the kitchen to see the action when she could not believe her ears.

Jacob ran back into the kitchen and yelled, 'Have you seen my roller skates?'

Renee closed her eyes and felt a headache coming on at the mere thought of Jacob's calamitous roller skates. They were the worst gift idea she'd ever conceived. She still felt slightly groggy from the previous night's Christmas party at Blaise's Tavern. Ray had had only a few drinks, but Renee had had five cocktails, enough to make her a little slow that morning. She had only ordered the cocktails because there was an open bar – she never would have spent money on more than one drink. She rarely went out at night.

She looked out the window with her back to Jacob.

'It's too early for roller skates, honey.'

'I just want to know where they are . . . for later.'

'For later, sure. How about you help me decorate Christmas cookies today?'

He pondered the invitation. 'I think I can do that.' After all, he had decorated cookies when he was a seed. 'What time do you want me to help you, Mommy?'

She turned around. 'Do you have a schedule to keep? Do you think you can pencil me in around one o'clock, or should I call your secretary?'

Jacob leaned against her waist and smiled at her. 'You can call my secretary.'

The front door slammed shut as Ethan entered the house.

Jacob looked into the mudroom. 'Here comes my secretary now!'

Ethan put his boots in line and put the wet clothes on hooks that jutted out over a heat vent in the floor.

'Ethan, is that you?'

'Yes, Mom.'

She was relieved that Ray and Joke had not come in yet as she had not yet started cooking breakfast.

'Well, what's the fishing report?' Renee asked.

He walked into the kitchen and showed her a thumbs-down. Even if he had caught a fish, Ethan knew better than to say anything that could spawn a conversation about the pond. Telling her nothing meant not having to lie. Future fishing outings, especially outings without adult supervision, depended on keeping Jacob quiet. He didn't want to lose the independence he had earned.

Renee transferred a plate of shredded potatoes to the hot skillet on the stovetop and a wet sizzle filled the kitchen. She lit two more gas burners on the stove and unrolled a pound of sausage. She made patties and placed them in a second sizzling skillet.

'Want me to make toast, Mom, or beat the eggs?'

'Oh, you're a good boy—' Renee corrected herself: 'You're *both* good boys. But not yet, Ethan. Why don't you two go watch cartoons for a while? Relax – you had a big morning of fishing and no luck. Isn't *Mighty Mouse* on at this time?'

'No it's *G.I. Joe* right now,' Ethan said. '*Mighty Mouse* is over. Come on, Jacob, let's go watch TV.' Ethan grabbed Jacob by the arm and led him into the living room.

'Ouch,' Jacob said, wincing. 'You're my secretary. I tell you what to do.'

Jacob's playful mood irked Ethan, since he had exhausted himself saving him. He glared at his brother. 'Why would I be the secretary?'

Jacob ignored the question and changed the subject. 'You know, when I was a seed, I used to catch walleye.'

Ethan rolled his eyes. 'There aren't any walleye. There's only bullheads.'

'When I was a seed I used to walk into the water and pull walleye out by the tail while they were still flipping.'

'You couldn't catch a flippin' disease.'

Renee listened to her boys argue and smiled at their endless battles. The obsession with seeds amused her as much as it irritated Ray. It helped Jacob create a whole world, one that amazed Renee, and made her reluctant to correct him. With the best intentions, Ethan had tried to explain the birds and the bees to Jacob, even showing him the anatomical drawing in the family encyclopedia, but Jacob thought it was inconceivable that a baby was born from a woman's ear. Renee tried to the laugh as Ethan explained the diagram, with full assurance, and when she looked at the drawing, it did in fact look like an ear. Renee corrected Ethan, but couldn't tell Jacob the truth because his seed notion seemed to make him so happy. He believed that his mother planted him in the ground and he grew into a boy. The seed fantasy became his security blanket and Renee decided that the plain, confusing truth of the real birds and the bees could wait.

'Did you put your shoes in place, Jacob?'

Jacob mumbled, 'When I was a seed I never had to put my shoes in place.'

'Lucky for seeds, they don't wear shoes.'

Once his shoes were in place, Jacob joined Ethan in front of the TV, but he did not sit still for long. He was thinking about the idea of having a secretary, and the urge to become businesslike overcame him, so he left the TV room and went into the bathroom to find products to sell to his mother.

On the bathroom floor, kneeling beneath the window that he used when he needed to go out at night for something – nightcrawlers, or to visit Tippy in the doghouse – Jacob opened all the bottles and packages he could reach, sniffing, squirting, spraying. He settled on a bottle of Bausch & Lomb saline solution, a stick of Old Spice, a bottle of Suave shampoo, a box of Band-Aids, a bottle of hydrogen peroxide and a make-up compact. He carried the products back to the kitchen.

'Mommy, I think I have something for you to buy.'

Renee had finished setting the table. He placed his wares on a chair, out of her view. She tended to the crackling skillets and listened as Jacob started an impromptu sales patter.

He set up his product with compliments. 'You seem to need a few things around the house, Mommy, things that no one should be without, especially a pretty lady like you. Things that if you had them, I'm sure your life would be better. Let me just say – you would be very happy, Mrs Marak. I am happier using these things. Really, I don't think

I could live without them. Do you think you might be interested in these things?'

Eager to see what Jacob was up to, she answered, 'I am rapt with attention. Please, tell me more about these *things*.'

The sound of the front door startled Jacob. Ray and Joke kicked off their boots in the mudroom. They had finished the morning work and expected breakfast. Renee heard them washing their hands, laughing with one another at the sink in the mudroom. Renee felt that the sound of deep voices added a certain comfort to the house in the morning. They brought the smells and the sounds of work with them.

Jacob went on with his pitch, placing his first product on the table for display. Ray and Joke quieted down to hear what was going on.

'You can see this is a bottle. It is a plain white bottle. There are some large words on the side. This is what we salesmen call "Bos-chuh and Lom-buh" water. I use it every day, and you can see how clean I am – it works very, very good. Please watch as I flip open the cap and show you the bottle that squirts. And it squirts very fast, which is why I am so clean.'

Renee pre-empted Jacob's demonstration by whispering, 'You don't have to squirt it, Jacob. I trust you.'

'Every morning I squirt myself with at least, I'm telling the truth, at least three bottles of this water. You can look behind my ears. I am as clean as the forks, Mrs Marak. Clean as the cups in your cupboard. Do you think you might want to purchase this bottle from me, Mom?'

Renee acted nervous and touched her cheek. 'Well, I don't know. It just sounds so expensive.' Ray and Joke came into the entryway and listened. Jacob became nervous, having his father near, but he went on selling anyway. Joke sat down at the table across from Jacob and winked encouragement.

Jacob sensed his father's approval and felt more at ease.

'Well, that's the thing about Bos-chuh and Lom-buh. It's really a very good deal. They are good people at Bos-chuh and Lom-buh. They don't sell water in a squirt bottle just to get rich like bankers. They want you to feel clean. You can buy this bottle from me right now for only three hundred dollars.'

'Three hundred dollars?' Ray repeated. 'I'll take two of them at that price!'

'Thank you, Dad. Now if you'll go into the living room behind me, my secretary will meet with you. His name is Ethan and he is very helpful.'

The adults all laughed at the punchline. Ethan sat quietly in the living room watching cartoons alone, exhausted. Jacob had caused the ice to break and ruined the fishing, and now Ethan had no energy. He had spent his morning sprinting back and forth over the snow to correct Jacob's error – to the pond and back to the farm, to the pond and back again, to the house and back to the shed, to the barn and back again. Jacob carried on in the kitchen and the family lapped it up, with Ethan as the butt of the joke. He wanted to tattle, to let his parents know the truth, but he dozed off instead.

Renee stopped laughing first. She said, 'Don't you mean that Ethan is your "partner"? No good salesman works alone.'

'Yes, he is a little of both, I guess.' Jacob nodded. 'But mostly he stays in the office.'

Joke played along. 'Well, let's say I have a dirty mind and don't want to be cleansed by Bos-chuh and Lom-buh water. What else are you selling?'

'Careful there, Joachim,' warned Renee. 'What kind of "dirty" are you talking about?'

Joke winked at Renee. She returned a serious look that scared the smile off his face, like a rabbit darting into bushes. Averting his eyes, he straightened up in his chair.

'I have just the thing for a slob like you, Joke.' Jacob looked down at the products sitting on the chair. Feeling the silence last a little too long, he picked one at random and set it on the table.

'Hydroggen Perziddy. This is the product for you, Joke. As you can see, it's in a brown bottle, the same colour of your hands.' Jacob examined the bottle. 'There is not much to the outside of the bottle. It doesn't squirt, either. But inside it is a special water – one that you drink before bedtime, and then you don't have to say your prayers *or* brush your teeth. It's holy water. Many of my customers drink it on Sunday morning, and that's why the church is never full. Drink Hydroggen Perziddy, and you have said the rosary five times. Father Dimer gargles it every morning before he gives communion. I've even heard him say it can be used in place of confessions. That way Father Dimer can golf more often.'

Joke said, 'That's exactly what I need.'

Jacob had recently performed his first confession with the local priest, and he had enjoyed recounting his sins much more than he was supposed to.

After they stopped laughing, Ray and Renee exchanged expressions of embarrassment. Jacob had never even seen a golf club or a golf course. It was an echo of their gossip, returned in an eight-year-old voice. During meals, they sometimes talked about who had missed church and other tiny scandals that flitted through Immaculate, and now they realized what they sounded like.

'Okay, Jacob,' said Ray, 'what's the next product?'

Jacob looked at his remaining items. The little ship on the Old Spice label seemed encouraging, but Jacob was more intrigued by the compact because it looked like a clam. He opened the compact and his eyes widened when he saw pearls inside – or, better yet, *seeds*. He decided to call them pearls, since his dad might object to seeds.

He kept the compact hidden on the chair while he whetted the audience. 'Mrs Marak, could you use a few extra dollar bills from time to time?'

'Well, of course, sir.'

Jacob turned to his father and Joke. Ray squinted at Jacob and listened. 'Dad, Joke: let me tell you. Times are hard. That's what they say at the feed store. Jerry rubs his tummy and pulls at his pants and says, "These are hard times." So, don't you think, maybe, wouldn't it be nice to have, say, lots of money?'

Joke said, 'It would, Jacob,' and clearing his throat loudly, turned his body and chair towards Ray. 'Boy, would it ever. Ahem!'

'Well, then,' Jacob said, bringing the compact into view, 'this is for you.' Jacob flipped open the compact and held it in his palm at shoulder height, turning it slowly for all in the room to see. The contents glinted in the kitchen light.

First Renee laughed, but paled when she saw what Jacob had in his hand.

'What you need is a money tree, lady and gentlemen.' Jacob was beaming. 'And here are the pearls that will solve your problems.'

Ray clapped and laughed, but slowly realized what Jacob was holding. Renee watched his smile flatten. When he recognized the pills, a secret of five years ended. Steeped in Catholicism, Ray rejected the use of birth control and had explicitly told Renee not to ask the doctor for them. To keep Ray from taking the pills and flushing them down the toilet, Renee snatched them from Jacob's hand.

'Sold! I'll take those off your hands, sir.' She pushed her hair out of her face and blushed. 'How much are they?'

'Hmm . . . three hundred dollars.'

Ray scoffed. 'I wouldn't doubt it.'

'Not even close,' Renee said, staring in defiance at Ray, 'but worth every penny.'

She pretended to hand out money to Jacob. 'Here you are – one hundred, two hundred, three hundred.' She took the compact and made sure no pills were missing. 'Hey, Mr Salesman, these aren't pearls. These are dragon's teeth! I'd better not plant these, after all.'

Having no idea what birth control pills looked like, Joke missed the moment. He added, 'Hold on, Mr Salesman. Wait just a minute. If these are money tree pearls why don't you use them yourself?'

Jacob shrugged.

Renee moved the morning forward before the argument

could put its claws into the day. 'Ethan! Time to eat. We're hungry. Yes we are.'

'What about my other products?'

'We've seen enough,' Ray said. 'You are quite the sales-man, Jacob. God only knows what else you have sitting on that chair back there.'

Joke continued to laugh and asked Jacob more questions about the money tree pearls. Everyone else ate in silence. Ethan ate ravenously, and Ray and Renee, both wearing red faces, needed plenty of salt to taste their food.

3

The nameplate on the desk needed dusting.

Customers recognize that sort of thing, Josh Werther told himself. Then he realized that a nameplate that was too clean was not necessarily good either: most of his clients farmed for a living and sat across his desk wearing cow manure on their pants. This was the Immaculate State Bank, not the Federal Reserve, and Christmas Eve was too late to worry about dusting.

As he looked at the knick-knacks scattered on the four corners of his large desk, he saw a snapshot of his adult life. He smiled weakly and wondered how he hadn't noticed it before. He had his 'ISB Campaign' trinkets organized by year across his desk. Nearest to the right side of his chair was the 1970 'I AM the Customer' snowglobe, given to all employees by the bank's morale officer. Inside the globe were pine trees and a tiny running man with his scarf flailing behind him in the wind. He carried a package, as if late for something or outrunning the snowstorm. However, with the snow in the globe as static as the dust on the nameplate, the man seemed to run for no reason. Josh recalled the radio ads of that year, when he and his co-workers laughed together: 'I AM . . . your personalized customer service. I AM . . . your home loan. I AM . . . going out of my way for your business. I AM . . . Immaculate State Bank.' In 1970 he worked at the bank during breaks in his college schedule. The memory of that summer always made him smile. Even work was enjoyable. Each employee had to memorize three 'I AM . . .' statements, but it took weeks to get everyone to say them with a straight face because the inside jokes thickened with each passing day.

He moved on to another trinket: 1975 – the 'ONE' campaign: 'ONE stop for all your banking needs. ONE place for farm and home loans.' Josh clasped his hands on his freshly trimmed nape and placed his elbows on the desk. He smiled – most of the mottoes were simply rearrangements of previous mottoes – but the more he thought about the trinkets and campaigns, the more his smile tapered.

As organizer of the campaign for the past two years, Josh had tried to keep it fun. In 1980 he did had done a *Rocky* parody, and given a little pair of gold boxing gloves to each employee. For the current campaign he'd coordinated a *Superman* theme, creating Superman T-shirts with 'ISB' on the front: 'Immaculate *Super* Bank'. He realized that he had overstepped numerous copyrights in producing the radio ads, and for a moment he had the foolish notion that some Hollywood lawyer might have actually cared.

Josh counted the trinkets and arrived at the number twelve. He had not taken an inventory of his life for some time.

Instead of going to lunch as he had planned, he counted to twelve again, then inhaled and held his breath and leaned back in his chair.

Twelve years, twelve trinkets, and now twelve Christmas Eves alone. Not that he wanted to be alone, he'd simply ended up thirty and single. He wondered how he stayed busy enough not to notice the years passing. The bank had kept him busy once, and until recently he had enjoyed his work. Until recently, he hadn't had to be the enforcer of foreclosures. Agriculture was in the middle of an adjustment after years of controversial financial policies set forth by the federal government. But when Josh had to assist in the repossession of cattle and gasoline, he could not help but harden his heart towards his work and clients. The best days were in the past. The market had been fat and bloated for too long and too many hands had reached into the government coffers. Friends and relatives sometimes blamed Josh personally for foreclosures and auctions, and, as a result, his compassion for the farmers waned. His bank's role in the machine was small: the Immaculate State Bank just followed the rules handed down by the policymakers and doled out the money from legislated pork-barrels. Every borrower and lender played the game by his own volition. Those who defaulted sometimes had malice towards the banker, as if he set the market himself. Josh worried about repercussions, especially after a colleague in Iowa received death threats because of a foreclosure. The times made for nervous bankers.

What he missed most was the camaraderie he once had with his clients, when customers came into his office just to chat, when he gladly stayed past quitting time, and when handshakes and smiles didn't feel forced. Now he dreaded even picking up the phone. Farmers he had once considered close friends now treated Josh as if he had signed them into indentured servitude. He felt worn out from 1981, and tired of business. He entertained old dreams that had neither lived nor died: starting his own business, finding a job at a bigger bank, in Minneapolis or St Paul. Josh reviewed his musty dreams with melancholy.

Again he counted the objects on the desk. One of the campaigns he did not recognize and the trinket lacked a date. He examined it closely until he realized it was from 1974. He racked his brain to remember the campaign of '74. With a wan expression on his face, he arrived at a conclusion.

'I need to get out of Immaculate,' he mumbled.

A teller named Kathy McKay walked by his office as he spoke, but she heard only the word 'Immaculate'. She stopped and said to Josh, 'Talking to yourself, are you now?'

His crisis ended upon hearing Kathy's voice. Josh snapped into business mode.

'Who doesn't talk to himself in this nuthouse? I mean, we are working on Christmas Eve.'

'Aren't you the boss around here today? Just leave.' Kathy winked at Josh and moved on, her ponytail swaying back and forth in opposition to the motion of her hips. Josh flinched at the wink, was taken aback by it. She was only twenty-two years old and he hadn't had a wink from a woman that young in a while – at least a year. A surge of confident energy came into him. He considered asking Kathy out for a drink but then thought better of it. He usually avoided dating employees, though he had made two exceptions in the past. He imagined being in a relationship with Kathy – and in bed. Perhaps the time had come to learn to date again, if such a thing could ever really be learned. He hadn't dated anyone seriously in nearly two years, though he had plenty of old flames in nearby Tonnamowoc, where he stowed his personal life. But those old relationships had long since turned mechanical, with everything, from the dates to the sex, feeling like work on an assembly-line. The flames of recent history were snuffed, but here something yet unstructured tempted him.

He heard Kathy's footsteps coming back down the hall towards his office. He grabbed a pen and pretended to write something on his desktop calendar. As Kathy passed the doorway, she glanced sideways into the office and wore an expression he'd seen before. The look erased the crisis of trinkets from his mind. This was a more acute matter, one of delight and nervousness. Normally level-headed and cool, Josh felt his senses consumed by the look of the younger woman. He would take the rest of the day off. Everyone else in town, out of tradition, had already quit work for the day to drink Tom and Jerrys at the American Legion, and so would he.

He stood to put on his winter jacket. His work ethic gnawed at him to sit back down and finish the day, but he stifled the notion. The bank president's decision to keep the bank open on Christmas Eve, a Thursday, upset some of the customers. Many people in Immaculate felt that Christmas falling on a Friday meant a three-day Sabbath. But that era was over. Already, in business journals, Josh read about banks in the larger cities staying open every day of the week, improving customer satisfaction and thereby profits as well. The Immaculate bank president felt that his bank's hours should reflect the stock market's, and so Wall Street's rules trumped the Gospels on the matter of holidays.

Josh started to slink out of his office but straightened up as he realized that the only way to take a half-day was emphatically and in full view of his colleagues so that no unnecessary break-room gossip undermined him. He walked out behind the counter and saw two tellers waiting on a single customer, an old man who frequently visited the bank, often for no apparent reason other than to socialize. Kathy's line was empty. She stood with her back towards Josh as she counted through receipts to total her drawer for the day. As she counted, her brunette ponytail bounced up and down. She had placed one of her feet on a stool. Josh, trying not to watch too carefully, watched carefully. She reached a count of fifty and whirled ninety degrees with the stack of receipts, causing her skirt to rise slightly. She opened a drawer and dropped the paper in and when she turned, the hem of her skirt became caught in the corner of the drawer. Unaware of the snag, she started to count another fifty receipts.

Josh noticed the hem. 'Don't move an inch, Kathy.'

Kathy froze. 'Is this a hold-up, Josh?' She put her hands up.

'Sort of.' Josh laughed. 'A hold-up for you.'

'For me? Just me?'

The other teller, an elderly woman named Helen Grossman, ignored the customer to listen in on what Josh was talking about.

'Your skirt is in a hold-up – I mean, ah . . . your clothes are stuck.'

Kathy, putting her arms down, asked, 'What is this, a riddle?' Then she turned to look at Josh.

'No, don't move—!'

The hem ripped. Kathy gasped at the noise. 'Oh, shit! Josh, why didn't you say something?'

Josh held his hand out to her. 'Well, that's what I was trying to tell you. I was getting to it.'

'Well, you shouldn't have said anything then.'

Helen rushed over to look at the skirt and found that it had only torn slightly along the seam, meaning that no irreparable damage was done.

'Damn it, Josh.'

'I'm sorry. I guess I should have stayed in my office.' He suddenly felt reluctant to announce his decision to quit early for the day.

'Really, Josh,' Helen said, 'you had better make it up to her.'

Kathy relented. 'Oh, it's not his fault.'

The opportunity had presented itself so naturally, so readily, that he didn't have enough time to hold back.

'How about I buy you a Tom and Jerry at the Legion.'

Holding her skirt, Kathy said, 'I have to change.'

'No you don't.' Feeling increasingly fluid, Josh said, 'It's the Legion, not the supper club. We'll go straight over. What time is it?' He looked at his watch. 'It's twelve-thirty. The place will be filling up soon. We'll get in and out of there before the afternoon crowd.'

'And who will stay here?' asked Kathy.

Helen said, 'Oh, go ahead, Kathy. I think we'll be shutting the doors soon anyway, won't we, Josh?'

Josh nodded. Kathy capitulated with feigned reluctance.

'Okay, what the hell. Let me count down this drawer. I'm nearly finished.'

She finished counting and gathered her purse and car keys. Only when they walked out of the bank into the cold air did Josh realize how this might look. Attending the Immaculate American Legion with a co-worker, for a drink – well, that was just inviting a scandal. To be seen with Kathy on the street and then drinking without a token family member or friend present would certainly ripen quickly on the grapevine into a hot date. Josh considered returning to the bank to find another co-worker to make a trio, but he looked at Kathy's face and felt an attraction to her again. She smiled at him. Afflicted by chronic but moderate paranoia, Josh wondered if he had been tricked into a date, even though he knew the tearing of the skirt could not have been planned.

He was right to be paranoid. Kathy had a standing crush on Josh and laughed at even his feeblest jokes. For months she had timed her breaks and invented other reasons to bump into Josh. The actual invitation to the Legion thrilled and worried her because she half-expected Josh to admonish her for flirting in the bank. She sometimes regretted her pursuit. Josh was much older than her, after all. However, Josh Werther was handsome and carried himself differently from the other men of Immaculate, whom she found to be gruff, insensitive and too much in love with liquor, cows, or both.

In the bank's parking lot Josh opened the passenger door for Kathy. He scanned the vicinity to see if anyone had noticed them.

He got into the car and said awkwardly, 'Okay, here we go.' He turned the key in the ignition, but the freezing tem-peratures meant he drained his battery in three attempts. The crankshaft lurched several times before it came to an impotent halt.

'Piece of crap! It's not even that cold out. My battery must be shot.'

'Maybe your antifreeze is bad.'

'I don't think so.'

The engine chugged as Josh turned the key again. The harmonic lurch of the engine slowed to a standstill.

'I can jump you if you'd like.' She bit her lip, and quickly added, 'I mean, my car is right over there.' She wondered if her second statement only made her first worse.

'You know what?' Josh said. 'The Legion is only four blocks away. Why are we trying to drive? Let's walk. We'll worry about the car later.'

They got out and walked towards the Legion, both with their hands stuffed in their jacket pockets, neither saying anything. Conscious of her torn skirt, Kathy walked on the inside of the sidewalk past the barber's window, and as they passed, the barber was kind enough to wave, though not kind enough to clear the walkway of snow. They moved swiftly to get out of the cold and indoors with a warm mug of rum.

They entered the American Legion's dark lounge and shook their arms to dispel the cold that had already permeated their zipped jackets. The Legion regulars and Christmas crowd paused for a moment to see who had entered. When satisfied that Josh the Banker was out on a date with the young McKay girl, they noted the liaison for future gossip and went back to their discussions. Josh tried his best to ignore the stares while Kathy hardly noticed, more concerned about someone seeing the tear in her skirt. She pressed the skirt to her leg to cover the rip but the lighting in the lounge barely allowed the reading of a newspaper. Josh led Kathy through the blue haze of cigarette smoke that hung from the ceiling. Each table had a red candle in a red, tempered glass candle-holder, surrounded by a small advent wreath.

As Josh and Kathy crossed the room they nodded and said hello to nearly everyone who looked at them. In Minnesota fashion, even those individuals with grudges against Josh said hello. Likewise, Josh exchanged the warmest greetings with the people he loathed the most. Two of Josh's friends from high school, Tommy Blanks and Hank Murphy, shouted and whistled when they saw him with Kathy. Josh cringed.

'Way to go, Josh!' said Hank. 'Hi, Kathy! There's a table open in the corner.'

Josh said to Kathy, 'Those two guys, I tell you what. Same age as me, can you believe that?'

Kathy and Josh slid into a booth. She pulled out her Marlboros and offered one to Josh. He declined.

'I'm quitting,' said Kathy.

'I've heard it's the hardest thing you will ever give up.'

'Oh, not at all,' Kathy said, striking her lighter. 'I've quit hundreds of times.'

A waitress with a double chin, deep laughter-lines and a smoky voice approached the booth with two thick porcelain mugs, and said, 'Do I even need to ask what you want to drink?'

'Yes, thank you,' Josh joked, 'I'll have a foo-foo spritzer, please.'

'Foo-foo, my ass,' said the waitress. 'Merry Christmas,

you two.' She set the mugs down with a thud on the table and left. Kathy reached for her mug but Josh grabbed her arm and said, 'Not yet. Wait until it stops boiling first.'

She looked up at him. As if startled, Josh removed his hand from her arm and looked away, pretending to search the bar, looking for a subject to discuss. She kept staring ahead, waiting for his eyes to return.

The look made Josh nervous and he felt trapped in the booth. He did not want to be seen making bedroom eyes at Kathy. His reputation as the playboy of Immaculate had followed him since high school. With the majority of Josh's clientele being married religious couples, his standing as resident womanizer and swinging bachelor stuck with him, almost forcing him to find dates down the road in Tonnamowoc. The majority of the women he dated ended up moving away from Immaculate; they already had one foot out the door, towards Minneapolis or California. Until they found their means of escape, Josh acted as their local surrogate. One ex-girlfriend had even told Josh that he seemed *less Immaculate* than other guys.

But nearly every one of Josh's relationships ended due to his unwillingness to say three words. He drifted out of relationships, unable to lie about love, for it seemed a betrayal to his one love that never died, like a branding that forever after smouldered.

Kathy stirred her steaming drink. She began to feel uncomfortable with Josh sitting quietly on the other side of the table. Josh noticed she had stopped tracking his eyes so doggishly.

'What Mass will you be attending tonight?' he said.

Surprised by the question, Kathy said, 'Midnight, of course. What else?'

Awkwardly, Josh asked, 'Do you always attend the midnight Mass?'

'Of course. I went to the morning Mass, too. Mom dragged my ass out of bed. Come to think of it . . . I'm not sure that I saw you at church last Christmas.'

'Never!' Josh scoffed. 'I always attend Mass. Last year I went to the midnight Mass. I saw you there.'

'Oh really. So you were watching me then? Tsk tsk.'

'No, I wasn't . . . watching you.' Hearing his voice, he recognized and felt disgusted with the dumbspeak of flirting.

'I think you're lying. You weren't there at all,' Kathy said with a smile.

'Lying?' Josh became more irritated. 'I've never missed a year in my life. I'm sure I saw you.'

'Do you always check out women at church?' She let her mouth hang open as she waited for him to respond.

He tried to discern if she was serious or not, but then passed. 'Okay, next subject. You really had me going.' He laughed, but he bristled at her way of speaking.

Kathy laughed and then put Josh in another spot. 'Well, I could pick you up for church tonight, and we could go together.'

'Hmm . . . that's a thought.'

'I could make certain you attend, so you don't just say you went and sit around drinking egg nog.'

Josh weighed an answer, feeling trapped again. Kathy was proposing a church date – a second date in the same day. He watched her make circles with her finger on the rim of the mug as she awaited his reply. Her lips and eyes almost dared him to wager a 'Yes'.

'I'll have to think about it,' he said. 'I usually go alone.'

'I know you do. Why not go with me?'

'Because I'm a loner.' He leaned back in his seat. 'Haven't you heard? I'm the original rebel.'

'I don't remember James Dean being a bean-counter.'

'If he would have lived, I'm certain that he would have been. Rebel doesn't pay very well.'

Kathy paused, and then asked again. 'So what do you say? How about this: you call me at nine o'clock tonight and let me know what you decide.'

'Fair enough,' answered Josh, with relief. 'All right, I'll think about it. Let's give these drinks a chance. Cheers.' He lifted his mug towards Kathy. The mugs clinked together and they carefully sipped the thick Christmas elixir that painted their internals with a rosy warmth. Kathy had never experienced a Tom and Jerry before and the amount of rum and spice overwhelmed her. It tasted blissful, yet revolting. The rum slowly rolled down her throat, and then a rush ran up to the top of her head like a whale spout. She did not expect to be toppled by one sip. It felt like Christmas.

Hank Murphy and Tommy Blanks stood at the bar with the older generation of Legionnaires, most of whom were veterans who held court on stools custom-fitted to their bodies from overuse. 'Hank and Blanks', as they were commonly referred to, regaled the older men with fresh comments and crude anecdotes, and were so well liked at the Legion that they had managed to obtain lifetime memberships from the

Post Commander, despite the fact that neither of them had served in any branch of the armed forces. As the world wars moved further from the present, and the regular Legion members became more wrinkled every year, the Post Commander did what he could to boost the waning enrolment. Some people suspected that he even paid dead veterans' dues in order to keep enrolment high enough to feed his hopes of becoming a National Legion Delegate.

The leather dice box changed hands every minute as the next gambler standing along the bar took his turn slamming the box upside down on the bar.

The dice spilled out and scattered across the bar. The retired doctor said, '6–5–4, right away.'

'Right away, nice roll,' said a mechanic, who leaned over the doctor's shoulder.

Tommy Blanks interrupted his conversation with the bartender to irritate another. 'Hey, doc, quick reminder: you might want to write a prescription for boxcars,' said Blanks, 'because I'm in the lead right now with eleven.'

Lacking any semblance of gambling etiquette, Blanks revelled in taunting the doctor. The doctor rolled the dice again.

'Not bad, doc. Nothing to drag your tail over. One more roll.'

The doctor rolled again.

'Let's see, that adds up to two, six, *loser*.' Blanks collected the pot. 'Jesus, I need a rake.'

The doctor said, 'That's the third time in a row.'

'You should have practised dice instead of medicine.'

'Wise ass,' the doctor grumbled. 'Whose dice are these?'

Blanks cut him off. 'Oh sure, call us cheaters. Now he wants to be Gaming Commissioner.'

The other players nominated and appointed the doctor to a mock office. The doctor did not reply, aware that bar wit did not become him. He leaned his elbow on the bar and propped his chin on his hand. His previous bouts with Blanks had not ended well. His tongue was not as sharp or as loose. The doctor quietly faded into the background, but did not take offence; he just took the insult. He enjoyed the company of Blanks almost as much as he wanted to choke him.

Hank Murphy and Tommy Blanks held the proud distinction of being the most successful former juvenile delinquents in town. Blanks's dream was to find a cow that had the image of Christ on its side, so that he could tour every county fair and trade show in the United States and charge a dollar for admission to look at the Holy Cow. In search of this cash cow, he drove slowly past farms. In the meantime, Hank and Blanks owned and operated the Immaculate Snowplow Company, which had won the snow removal contract for the county for five years running. They were not wealthy, but they had succeeded far beyond their own expectations and infinitely beyond the townspeople's. Everyone knew a Hank and Blanks story that was ribald, reckless and either offensive or hilarious, depending on the listener. Until they started their own business they had stuffed themselves with experiences as if life were a buffet. Their exploits with motorcycles and watercraft served as an informal and expensive education for snowplough driving. They had the ability to drive in blinding, hypnotizing night snowfalls and could feel the road in places where no road appeared at all. In contrast to their history of borderline lunacy was their company's safety record and reputation, which they went to great lengths to keep intact and broadcast to their customers. The slightest malfunction or repair got logged, posted and serviced immediately. They took pride in the company's safety record of four thousand continuous hours without a single accident. (They did not count mailbox-pluckings as accidents, filing those incidents as a humorous type of collateral damage.) They ploughed every farm driveway no matter how remote, and even the dead-end roads. Immaculate Snowplow had a fleet of fifteen trucks to cover one sparsely populated county. They had the same number of seasonal employees, most of whom were farmers of one of two types: solvent or bankrupt.

Hank and Blanks ran the summer baseball programme for kids. Neither man had any sort of real money to spend, but their donations of time and labour to the town of Immaculate were conspicuous. In reality they volunteered for two reasons: the improvement of the Immaculate community and (the principal reason) the procurement of the annual ploughing contract.

Sitting next to Hank was Renee Marak's father, Ben Masterson, a lean sixty-five-year-old with a leather neck, who in the winter drove a snowplough and in the summer farmed part-time. The skin on his hands and face was thick enough to push a thumbtack to the hilt without hitting a nerve. He had come to the Legion with Hank Murphy after doing maintenance on one of the ploughs, and expected to meet up with Ray, Renee and his grandsons.

Hank said, 'Where's that daughter of yours, Ben?'

Ben held a toothpick between his teeth as he spoke. He shook his head, 'Ray's probably working on something. Thought they would be here by now.'

Hank nudged Ben. 'Ray's probably got her out pitching shit.'

'Could be.' Ben laughed. 'Ray doesn't know when to call it a day sometimes. I think he works just to work.'

'I worked a concrete job with Ray – did I tell you this yet? – for a few weeks, before I got fired. Was it 1972?'

Ben said in monotone, 'Weren't you on dope that year?'

'And then some! But I remember standing on the scaffolding above Ray, and he slung mud and mortar uphill all day, lifting pails up to me. You don't need a machine with him around. God dammit, every time he went down the ladder, he'd come back up with four blocks, fifty fuckin' pounds apiece, two in each hand. We did a whole wall that day. It's hard to have a hangover around that guy.'

Ben laughed. 'Yeah.' He shook his head. 'Yeah, he's just strong. Last spring, I helped him put a homemade fertilizer tank on the three-point hitch of his John Deere. The tank weighed a ton. Like dumbasses, we had it propped up with a two-by-four and it started to slip. Of course, I was standing behind it, and just to keep the tank from falling I leaned into it with all my strength. I was straining at the seams. And then Ray casually walked over, put one hand on the tank, and pushed it up. When I realized I wasn't holding up any weight, I took my hands off. I just looked at him. He stood there holding it with one arm, and said, "Now go get me a hacksaw." And I said, "Yes, sir." And off I went, like a kid.' Ben did a mock salute.

Hank said, 'Some father-in-law you are. You're supposed to intimidate your daughter's husband, not roll over. But don't let me tell you any lies: I've done the same thing. I tell you what, Ray showed me the way.' Hank sipped his rum.

Ben raised an eyebrow, causing the lines in his forehead to curve like snakes. 'Oh yeah, how's that?'

'Oh, you probably don't want to know, Ben.'

'You don't say something like that and drop it.'

'Well, it's an old story. You've probably already heard it. With the way news travels in this town. Happened a long time ago, back when Renee and Ray were dating. Ancient news.'

Ben's expression changed and the contours on his weathered forehead deepened. 'Oh, Christ. Your stories are better when they concern other people's families.' He turned towards Hank, bracing his body for a shock. 'Okay, let's hear it.'

Likewise, Hank turned towards Ben, getting in a good position to tell his story. Hank Murphy was one of the few people in town who openly spoke about skeletons in his closet. His closet had no door. He didn't care what the Immaculate moralists said about him. But in this case, he spoke quietly, since the story involved Renee. '1969. I think it was 1969 anyway. Ray was back from his first tour in Vietnam. You know how big he was in high school, like an ox. He was always quiet and nobody really messed with him. It's funny, the one person I ever saw pick a fight with Ray in high school ended up sailing into a dumpster behind the wood shop.' Hank raised his voice. 'Isn't that right, Blanks?'

A few barstools away, Blanks turned his neck. 'Your what hurts?'

'Remember when Ray threw you in the dumpster?'

'I, ah . . . ahem,' Blanks cleared his throat, 'remember something about that. Yeah, now it's coming back to me. I remember winning that fight.'

'You hear that?' Hank smiled at Ben. 'That tells you how hard his grape hit the damn dumpster. That fool, I tell you what: he was a one-legged man in an ass-kicking contest. I had one of the best laughs of my life that day. But back to the night. That night Ray and Renee were out on a date of sorts and – Ben, don't take offence – she looked . . . wow . . . great. I mean, what I wouldn't have given—'

'On with the story, please.'

'Right. Whew. You may or may not know this, but back in the day, I had a thing for Renee. She was the best-looking girl in town. She's still the best-looking woman in town.'

'Hank,' Ben said, while gently placing his fist on the bar, 'you've had a thing for every woman in town at one time or another.'

'It's true. Oh, Lord, it's true. Have mercy on me on Judgement Day.' Hank made the sign of the cross upside down and with his left hand. 'The flesh is weak and the mind is, too – thank God for that or I'd never get laid. But anyway, Ray and Renee were sitting right over there, in that same booth that Josh is in right now with Kathy. (Must be his flavour of the week, what do you think?) But Ray and Renee, they sat without saying much. I imagine it was a stressful time for the two of them, knowing that he was leaving again in a few days to catch a plane back overseas. Then a crusty old veteran started harassing Ray about the war, like it was Ray's decision we were in Vietnam. You remember Kurt Lee? He was up in Ray's face, sat right in the booth next to Ray. By that time, half the country had stopped supporting the war, including me, but that old Legion barnacle hated the idea of losing the war, or exiting without a clear victory.'

Ben, a Korean War veteran, asked, 'What did Kurt say?'

'Oh, all kinds of shit, Ben. Like, "We sent you boys over there for a little police action and look at the mess you made." That sort of thing. And, "Your generation is a bunch of lazy men and easy women," and he said that little nugget while staring right at Renee. He said it nice and loud, too, so that everyone could hear it, plain as day, and I could see Ray taking it all in, like he always does, but I knew he was foaming over his beer. Blanks yelled across the bar, told Kurt to shut his cocktrap, but that was the only protest. I admit it: I wanted to see a fight. Ray only weighed about a hundred-fifty pounds at the time. His skin and bones were strewn between here, Fort Bliss and Hanoi. His shoulders looked about like mine.'

'Girlish?'

'Oh, a comeback! Keep drinking, you old sack. No, Ray didn't look *that* pathetic. Kurt Lee kept on talking, making noise, and bringing all the stares in the bar down to that booth. Ray was on the spot, right. If he didn't respond, somehow, he would have felt soft, weak, you know? Especially since Kurt insulted Renee in such a less-than-subtle way. Renee looked like she was about to cry, or maybe bust a bottle over his head. Then Kurt made his last mistake. He wadded up a cocktail napkin and tossed it at Renee.' Hank

49

flicked his fingers at Ben. 'And before that napkin was halfway across the table, Ray had his elbow rammed up in Kurt's throat. They tumbled out of the booth, ass-over-teakettle. Then before that napkin even started to uncrinkle, Kurt was being carried out of the bar like a bale of straw. Ray had the belt of Kurt's pants in one hand and his scalp in the other. Ray opened the door with Kurt's forehead. Then there was a whimper, followed by the outer door opening, and then another whimper. Everybody filed outside to break up the fight, but Ray held the outer door shut with one leg so he could he trounce Kurt in peace. He left that old man crumpled on the stoop. By the end of it, the napkin Kurt had tossed at Renee looked better than he did. And I have to tell you: it was awesome. After that, Ray walked down the sidewalk and no one saw him the rest of the night. But he was ready to tear fucking trees out of the earth. Blanks tried to find Ray, but you know Blanks, he couldn't find his asshole with a flashlight and both hands. Dumb as a box, that poor guy. Look at him over there.'

Hank paused to watch Blanks roll the dice. When the dice spilled out, Blanks pointed at the dice and shouted, 'Stupid dice! Why can't one of you be a three?'

Ben laughed, 'Right on cue.'

'Did you know that he's a bedwetter?'

Ben stopped smiling. 'You're kidding me.'

'Well, it would be a fun rumour to start. We should do that this afternoon, once everyone has gathered at the garage. Anyway, back to the story. Turns out Ray walked all the way to his parents' farm that night, in the cold, wearing a T-shirt and the blood of Kurt Lee. Now that's about a ten-mile hike, and it was N.H.O. cold.'

Ben went to put a toothpick in his mouth, but stopped. 'N.H.O.?'

With his index fingers, Hank drew circles on each of his shirt pockets over his breasts.

Ben said, 'Don't tell me what it means. Please. I'm fine not knowing.'

Hank stopped rubbing his chest. 'Kurt Lee deserved it, too.'

'But Kurt was always that way.' Ben waved the toothpick at Hank. 'Right up 'til he croaked, he was a loudmouth. And of all people to talk: he never even left the States during World War Two. He was a supply clerk, for Christ's sake. A warhawk that never saw a war.' Ben shook his head. 'Fuckin' pisses me off. I don't want to think about it. Is that the end?'

'No, it's halftime.' Hank sipped on the rum. 'Jesus, these drinks get stiffer every year. This one is stiff as my new mattress. Speaking of which, I need a girlfriend.'

'Don't look at me.'

'Pity me, Ben. The only thighs I've seen since August were on the Thanksgiving turkey.'

Ben frowned and looped his finger in the air, to keep Hank on track.

'Okay, fine. So Ray walked home. In the meantime, you know me, Ben: I was drunker than six Indians that night. Now that Renee was alone in the bar, I started checking her out, thinking I might get lucky and score the rebound. (Sorry, Ben, but you asked.) I tried to comfort her and cheer her up, you know – take her home. Hell, I just wanted a date with her because she was out of my league. I mean, I'm a catch, but I just don't have it all. I've often wished that I had been born rich instead of just good-looking. And I imagined if I could get my foot in the door with Renee I would surely hit it off with her father.'

Ben shuddered at the thought. 'I'd have broke your foot off.'

'But I was hitting on her, plain for all to see, particularly since Renee had become the centre of attention. I ended up giving her a ride out to your place that night, drunk as I was. I tried to put the moves on halfway there and she slippered me. Literally. She took her shoe off and hit me with it. Talk about degrading. So much for my initial approach. I recircled for a second groping and she whacked me again. Twice she slippered me.'

'Good girl! What else?'

'She got out of my truck and started walking to your place. She called me a few names I hadn't heard before, so I followed her for awhile, drove two miles an hour behind her until your farm came into view, and then I rolled down the window and apologized. She said, "Wait until Ray hears about this." Well, that injected reality back into my night. I didn't know whether to shit or go blind. I mean, I'd just watched skinny Ray Marak mop the floor with Kurt Lee, and even though I imagined myself to be a good fighter, I was already nervous.'

'Did she tell him?'

'I don't know if Renee told Ray or the grapevine did. But the next day I was in the feed store parking lot when Ray and his old man pulled up in a truck. Ray's dad went inside, but

Ray, he lingered outside to talk to me. Oh, man, he walked towards me and I puffed up like a cat in front of a German Shepherd. I said – I said, "Ray, nothing happened, but if you want to make a big deal of it, we can deal with it right here." Ray acted cool: "No big deal." He said, "Just don't let it happen again," and he reached out his giant hoof to shake my hand. Even when he was skinny he had those big hands, like vices hanging on his wrists. I reached out to shake and he pulled me towards him in some crazy police manoeuvre. My wrist, oh, Ben: my wrist. I don't know if I can tell the rest and maintain my manhood.'

'How does that apply to you?'

'Do I have to show you?'

Ben waved his hand and then shielded his eyes. 'Spare me.'

'Okay. Well, in the parking lot, I dropped to my knees and begged for mercy. Ray smiled at me and said, "This is what you call a 'Z-Lock'. Hurts, don't it?" I thought my wrist bones were crushed and I'd never have the pleasure of my right hand again. I begged, and it hurt so bad that I started reciting the Act of Contrition. Yes, that's right, I said it. Seeing me pray must have tickled Ray, that bastard, because he said he'd let go, but only if I recited the Twenty-Third Psalm. Can you believe that? I was kneeling on grass, and it gave him a good hearty laugh when I said, "He makes me lie down in green pastures." I'll never forget it.'

Ben's whole body bounced as he silently chuckled. 'That's a funny picture. Ray's a good man.' Then Ben put his hand on Hank's shoulder and said, 'And thank goodness Renee didn't bring you home as a boyfriend. I'd have killed you.'

'I've seen a few shotguns in my day. Carl Stahling chased me with a crowbar once. To think, I could have been your son-in-law.'

'Hey, Sharon, I need another drink here.' Ben said quietly to Hank, 'Just thinking about it hurts my ass.'

From the booth, Josh heard the name Ray come from the conversation between Hank and Ben. Josh was reminded of Ray's financial problems. Just a few days earlier Josh had reviewed Ray's accounts with the bank. Ray was close to insolvency, again. His borrowing capacity already exceeded the bank's acceptable debt ratio, meaning that Ray had no more wiggle room. As Signer on the loans, Josh put himself at risk. Ray was fifty thousand dollars over the limit. Josh tried to be generous and no one did he show more generosity to than Ray, who seemed to think that money problems could not touch him so long as his farm kept producing milk. The concepts of the market bounced right off him. Ray's problem would never be work or production. The thing about Ray that irked Josh most was his lack of attention to detail. Josh and Ray had a long history and that skewed the business relationship. They played football, hockey and baseball together. They were never friends exactly but they crossed domains often. He simply knew the Maraks too well to be reasonable, but he also silently wished that the farm or marriage would some day collapse.

4

In the garage, Jacob said, 'Can we please go to the bar, Dad?'

Renee said to her husband, 'Oh that's wonderful. That's *real* encouraging. Eight years old and he wants to go to the bar.'

'He likes the Shirley Temples,' Ray said. 'Don't you, Jacob?'

Jacob opened his mouth like he was going to respond, but then burped.

'Gross, Jacob,' Renee scolded. 'Now what do you say?'

'Thank you.'

She pursed her lips and widened her eyes.

He immediately recanted. 'I mean, excuse me.'

Without exchanging a word, Ray and Renee had agreed to postpone their argument over the birth control pills until after Christmas, or at least until the first moment they were alone. The family piled into the front of a Ford pickup. Tippy, a pedigree of two yellow mutts, tried to jump into the truck as well but rebounded off of Renee's leg back to the ground.

'Stay here, Tippy.'

Jacob yelled, ''Bye, Tippy. Remember what I told you about the . . . shhh! Keep it quiet!'

Tippy barked at Jacob and seemed to smile, while Ethan scowled at his brother's stupid secret with the dog, which changed every day. Ethan still felt grumpy and groggy from the incident at the pond. When he'd first heard the parable of the Prodigal Son in church, he'd felt certain that it was expressly meant for him.

The diesel truck grunted to life and started down the narrow snow-covered driveway. The Maraks had to drive two miles from the farm to reach asphalt.

Jacob said to his father, 'Can we get some candy cigarettes for when we go to the bar? Ethan and I want some.'

Ethan frowned. 'I never said that.'

Renee covered her ears, 'Jacob, I'm going to pretend I didn't hear that.'

'But Dad smokes.'

'Dad's quitting, aren't you, Dad?'

'That's right,' Ray lied, 'I haven't had one in two weeks.'

'Really?' said Jacob.

'That's right.'

'Huh,' Jacob said. 'Then I wonder if Joke smokes? 'Cause I found a pack of the Camels in the tool shed yesterday.'

Renee's jaw dropped at the revelation, but her expression turned into a smile as she felt partially vindicated for hiding the birth control pills. Now she had a weapon: 'A lie is a lie is a lie.' Ray stared straight ahead into the windshield, not moving a muscle.

'I'll have to have a talk with that boy,' he said. 'He shouldn't be smoking.'

Already Ray mourned the loss of his morning cigarette – one lousy damn cigarette a day. He understood the health risks, but one cigarette a day seemed harmless, about like having one drink a day. At least that was his latest reason, with the addiction acting like a lawyer in his head, always seeking loopholes in logic to ensure the continuation of the vice.

Ethan could sense the tension between his parents but was consumed with thoughts of his morning heroics at the pond. What if Jacob had drowned? Then they would be crying and saying, 'Ethan, why didn't you save him?' Whatever Santa was bringing had better be good.

After a quiet ride to town, with only Burl Ives on the radio to break the silence, Ray announced that he needed to stop at the feed store before it closed. Ethan brightened at the announcement. The smell of the cooperative feed store alone made visiting a pleasure. The synergy of pure grains and proteins filled the air.

Ethan and Jacob ran from the truck to the front door, yelling, 'Feed Man!' The clerk, Jerry, always had a treat or a new joke for the boys. Jerry was flighty but Ray respected his ability to entertain children.

Hearing the voices, the Feed Man reacted quickly. He put on a long white beard and kicked off one of his shoes. Over his plaid flannel shirt he wore red suspenders. His thin glasses and balding head, with the white beard, made him a plausible enough Santa for his annual Christmas Eve charade. Once in costume, he sat quietly behind his desk and pretended to fill out paperwork.

When Ethan and Jacob opened the office door, Jerry acted surprised to see the children and, doing his best impression of an elderly man, said, 'Well, now, what in blazes? Wh-wh-what are you children doing here so early? I have to get ready for Christmas. And you caught me without my red suit on!'

'You're not Santa!' yelled Jacob.

Ethan said, 'You're too skinny to be Santa!'

'And you're so bald!'

The Feed Man took offence. 'But Santa *is* bald. I am so Santa Claus! Didn't you see my sleigh out in the parking lot? I was on my way to the North Pole and I had to stop by Immaculate. You see, I have a terrible problem with my toe, and, I'm sorry, boys, but I don't know if I'll be able to deliver presents this year to all the children of the world. There's a problem with Rudolph, and, well, it's all very hard to explain.'

Ray and Renee entered the office. Renee stifled her laughter so that the boys could enjoy the show. Ray took a seat near the door and smiled.

Jacob asked, 'What's wrong with Rudolph?'

'Oh, boys,' said Jerry, 'you don't want to know.' Without letting the boys see his hands moving behind the desk, Jerry grabbed a red clown nose out of a drawer and placed it over his big toe. 'Rudolph's nose . . . it's . . . it's terrible. He's lost his nose, I'm afraid. I might need your help. You see, his nose is stuck on my toe!' Jerry held his leg in the air and the boys ran around the desk to help save Rudolph's nose.

'Now careful, boys. We'll do it on three. Give me a hand now. Are you ready? One, two, three!'

The boys pulled the nose and fell backwards to the floor, while Jerry simulated extreme pain from the amputation. 'Oh, thank you, boys! Now go see if you can find Rudolph back in the warehouse. He's in there somewhere. Oh, the pain!'

The boys ran into the warehouse to search for Rudolph.

Jerry always sent the boys to wander the warehouse while he and Ray discussed business.

'Good show, Jerry,' said Ray. 'I don't know how you come up with it.'

Jerry pulled off his beard and thanked Ray for the compliment.

'I need ten bags of barn lime.'

'Is that all?' Jerry picked up his pen.

'That's it.'

Jerry looked Ray in the eye. 'Do you have a cheque for me?'

Ray fumbled in his pocket and produced a cheque made out for fifty dollars. Jerry reviewed it carefully. Over the past few years he had become wary of cheques that were unsigned, or sloppily written, or made out for two different amounts.

'Come on now, drop it on the desk and see if it bounces,' said Ray.

Jerry let the cheque float down to his desk. 'Ah, it passed the test. Do you want your account balance?'

Ray nodded. Jerry opened a ledger and scribbled in the number 50 and subtracted from it the cost of ten bags of lime. The mere sight of the ledger aggravated Ray. Jerry wrote the balance down on a receipt and added a reminder in red ink about the payment due on 1 January 1982.

Renee pretended to be reading an auction bill on the wall, though she listened intently. She yearned to know the number at the bottom of the receipt, to know how tight the purse strings would need to be for the next few weeks.

Jerry said, 'Did you hear about Ross O'Brien?'

Ray shook his head.

Jerry closed the ledger. Like the Legion, the feed store was a gossip depot. 'I guess he and his wife are getting divorced. She's got some man in Sharpsboro.'

'You're joking!' Renee whirled around to face Jerry.

'That's just what I heard.' He held up his hand as if swearing on the Bible. 'I wouldn't make it up.'

Renee, suddenly full of conversation, began to interview Jerry about the details. Divorce was still a radical idea in Immaculate. It happened once a year at the most. Ray and Renee had played cards on several occasions with the O'Brien couple and noticed that the two of them tended to drink a little too much, but the idea that they could not work things out – it seemed impossible. Renee felt disgusted by Jerry's glibness.

'I'm just the messenger. I'm not happy about it, Renee.'

'It's awful.'

'These are tough times. Money. You folks know that it's not easy.'

Ray nodded, but didn't care for the comment.

With all of her reading and self-education, Renee still considered divorce alien to Immaculate, although on two occasions she had nearly left Ray. Her bags had been packed and the threat had been real. The threat of leaving had proved to be great leverage in an argument, and in both cases Ray had relented first, with her following his lead shortly thereafter. Renee believed that everyone thought about leaving, but she could not imagine taking the final step. She thought of herself as a liberal Catholic, but when the realities of modern America came into her town, she balked. Staying committed to the family superseded all, even if it meant suffering, because continuity of family and home was the foundation of life. She had constructed her values on that rock. Hindsight convinced her that all adversity in a marriage was surmountable. The first several years of her marriage to Ray had been very unstable, but they had managed; thus she felt that all couples should and could do the same – for better or worse.

Ray felt the receipt in his hand and casually looked down to see the number beside his name. $5,562.32. The figure somehow came as a surprise to Ray, as if the amount he had borrowed from the Immaculate Farmers' Cooperative had accumulated overnight. The receipt suddenly felt like a brick in his hand. He felt his neck grow hot, and he gripped the receipt tightly between his thumb and forefinger. He hated money and budgeting and was too stubborn to let Renee manage the finances. But his wife knew more about the situation than Ray imagined.

Ray felt the need to get out of the feed store. 'I'm going to find the boys.'

He walked into the warehouse to mull his debt and the 1 January deadline, muttering as he walked down an aisle of stacked grain pallets. The warehouse provided good hiding places for his sons. Ray turned down an aisle and caught a glimpse of a pair of feet running across an aisle. From behind a pallet came a short laugh that sounded like Ethan's. Temporarily forgetting about the receipt burning in his hand, Ray began to step quietly through the aisles, hoping to surprise Ethan from behind. Turning down an aisle towards the laughter, he walked several steps and climbed on to a short stack of feed.

Meanwhile Ethan inched along with caution, checking each angle before moving from one alley into the next. Each time he stopped, he pressed his body near the stack of feed and inhaled deeply, enjoying the rich and condensed smells of small grains, sorghums and protein supplements.

Ray stood on the stack and searched for his son, listening for the crackle of feed sacks and looking for the flash of sneakers. While Ray scanned the pallets, Ethan continued moving through the warehouse, staying low, dashing across aisles. Before long, Ray gave up looking and shrugged his shoulders. As he prepared to leap to the ground, Ray paused and listened one last time, but he did not hear his son. Ray then jumped to the ground and landed with his back to Ethan.

Standing as still as a deer, Ethan froze with his nose pressed to the stack. In his periphery, he saw Ray's shoulder and decided to take a chance and scare his father. However, they turned at the same time, and terrified each other. Ray flinched when Ethan said, 'Boo!' Ray returned a much louder and convincing roar at Ethan, thrilling him with fear. They laughed together.

Ethan said with wide eyes, 'Wow, where did you jump from, the ceiling?'

'I'm trying to figure out how you got behind me!' Ray laughed and looked around. 'Where's Jacob?'

Ethan shrugged.

'Okay,' Ray said, sighing. 'Let's find out what goofy is up to.' He tucked the receipt into the back pocket of his jeans.

Together they moved down the aisles of the warehouse calling for Jacob. Ray separated from Ethan to check out the rear of the warehouse, which connected to a climate-controlled partition that housed chemical products. He reached the corner of the warehouse and opened the door to the partition. He looked to his right and saw nothing, then looked to his left and found Jacob unscrewing the cap of a herbicide container.

'Jacob, knock it off right now!'

'Why?' Jacob whined. 'It's good for my collection.' He pointed to a small pile of watermelon seeds, sunflower seeds and kernels of corn, which he had carried in his pockets to town.

'That stuff will kill you,' Ray said, 'or give you a very short life. It will kill your seeds, too.'

Jacob whined, 'But it says right here, "Protect your seeds with 24-D." It says, "A little goes a long way." I just wanted to put a little bit on them.'

Ray nearly slapped himself. 'Jacob, it should also say "Hazardous to your health" somewhere on the label. And that it will give you a tumour. You can't even touch that stuff unless you have gloves on.' He snatched Jacob by the arm and pulled him away. 'Did you open anything in here?'

Jacob shook his head.

'You had better not lie to me. Did you open anything? Anything at all?'

'No.'

'Because if you did open anything, I have to pay for it, and then we can't go to see Grandpa at the Legion. Plus, Santa will know if you don't tell the truth.'

'I promise, Dad!' Jacob pleaded. 'I didn't open anything.

I just wanted to protect my seeds so that I can plant them in the spring!'

Ray tried to read the label: '2,4-dichlorophenoxy . . . acid. Kills broad-leaf, protects seeds.' He shook his head and put the container back on the shelf. Ray used the herbicide on his land out of necessity. His father used to say, 'Avoid things you can't read or pronounce.' But nearly every farm used chemicals. One bad crop almost guaranteed an auction and a career change. At first Ray felt guilty about using the chemicals, but when the yields increased dramatically, like so many other farmers, he was simply won over. He knew that if his father were alive, even he would reconsider his principles, if it meant staying in business. It was a fact, graphed out and explained by many salesmen spreading cost-benefit brochures, like tablets carried down from Mount Cargill: every one dollar spent on herbicides earned three dollars in return.

Jacob crouched to pick up his seeds from the floor but Ray stopped him. 'No, Jacob.'

'But these are my lucky seeds. I've had them for ever!'

Renee often commented on the amount of seed that came out of Jacob's pants in the laundry.

He grabbed his son's arm. 'Let's go.'

Renee was waiting in the truck. She watched her husband shake his head and assumed it was the receipt that was causing his frustration. The gifts she had bought for Christmas seemed inadequate and she worried that the boys would be disappointed. To save money she'd become creative and researched do-it-yourself gifts that she could make at home. She looked at the patched jeans that Jacob and Ethan wore, and shuddered to think that they would have to wait until spring for new clothes.

Ray got into the truck and looked at Renee under a furrowed brow. She returned the look, as if to say, 'Don't worry, Ray.' She reached across the bench seat and squeezed his shoulder, bringing a sickly smile to her husband's face. He reached over to thank her, his rough hand softening on her neck.

Jerry, the feed man, waited on the loading dock with a hand cart stacked with ten bags of barn lime. As Ray backed up his truck, Jerry mumbled, 'Damn, I could have talked to her all day. Too bad she ended up with *him*.'

5

The family arrived at the American Legion and walked inside to meet with Ben Masterson. The patrons paused to see who had entered, taking mental notes for their personal inventories of those who were present. Satisfied that the Ray Marak family could be checked off, they returned to their conversations and their rum, though men and women alike paused a little longer than usual to take an extra look at Renee. She was wearing a pair of bargain jeans and a red and green sweatshirt. Some of the men wanted to see Renee in a dress and some of the women would have preferred her in work boots and flannel. She had stopped seeking attention long ago but, although the townspeople treated her with respect and seemed to go out their way for her friendship, sometimes she felt contemptuous eyes on her.

Tommy Blanks noticed the Marak family standing in the doorway and yelled, 'Marak, get your ass over here! We want your money.'

Ray said to Renee, 'Looks like some people have been here since breakfast.'

'Blanks probably never left last night.'

The family made their way through the dark lounge towards Ben, who was still standing at the bar with Hank Murphy. When Ben saw the family he swelled with pride and ended his conversation with Hank without pausing to excuse himself.

Jacob said, 'I'll have what my grandpa is having.'

'Oh no you won't, little fella!' Ben lifted Jacob into the air with his rough hands. He said to the other boy, 'Ethan, I think you're almost too big for old Grandpa to pick up now. You are growing like a weed. You might have to play basketball instead of hockey.'

'No way!' Ethan's face soured. '*Basketball?*'

Ray shook hands with the men at the bar and turned down invitations to join the dice game. The players knew he wasn't exactly thriving in the dairy business at the moment. Most of the players had little money to gamble with, but that didn't stop them from rolling the dice.

Tommy Blanks paid for the drinks before Ray could get out his wallet. 'Your money's no good here, Ray.'

Ray thanked Blanks, although the offer seemed like charity. Blanks clapped Ray on the shoulder and threw a five-dollar bill into the pot on his behalf. Ray recoiled with excuses but Hank Murphy handed him the dice box anyway.

'Roll, you cheap bastard.'

'The game is 6–5–4, Ray,' said Blanks. 'Roll those ice cubes. Doc keeps 'em cold. He's like liquid nitrogen.'

Renee ignored the game. Ray slammed the dice box upside down on the bar top and lifted it to uncover a lucky roll. The sight brought a shout from the onlookers about beginner's luck. Ray separated out three dice and rolled a second time for points.

'Boxcars!' Ray shouted when he saw two sixes showing on the bar. The players yelled protests.

'You just won the pot,' Blanks said with disappointment. 'Forty bucks. How do you like that? That's the last time I stake anyone.'

Suddenly Ray had money to continue playing. Feeling lucky, he threw a five-dollar bill from his winnings into the pot for the next round.

Ben, Renee and the two boys moved to a quiet table away from the bar. Jacob and Ethan looked around for other kids to play with but the other children in the bar were sitting quietly with their families, itching to escape. The waitress delivered Shirley Temples to the table while Jacob and Ethan answered Grandpa's questions. After quizzing the boys, Ben turned his attention to Renee and wheedled her about the state of affairs in the House of Marak. Renee took it as snooping. Ben missed seeing her on a regular basis. His two sons were en route to Immaculate, but Renee showed little enthusiasm about their homecoming. Ben valued nothing more than the few days of Christmas when his family came together. Success for him was his healthy and well-adjusted family, even if his sons wanted to live elsewhere. The only person missing was his wife. Since her death, Ben had clung to Renee, but during the holidays he could not hide his excitement at the thought of seeing his sons.

More than once, Renee had had to push her father away. She had tried to play matchmaker by arranging surprise dates with women his age, but Ben hated the idea of dating or marrying again.

'So, you have everything you need for tomorrow?' asked Ben. 'You don't need . . . a booster . . . or . . . anything?'

'Do you mean money?'

'Well,' Ben said, 'not *just* money.'

'I don't balance the chequebook, Dad, if that's what you want to know.'

'Oh, now, honey! I never said such a thing. I'm just wondering if you need anything . . . *special* for Christmas this year. I thought about getting you and Ray a weekend trip to Duluth.'

'Ha! When?' Renee laughed. 'When would we go? Who would milk the cows?'

'Well, I could. I'm old, not dead.'

Renee stirred her Tom and Jerry and said, 'You'll have to talk to Mr Marak about that, Dad. I swear he's too in love with those cows to leave them for a day.'

'As it should be,' said Ben. 'As long he doesn't love them more than he loves you.'

'Ray loves me Ray's way.'

'Okay then. How about April for a trip then, eh?'

'Oh, God,' Renee groaned, 'I don't know, Dad.'

'Duluth.' Ben plugged his idea again. 'The North Shore is a lovely place.'

'When was the last time you were there?'

'Let's see.' Ben scratched his forehead. 'Must have been in '74.'

'It's that good, huh?' Renee smiled and looked down at her drink. She turned her head and noticed Jacob had disappeared from his seat with his cocktail. She looked around, as she had done so many times, and discovered him standing near the booth where Kathy and Josh sat.

Jacob immediately started a conversation with them.

'Are you guys married?'

Renee blushed with embarrassment and said, 'Jacob, come over here. Let those nice people enjoy themselves.'

'He's no trouble at all,' said Kathy, while Josh sank into his chair. 'What a little sweetie he is! He can join us for a bit, if that's okay with you.'

Josh glanced at Renee and looked away.

'He's the dickens,' Renee replied. 'Come back here, Jacob.'

Jacob shuffled back to his seat as if laden with log chains. He plopped into his chair and made faces at Kathy.

Renee asked her father about the evening's weather. The topic transformed Ben as he began to describe the forecast in excessive detail. The TV weatherman had been rather vague, so Ben gave a long-winded answer that boiled down to a sixty per cent chance of snow. There was even a chance of a winter storm if an Alberta Clipper shifted direction dramatically. He explained that several large air masses could impact anywhere from Albert Lea to International Falls to Kenora, depending on the ingredients in the atmospheric soup.

'Really,' Ben said, 'it all depends if we get the Arctic blast or not. That's it in a nutshell.'

Renee nodded without paying attention, letting the weather fill the gap in conversation, as talk of weather tends to. The people of Immaculate appreciated weather as both an essential part of their lives and a polite way of interacting while saying nothing. Many men, notably the older weather pontiffs like Ben Masterson, had an honest interest in meteorology, since their lives meshed so closely with wind, sun and rain.

Another shout rose from the men surrounding the dice

game at the bar as three hands at once slapped Ray on the back. Since Ray appeared to be winning, Renee watched the scene with tempered disapproval. She heard Ray say, 'Keep a five in there for me,' meaning that the betting ante stood at five dollars, an amount that did not sit well with her. Winning money was fine, but if Ray slouched to their table without the money he had brought she would be irritated.

He turned towards Renee and winked at her, but she showed him a curt smile.

Josh overheard Ray winning at the bar and muttered under his breath, 'You better win every game, Marak.'

Kathy asked, 'What was that?'

'Oh, nothing,' Josh answered.

She had heard enough to understand. 'Did I hear a little insider information just now?'

Josh ignored her. Kathy tried to look him in the eye but he would not look back at her. She moved her head from side to side to entice him but he did not say a word. He felt that he had divulged too much information already. Watching Ray gamble annoyed him. Not being invited seemed like a gesture of exclusion, although he knew that, if he simply asked to play, no one would reject him. Nevertheless he allowed himself to wallow for a moment in self-pity.

Undaunted, Kathy continued batting her eyes. Seeing that he intended to continue ignoring her, she placed her hand on his thigh, which startled Josh so much that he stood up and nearly knocked his mug off the table.

'Excuse me, I'm going to use the bathroom.'

Backing away from the booth, he bumped into Renee

Marak. Turning around, she said, 'Careful there,' and then seeing that it was Josh, quickly turned back to her table.

Ben said, 'One too many for you, Josh?'

Josh stuttered, 'Pardon me, Ren. Ah . . . no, Ben, just getting started!' He laughed nervously before quickly moving away from the lounge. He felt his ears burning as he descended the staircase into the dance hall and bathroom area.

'That Josh Werther is a decent guy,' Ben said. 'You know . . . for a banker.'

Renee didn't respond.

Seeing the empty seat, Jacob got up from his chair and climbed into Josh's seat across from Kathy.

Kathy said, 'Well, hello. What is that you're drinking?'

'Shirley Temple,' Jacob said. 'Still working on my first one.'

'Oh really?'

'Can I try yours?'

'No, these are for big kids. Is your name Ethan?'

'Jacob. That's my brother Ethan over there, and that's my mom who is looking at me right now like she ate something that didn't taste very good.'

Renee said, 'Hi again, Kathy. Just send him back over if he gets troublesome. He can be a real monkey.'

'Is that true? You don't look like a monkey.' Kathy mussed his hair. 'Oh wait, yes you do!'

Ethan moved into Jacob's chair to sit next to his mother and whispered to her, 'I have to use the bathroom, Mom.'

Renee told Ethan how to find the bathroom and he left the lounge. As Ethan walked under a doorway, the priest of the country church, Father Dimer, entered in his black shirt and white collar. He said hello to Ethan in passing.

Holding his hat in his hands, the priest entered the bar area and broadcast his smile to everyone at once. In the middle of Ray's roll of the dice, Blanks shouted, 'Hello, Father! Merry Christmas.'

Ray spilled the dice on to the floor, and then bent over to pick them up. It was too late to disassociate himself from the game in the presence of the priest. Father Dimer came over to offer his hello to Blanks and the other men gambling at the bar.

The priest said, 'Merry Christmas, gentlemen. Looks like you got a good little game going here. Who's winning?'

'Ray is cleaning house. Pray for us sinners, Father.'

Ray looked at his pile of winnings and wished to be invisible. Father Dimer eyed the money and said, 'Thataway, Ray. Take him for all he's worth.'

The priest smiled. A large crack in his lower lip had a permanent wine stain from the daily Communion and his nightly nip. Father Dimer knew every game in *Hoyle's Book of Rules* and played nickel stakes with old ladies at the nursing home three mornings a week. He would have joined the dice game if it weren't for the pressing news he needed to announce.

The waitress asked, 'Can I get you anything, Father?'

'No, but thank you, Ms Carter. Nothing for me. I just wanted to stop in to say Merry Christmas to you all and to make an announcement. It seems the weather has taken a turn for the worse.'

Hank and Blanks straightened up and pushed their mugs to the bar rail to indicate that they had finished drinking for the day. The statement surprised them, since they listened to the morning weather as intently as Ray listened to the Sunday homily.

'What's the forecast now, Father?' asked Blanks.

'Sounds like a big storm is headed this way. Maybe I had better tell everyone all at once.'

The bartender shouted, 'Listen up, everyone!'

'Thank you, Vern. Ah, well, hello, everyone! Pardon me for interrupting your socializing, but I wanted to stop by and pass along a bit of news. I was at the church getting ready for this evening and at the same time I was listening to the weather report. It seems the storm they originally predicted as only being a slight possibility is now inevitable and heading for our region.'

Ben Masterson nodded with approval as if he had predicted it.

The priest went on, 'From the looks of it, by eight o'clock tonight we will be under the brunt of the storm and the prediction is snow – lots of snow. Lots of wind, lots of drifting, and of course a lot of bad roads. That is, until Hank and Blanks take care of it for us, as they always do. However, after hearing what the WCCO weatherman is predicting, I want to say to you all that although I still intend to hold the midnight Mass this evening, please do not venture out if the roads are drifting.'

A din of disagreement came up from the crowd.

'I appreciate your dedication,' said Father Dimer, 'but the last thing I want is for anyone to run into trouble trying to get to church in the middle of the night. Tonight is meant to be spent enjoying the company of your families in warm houses, not digging your loved ones out of a snow bank somewhere and freezing your fingers. The Mass scheduled for tomorrow morning will go as planned if you cannot make it tonight. The weatherman said the temperature could be forty below zero and the winds could be up to fifty miles an hour. He also said that the storm could last all night, so if tomorrow you wake up and the storm is still upon us, the same applies. My advice is to only venture out if the storm has stopped and the roads are clear. Don't worry if you can't make it. I know that some of you have never missed a midnight Mass and probably never intend to, and I thank you for that, but we may never see a storm like this again on Christmas Eve. I certainly would not want any of us to miss our great annual tradition unless it was for something serious, and I believe that tonight's weather will be serious. We've all seen how fast these Immaculate storms can paralyse our travels. For those of you with generators, this afternoon might be a good time to make sure they are ready to go in the event you need them. The power company and the phone company have their employees on standby, but you know how it is – Immaculate usually gets its services back up and running after everyone else in the state.'

The bartender asked, 'What about Communion, Father?'

'If you would like to stop by the church this afternoon, I could offer Communion. However, I think the wisest thing is to go home and get out the candles and lanterns, make sure you have firewood and other necessities. Maybe do chores a little early and get the cows inside the barns. If you can't stand missing church tonight, you could say a rosary before you go to bed. God will be with you wherever you are. That's all I have to say, my good friends. I give you all my blessings, and will pray for us all. I'm making a few stops to pass the word along. I need to stop at the nursing home and deliver some gifts, so I'll take my leave of you.'

In a moment of glorious sanctimony, Tommy Blanks, the least religious man in the bar, said, 'How about a prayer, Father?'

More than a few eyes rolled at the request from Blanks, but all agreed that a prayer seemed appropriate.

One book of the Bible in particular stood out to Father Dimer when he thought of the word 'storm'.

'I think an excerpt from the book of Jonah will do, since we are being faced with a storm of, well, epic proportions, so far as we know right now. I once had this piece memorized, but bear with me if I skip a few words. Jonah was in the belly of the great fish for three days and nights when he cried out the Psalm of Thanksgiving:

Into the heart of the storm, the flood enveloped me,
All the breakers and billows passed over me,
The waters swirled about me, threatening my life;
The storm surrounded me.
Down I went and life was closing behind me forever,
When my soul fainted within me and I remembered you.
I cried out for help and you heard my voice.
And my prayer reached your merciful lips,
And you brought me up from that pit.'

The priest finished by saying, 'And after Jonah's prayer, the Lord delivered him from the storm and the great fish.

Thank goodness we only have small fish and big liars in Immaculate. Merry Christmas. Have a safe night.'

Father Dimer turned to go as the crowd said a broken 'Amen' and started to file out of the Legion to prepare for the storm.

Josh Werther washed his hands in the bathroom, shaking his head and cursing in the mirror. He felt his bad Christmas mood settling in against holiday loneliness. The season made him emotional. All day his nerves reacted to the slightest stimulus, and Kathy rubbing his leg and his bumping into Renee had flustered him. He looked in the mirror at his cheerless eyes and felt steam building up behind them. His face paled and his skin was clammy. He slapped water on his face and then scrubbed his hands violently with a bar of soap until a lather foamed. Gritting his teeth at his reflection, he snorted like a bull and built himself up, then suddenly stopped scrubbing and gripped the sides of the sink and hissed, 'What's wrong with you, dammit? Do we have to go through this every year? All because you were too much of a goddamn wimp to . . .'

Ethan Marak tramped into the bathroom but caught only the last few words. Accustomed to hearing cursing on the farm and from listening to stories told by Hank and Blanks, Ethan did not flinch. However, he had never seen anyone talk to himself, even in the mirror. The words sounded like whining to Ethan. Ray preached often and adamantly at Jacob on the subject of whining. But Ethan could not imagine what a banker could possibly have to whine about. He assumed that all bankers were rich because they simply collected money from farmers and people who worked. Ethan walked past and kept quiet.

Josh's eyes had become bloodshot in the two minutes between Kathy touching his leg and Ethan's appearance in the bathroom. Josh shook off the funk he was in and rinsed his hands. He snatched six paper towels out of the dispenser and dried his face aggressively, pressing the towels hard against his cheeks and pulling down on the flesh to look at his eyeballs, and then he scrubbed his forehead and chin.

Josh turned to leave, but paused when he saw Ethan standing at the urinal. The boy looked over at Josh for a split second, then looked back at the plaster in front of him as he finished.

Josh said, 'How are you doing, Ethan?'

'Fine.' Ethan stared at the tiles in the wall.

'Are you wrestling this year?'

Ethan buttoned his pants quickly and said, 'No, I'm a hockey player, not a wrestler.'

'Oh, sorry,' Josh said, nodding. 'I won't accuse you of that again. What about in the spring, what are you going to play? It won't be long now and you'll be in seventh grade, you know.'

Ethan replied, 'Baseball.'

'What position? Shortstop?'

Ethan relaxed. 'No, I can't play shortstop because I'm left-handed. My dad said I'll have to be a pitcher or an outfielder. I wish I was right-handed.'

'Oh? No, no. You've got it all wrong, Ethan. Everyone wants to be a lefty in baseball. Righties are a dime a dozen. Lefties have all the advantages. Your dad is right, you can't play shortstop or third base – but so what? Every other position is open to you: pitching, catching, first base, outfield. There are even some second basemen who are southpaws. And hitting as a lefty is easier. All those right-handed curve balls come towards you instead of away from you, so you can see the ball better. My dad was ready to tie my right arm down until he realized I was naturally left-handed. If nature hadn't made me a left-hander he was going to turn me into one.'

'You're left-handed, too? What do you play?'

Josh put his hands on his hips and inhaled proudly. 'Well, I don't play baseball any more, but I used to pitch and catch for Immaculate. I played baseball with your dad, you know. Now I just play softball, but I still pitch. It's the best place to be on the field. If you pitch or catch, you get to be involved in every single play. That's where all the action is at. If the pitcher and catcher do their job, the outfielders get to pick their nose and name the shapes of the clouds.'

'Pick their nose!' Ethan laughed. If that were the case, Jacob would some day be an All American outfielder.

'But you need good outfielders, too. Even the best pitcher can use a diving catch from time to time.'

Josh wanted to go on talking to Ethan but he heard a rumbling of feet overhead, as if everyone in the Legion bar had risen from their seats at once. Josh looked at the ceiling, then down at Ethan, who also seemed bewildered by the sound above. Together they made their way to the staircase to return upstairs. Josh put his arm on Ethan's shoulder as they walked.

Looking up, Josh said, 'I wonder what's going on.'

Ethan shrugged and assumed that Jacob had caused the commotion, perhaps with a fire. They ascended the stairs and in the doorway met a married couple wearing matching snow-mobiling jackets.

'Why is everyone leaving?' asked Josh.

The man, whose lapel read 'Eddie', was the acting leader of the snowmobile club. He puffed on a Swisher Sweet wood-tip cigar and said, 'Father Dimer just told us the weather report. Let me sum it up for you in one word: Terrible.'

'Oh yeah?'

'Times like this,' Eddie said, 'I'd rather live in Rio. Some day I'm going there for Christmas.'

Josh briefly wondered how Eddie knew of any city, state, or country beyond Immaculate. His entire impression of the man changed in an instant.

'I think I'll join you,' Josh said. 'Take care, Eddie.'

'You betcha.'

Ethan looked up at Josh with an admiring smile and said, 'See you later!'

Josh tousled his hair with his fingers and his eyes followed the boy with affection.

Hank Murphy pulled his jacket on as he walked towards the door and Blanks followed two steps behind. When Hank saw Ethan looking up at Josh, he paused for a moment and then staggered at the sight of the two together. Before he could place his thoughts, Blanks bumped into him from behind.

'Jumpin' Jesus, move your ass already.'

Father Dimer, on his way out the door, said, 'I heard that, Mr Blanks.'

'Sorry, Father.' Then to Hank, he said, 'Way to go, dip-shit. Now Father has to pray for me because of you.'

Father Dimer laughed and waved to the ploughmen. 'Be safe tonight.'

Hank started moving forward again but took his time to look down at Ethan as the boy swam against the current of adults heading to the exit. After Ethan passed, Hank moved towards Josh and looked closely at Josh's face. Josh returned the look, but Hank said nothing and brushed past his shoulder, although he could have avoided him. Josh moved aside to let Blanks pass. He seemed in a great hurry to leave.

Ray collected his winnings and stuffed the unclean money into his pocket with regret. He had won nearly every round.

'The weather made you lucky, Ray,' said the doctor. 'Or are you and Dimer working a racket together?'

Ray smiled and turned away from the bar to join his wife and Ben at the table. Renee picked up her jacket from the chair and gave her father a hug. She felt the extra squeeze and read his thoughts. She separated from him and held him by the arms and said, 'Everyone will make it home, Dad. We'll still have a good Christmas, I promise. They'll be here before the storm.'

Ben pulled Renee towards him for a second hug, then shook Ray's hand and said with damp eyes, 'Duty calls.'

Ray agreed in Immaculate terms. 'Yep. Yep.'

Renee said, 'Drive carefully, Dad.'

'Yep. I'll see you later.'

Ben Masterson walked towards the exit to catch up to Hank and Blanks, who were already waiting impatiently outside the front door in a grumbling Chevy pickup with custom red and white trim from bumper to bumper. It had a shiny red snowplough attached to the front and on the side door was written 'Immaculate Snowplow'.

6

The day quickened as the news of the storm passed from household to household. Storms brought to Immaculate a strange sense of isolation and connectedness. Each household huddled under the storm separately, but everyone suffered together. To the surrounding cities, Immaculate seemed like a place full of simpletons, a Catholic town twenty years behind the times. But the stubbornness that kept Immaculate behind the times also made its people resilient. Sons and daughters of Immaculate who ventured to Minneapolis often returned after feeling out of place, having bored their urban friends with tales made up in winter houses over card games, stories that pertained only to that tiny culture occupying twenty square miles of fields and lakes. And those who never ventured past the county line found it preferable for the surrounding world to think of Immaculate as backward and undesirable, because it kept the local hunting and fishing unspoiled.

In the first few hours after the priest's announcement, families visited those relatives they were still speaking to, particularly the elderly, to make sure they had candles and their windows were sealed. The younger generation disguised their inspections as holiday kindness, while the elderly rebuked their children for snooping and dusted off stories of storms, epic winds and snowdrifts that surely dwarfed whatever drizzle was on its way. Many of their stories came from the '30s and '40s, before the widespread use of generators and portable heaters: tales of entire families sleeping in a single bed, about whole herds of cattle flash-frozen to death, of finding deer hiding out in hog sheds. Whatever Immaculate was currently facing, surely they'd seen worse. The listeners nodded, doubtfully.

Endurance and perseverance were common themes in Father Dimer's sermons. Publicly and privately, he often said a short prayer of persistence. Before the storm, various people recited the prayer – some said only a single line, some said the whole thing. The brief verses had turned into local maxims, but the origin of the prayer was a grave secret, one that Father Dimer could never admit, least of all to his peers in the priesthood. The words came from Epicurus. Father Dimer said the prayer now, as he drove back to the church.

> 'Nothing to fear in God,
> Nothing to fear in death,
> Evil can be endured,
> Goodness can be attained:
> Jesus helps me and I am strong.'

The priest's little car wound along the thin roads leading from Immaculate to the country church. He passed a tractor pulling a manure spreader and gave a three-finger wave to the farmboy in the tractor cab. The farmboy returned the gesture, flinging mud from the tractor tyres on to the priest's windshield. A trail of mud clearly marked the tractor's route from the road to the field where he had spread his freight.

Another car passed Father Dimer, but the driver's failure to wave told the priest that he or she was from out of town, either lost, passing through, or home from afar for the holidays.

He arrived at the church and waved at the church caretaker, who stood on a stepladder and appeared to be checking the stained-glass windows for something. John Delaney was a mentally disabled man with one eyebrow protruding and a zipper scar down the left side of his chin. He had not always been the church caretaker, or mentally disabled. Five years before, he had been unloading corn into an auger connected to a spinning shaft on his tractor. He wore a hooded sweatshirt with shoestrings around the neck and when he leaned over the power take-off, one of the dangling shoestrings touched the spinning device and wound around the metal shaft as if it was a spool, and John wound around the shaft, too. In a split second his head struck the spinning shaft one, two, three, four, five times and he was knocked unconscious. The force ripped his sweatshirt in half and flung him on to the ground. The spinning steel had cut through his face like a blunt knife and had caused major trauma to his brain. John slept in a coma while his wounds healed. When he came to, his family's initial elation subsided as the change in his personality became apparent. Shortly after John returned home the farm was insolvent and his wife was on the verge of murder. Father Dimer, who foresaw the collapse, spent many hours with the Delaney family during the ordeal, and decided to hire John. His wife took a job at the Immaculate Bakery and stayed with John for a while, but he had a hard time remembering her or anything else and in the end she left town with the kids in tow, and never returned. Whether John noticed their departure Father Dimer couldn't be sure.

Under John's care, the church stayed spotless, despite being located at a point where five roads met. He painted the entire building twice a year, using his own money to put on the second coat. There was speculation that yet another coat might cause the church to fall in on itself. He willingly acted as janitor, maid, laundryman, interior designer and altar boy. A few women were upset by John's diligence (historically the women came together once a month to clean the church), but most were happy about it – as were the men to have been spared the painting of the exterior.

When John saw Father Dimer's car, he climbed down from the ladder and limped over to greet him.

'I was just checking for a draught on the third window there. Don't want people getting cold in here, now do I, Father?'

Father Dimer patted John on the shoulder. 'Good work, John. But I think it might be a small crowd tonight.'

'Small crowd?' John asked incredulously. 'But it's Christmas!'

The priest explained the coming storm and John fretted during the entire narration and became visibly agitated when the priest said he had advised the parish to stay in their homes for the night.

'But it can't be, Father. Not tonight.'

'It's unfortunate, yes. But we have to think of safety. Don't worry, John, there will still be Mass tonight, even if it's just you and me.'

The two of them went into the church, John following

Father Dimer's every footstep. Together they consecrated the hosts for those people who would be stopping by for Communion. Tired of him stepping on his feet, Father Dimer suggested that John finish decorating the manger scene while he finished up the consecration alone.

John wrung his hands and asked, 'Now there, Father, I know that I should know this, but . . . now there, I don't know the order of things for the manger.'

'What do you mean by "the order"?'

John's face turned red as he said, 'Now I don't know what to do at all. I don't know which is the order, and now there God help me if I'm not a sinner of the worst way for not knowing, since I've done it for years now there.'

Recalling last year's conversations with John, and well versed in his anxiety over the customs of the Roman Catholic Church, Father Dimer nodded and asked, 'Do you mean the placement of the statues?'

'That's it,' John said, frowning. 'That – and every other else about it. I mean now, look at all of these animals here, and where to begin wrangling them? See there, I don't want the Lord watching me put the donkey in the place of a Wise Man, or a Wise Man in the place of a donkey, and then when I die having to 'splain why I made a Wise Man into a ass, or I mean a barn animal, sir. You see now there, I started putting the sheep and cows in there, where they are supposed to be "lowing" and such, but I'm not sure what a cow is actually doing when she is lowing. See this feller cow here now – I put her in here and she's lowing as I imagine what lowing is. But then I stopped what I was doing to wait until you came back so that I wouldn't mess up the lowing or the swaddling or the waffling, and all those other words that only a holy man like yourself understands.'

'I think that is exactly where the cow was lowing when Jesus was born. Though perhaps not a Holstein like the statues we have.'

John brushed off the compliment and walked over to the manger scene with the priest following behind. Father Dimer couldn't help grinning while listening to John discuss the three-foot-tall statues.

'But Father, that cow over there is only one piece of the manger scene. I have four cows and ten sheep! Worse yet, which cow was closest to Jesus? Or was a sheep closer? Was there a sheep looking in at Jesus, standing very close, over there here now, wondering what was in the basket next to Mary? Maybe the sheep was just hungry? Or could the cows and sheep possibly be mingling around together? Not that I've ever seen sheep and cattle in cahoots. What kind of farmer would allow such a thing? A cow could kick a sheep and kill it. Not to mention a cow could bump into Mary, the ever-blessed Virgin. If I were Joseph, I would have chased all those damn cows outside, and the sheep too, cold or not – even chased the sheepherders out for bringing those damn animals in there at all. Pardon me, Father, but if God put me in that manger I would have bounced them all. Guess that's why it's a good thing I wasn't there when it happened, because the manger scene would have had only three people in it: Joseph, Mary and the baby Jesus, with me standing outside holding a pitchfork in the doorway. Look at this statue here now, Father. This one looks like the sheep is eating something. There isn't a trough or bucket anywhere to be found in the scene. I had a thought then, Father. Maybe the ten sheep mean somethin'– like the Ten Commandments, could it be now here? And the cows represent something else – four of something. Then I thought – the four Gospels of Matthew, Mark, Luke and John. So I thought I might put in front of each cow a little Bible opened to one of the Gospels. See this cow here kind of looks like Mark Spurlock, you know, who lives in town and only comes to church on Christmas and Easter, so I thought this cow could be reading the gospel of Mark. And this cow statue here is my favourite, so I thought maybe she could be lowing over the gospel of John. Lowing over John 3:16 maybe, now. I would say this cow is lowing, don't you think?'

Father Dimer rubbed his chin as if he were considering the options, though really he was using his hand to cover his bursting smile. With an air of authority, he said, 'No question about it. That cow is absolutely lowing.'

John continued. 'But the real reason I stopped setting up the manger, Father, is because I don't know who goes in first. I thought, there now for a minute, that maybe baby Jesus should be first in the manger, because he is the most important feller of all. But then I realized that really Jesus arrived last of all since he came with Mary, inside her now there, the blessed Virgin, of course. Now in town, at the feed store when I used to buy feed, they told me about "Last In, First Out" and "First In, First Out" so I tried to think of the order I would put them in so I could take them out, and Lord have mercy on me I don't want to muck it up and have a sheep getting kicked by a cow that's lowing over the Gospel, or have a hungry-looking sheep staring down at our Lord and Saviour infantile Jesus Christ.'

The priest put his head down on to his chest and his eyes danced, but he composed himself and walked past John to the manger scene. He folded his arms and put his fist up to his pursed lips and said, 'I have to tell you, John. I remember it distinctly now – *ahem* – the order, that is. I'm sorry I didn't tell you earlier, because the placement is very important. The order was declared many years ago, in a famous meeting that became known as the Swaddling Schism of 1517. It was very controversial and the argument has never truly been settled. They decided in the end that the order of placement is: Cows, Joseph, Mary, Jesus, Sheep, Sheepherders. And the Wise Men are last.'

John said in amazement, 'The Wise Men are last?'

'Well, they arrived after Jesus was born. Remember the star? They followed the star and . . .'

'Of course!' John replied. 'Oh shit, I'm a fool!'

'Now, John Delaney – we talked about you saying that word.'

'Pardon me, Father. I mean to say, "I'm forgetful on occasion."'

'That's right – just like everybody else. I'm forgetful, you're forgetful. Jesus was a person like us; he was probably a little forgetful, too. No one is a fool, John, unless he tells himself he is, and you are certainly not a fool. You are a smart man with a creative mind. The idea of four cows and four Gospels and ten sheep and the Ten Commandments was brilliant. Not many people could make that leap. But the cows actually do not need any little Bibles to read. The cows and sheep are reminders of humble beginnings for the son of God. And you know cows better than I do, John. They are happy to be sitting in a warm place with some hay. We'll just put some hay by their feet instead of Bibles.'

John said out loud while he pointed his finger, 'Cows, Joseph, Mary, Jesus, Sheepherders, Sheep, Wise Men.'

'Exactly.' Father Dimer lifted and dropped his hand. 'Perfect.'

John remained discontent and asked if the priest could use pennies to mark the individual spots for each statue, but Father Dimer encouraged him to get started and said he would come back to make any adjustments if needed.

'Now there, I don't know, now here.' John shook his head.

Father Dimer grabbed John's shoulders and said, 'John, you've done this for six years. You're a natural at setting up the manger scene. I receive many compliments on it every year.'

John smiled and repeated the order of characters as he carefully picked up a statue of a cow.

Father Dimer walked back to the altar and finished blessing the wine. As he raised the chalice to the heavens, he said the blessing quietly and lowered it back to the altar. Just as he finished his blessing, the front door of the church opened and in came the first family for early Communion. Father Dimer motioned them to come forward as he picked up the golden bowl that held the Communion hosts. It was Ray and Renee Marak with the two boys in tow.

7

'I need this tyre on this truck. Now, not later,' Hank Murphy said, raising his voice over the Led Zeppelin song on the radio.

'What's with you?' an employee answered. 'Why are you giving me such a hard time? I already greased every piece of equipment in here.'

Hank winked at the employee and yelled so that the others in the shop could hear, 'Because you're the only one here that has a clue about the price of goddamn tea in China.'

Ben Masterson slid out from under a dump truck to say, 'Hey! I resemble that.'

The first employee said, 'Or the price of rice in Russia.'

'Or shit from Shinola,' added Hank.

'What's *Shinola*?'

'It's boot polish,' said Hank. 'And real quick someone is going to have it on the seat of their trousers after my boot connects with his ass. Let's get this stuff done.'

The others protested in chorus that Hank Murphy of all people shouldn't complain about bad help, given his own employment history before he and Blanks had started Immaculate Snowplow. Several of his employees had worked on jobs with Hank. One of them said, 'Need I remind you of Bob Barry's pole shed?'

'That's completely different.' Hank laughed. 'I was under

the influence of lust. I was sixteen. And she was a good Christian girl. She was.' He nudged one of the guys standing next to him. 'But I'll tell you one thing: Miss Barry was so familiar with breaking bread that she quickly learned how to part buns.'

The others asked about Bob Barry's pole shed, but Hank directed their attention away from his prodigal adventures. The storm warning had changed his demeanour, and while he was still able to make jokes, he was nervous, thinking about the safety of his workers and the state of the equipment. Moreover, he wanted to handle the storm without error in order to seal future contracts and help expand the business. Over the years, business acumen had developed in Hank. But he remained deathly afraid of becoming an overbearing boss.

'I just want to get this stuff done so you all can get a few hours of sleep before tonight. Maybe a Christmas poke with your wives – who knows?'

One of the men asked, 'Is that us getting the poke or you?'

'Hey, come on now,' said Hank. 'I'm no swinger. Unless Shirley wants to. Has she said anything about me?'

The man held up a crescent wrench as if he were going to strike Hank with it. 'I should use this on you for that comment.'

Hank moved away quickly. 'Damn, you're sick, man. Use it on Shirley, poor girl. Count me out.'

The men laughed. A woman named Shelly also drove a plough for Hank and Blanks, and she laughed as much as any of the men. Shelly and Tommy Blanks had started dating recently and the two of them stood behind the group, playing with each other's hands and bumping hips. Blonde pigtails came down to her shoulders. She wore a flannel shirt and a puffy blaze-orange vest. She wore her hair in pigtails because Blanks had asked her to after they had showered together that morning.

Blanks stopped flirting for a moment and asked, 'Did anyone fix that gasket on number twelve yet?'

The muffled voice of Ben Masterson came from underneath the truck he would be driving that night. 'I fixed it.' Ben continued his inspection of the vehicle.

'Good man.'

Ben mumbled, 'I deserve a raise.'

'I want two inspections on each truck,' said Hank, turning serious again. 'Let's just do it and be done with it. Everybody has done their own truck inspection already, now everybody get under another truck and go through the checklist again. Tonight's not going to be an easy walk if you get marooned somewhere. Let's take twenty minutes to check everything over, and then we'll break until six o'clock.'

The crew grumbled and slowly dispersed. Tommy Blanks played buddy to Hank Murphy's leader, making an effective partnership, like a sergeant and a captain. Blanks was less confrontational than Hank and allowed him the final word in company decisions. He knew of Hank's plans to grow the business and pursue further city and county contracts. Immaculate Snowplow had come a long way since Hank and Blanks had used their Toyota pickups to plough driveways for extra beer money. The latest purchase, several new dump trucks, had doubled the company debt. Blanks ceased to concentrate on the costs of running the business and focused on scheduling and hiring. He asked only that Hank inform him if the business was going bankrupt so that he could flee to Mexico with a few thousand dollars. As both men aged, they started looking towards a future they had tried in earnest to avoid for most of their lives. Even retirement began to slip into their thoughts at night. Planning, hard work and responsibility – notions once anathema to them – were quickly becoming sacred. In some respects their former excesses had made them wise.

Wise in some ways. Blanks put his finger in the back belt loop of Shelly's pants and pulled her towards him. She smiled as he whispered in her ear, 'About our nap break – your place or mine?'

She smiled at him. 'Mine. Your place is a mess.'

'Well, you helped.'

Blanks beamed, unsure if it was love or infatuation that had him. He had survived love and its derivatives many times but marvelled every time at the feeling. Hank marvelled at how fast the fool could be smitten.

The men carried out their inspections and handed the inspection sheets to Hank, who looked them over meticulously before excusing each man. He addressed every detail on the inspection sheets and decided to stay and personally make the final adjustments to the trucks. He was surprised to see Blanks slipping out the back door with Shelly, ass in hand.

'Blanks!'

The door swung shut. Hank walked in the opposite direction, towards the front door, to catch the two lovebirds as they left the parking lot. When Shelly's Chevy Blazer came around the building, Hank put his hands up in the air to protest. Shelly stopped the vehicle and Blanks rolled down his window.

Hank said, 'Three words: W.T.F.?'

Blanks understood the abbreviation well (he had coined it). 'What do you mean?'

'I mean just that: W.T.F?'

'We're going on break. Aren't you?'

Hank shook his head, but relented. 'All right, fine. But be back in an hour or so. This is a big night. How we handle it means a lot.'

'Means a lot for who?' Blanks asked. 'The good people of Immaculate or for Immaculate Snowplow?'

'Oh, come on. You know better than to ask that.' Hank bobbed his head. 'For the children, of course.'

Blanks laughed and then turned his body to block the window so that only Hank could see his hands. He started by rubbing the tips of his index fingers together, then he pushed his palms together rhythmically, with his mouth open in ecstasy. Then he gave Hank a big nod followed by two thumbs up and a smile.

'I know what you're doing, Blanks,' Shelly said with bravado. 'You're so discreet.'

'What?' Blanks objected. 'We have a secret handshake!'

'Mm-hm,' Shelly said. 'I can hear your palms squishing together. And what the heck is "W.T.F.?" Is that some code for a threesome? You guys are sick.'

'No!' Blanks said, and then added, 'Why? Never mind. Let's go before Hank tries to climb in the truck.'

Shelly sped out of the parking lot, leaving Hank standing there.

*

Inside the pickup, Ray Marak passed his gambling winnings to Renee as if it were drug money. She rolled her eyes and knew that Ray's Catholic guilt was burning in him. The gambling itself did not bother Ray as much as getting caught by Father Dimer. Renee counted the bills, and Ray said, 'I don't even want to know how much.'

Renee said, 'Oh, good heavens, Ray. You had a lucky day. You should be happy! It's already a good Christmas with this.'

Ray said, 'We should give it to the church.'

'Ah – excuse me? How about we give it to the feed store, Ray?' She shot a piercing look at him. The money was enough to make the 1 January payment. Ray nodded and drove to the feed store. Renee handed the wad of bills back to her husband, and after running into the feed store, Ray drove straight to the church to receive early Communion, although he had every intention of getting his family to midnight Mass, even if it meant taking the tractor.

Jacob had fallen asleep in the truck almost instantly, finally exhausted. He dreamed about the seed planet. It was a place only he and Tippy knew about.

A cruel giant ruled the seed planet. He ruled over a group of turtles called Tumblers, and when the giant slept, the Tumblers stole seeds from him. They used the seeds as coins for gambling. All Tumblers, without exception, had bad habits. Every Tumbler had bloodshot eyes, as they never stopped for foolish things like sleep or church. They played games incessantly, games like Wolla-Wolla-Burr and Timber-bobble. They admired the best swindler. Late at night, the

Tumblers tended to grow increasingly irresponsible and squirrelly. And they were famous for their ability to fib, trick and sneak their way out of any trouble.

8

The Ford pickup vibrated on a washboard gravel road that led to the Solemnity of Mary Church. The boys sat between Ray and Renee in the front seat. The rattle awakened Jacob, who had drooled on Ethan's shoulder. When he tried to fall asleep again, the seed planet dream disappeared. Ray turned off the truck's engine. Renee tickled Jacob but he kept his eyes shut.

Renee said, 'Looks like one sleepyhead needs a good long nap when he gets home.'

'I'm awake.' He opened his eyes. 'Just pretending, Mommy.'

He crawled out of the truck and ran to catch up to Ethan, who had already started to climb the twenty-four steps to the arching doorway. Above it, engraved in stone, were the words 'Annunciation – Conception – Assumption', to remind those entering of the church's patron, the Virgin Mary. The spire of the steeple was fifty feet above the ground. An unspoken rule of earlier generations was that the church spire should be the high point of the region, but with the advent of farm silos the rule had been quietly forgotten.

Father Dimer motioned to the family to approach the altar. Renee snatched the hood of Jacob's jacket before he could run. Jacob choked and stuck his tongue out and she glared down at him with pursed lips. 'Santa saw that,' she whispered.

Jacob knew that the solemnity of the church prevented his parents from doling out punishment there and then, but he also knew that any misbehaviour would guarantee the heavy hand of his father later, and the fun was hardly worth the spanking.

Father Dimer said to Renee, 'The Body of Christ.'

'Amen.' She opened her mouth for the priest to set the host on her tongue.

The priest turned to Ray. 'The Body of Christ.'

'Amen.' Ray held his hands out, one on top of the other, to receive the host. The priest did the same for Ethan, and then turned to Jacob, who stood with his mouth wide open and his arms flat at his sides waiting for the priest to serve him. The priest gave Jacob a curious look and said, 'Did the dentist teach you that method of receiving Communion?'

Jacob said, 'Yes!' He left his mouth agape.

The priest said, 'Remember how we showed you to hold your hands? One on top of the other, like Ethan does.'

Jacob held his mouth open and averted his eyes to look at Ray and he saw a stare that preached hellfire. Jacob shut his teeth with a clatter and placed his hands in the proper position.

The priest said, 'The Body of Christ.'

'Amen!'

The priest set the host down gently on Jacob's palm and Jacob tossed it into his maw like a potato chip and gulped it down.

Father Dimer turned back to Ethan, who reminded the

priest of himself as a boy, quiet and bookish, serious in church and school – moderately depressed. He asked Ethan, 'Have you been enjoying your Christmas break?'

Ethan answered, 'Yep.'

'I suppose you have already received your report card, yes?'

'Yep.'

As Father Dimer tried to think of a more open-ended question for the laconic boy, a loud noise from the manger scene interrupted him. The priest, Ray and Renee all turned their attention away from Ethan to look at John Delaney.

Frowning, John picked up a cow statue he had knocked over. Father Dimer offered a reassuring look, and it dawned on him to let Ethan and Jacob assist with the manger scene, something the boys were more than happy to do.

Renee asked Father Dimer about the books he had read recently. Ray listened carefully, only showing interest when the priest showed interest. Ray hated to sit in one place and read. The priest named a few books he had finished recently, all of which Renee had read.

'I'm tackling Joyce again,' Father Dimer said. '*Ulysses*. It's my third attempt but I'm determined to suffer until I actually comprehend it or am committed to an institution.'

'Yuck,' said Renee. 'Why bother?'

'Well, I imagine myself pretending to enjoy it some day. But I have to read it in such small portions. I still can't decide if he was a genius or just nuts. The style is a real struggle for me, though I suppose I can appreciate the effort. I just assume I'm the one lacking imagination.'

'No,' Renee said, 'I think madness was clearly the case,

Father. Anyone who writes a forty-page sentence cannot be serious. What you should read instead is *The Shining*.'

The priest nodded. 'I'm trying to avoid Stephen King, but I may have to give it a try.'

'I love a straight story,' Renee said. 'I suffocate under symbols. I don't want to trade my story for symbols. With Jacob I can only keep one eye on the book and one eye on him. Everything has to be practical. Give me a story, entertain me, a little sugar – hold the sap. I read a lot, but I don't dig; I don't have the time for that.'

'I think I know what you mean.' Father Dimer chuckled. 'I do the same thing with the New Testament. Sometimes I feel that looking too deep, too far past the surface story makes fools of men, since the simple answer is usually floating on top. I don't expect to have all the answers when I am eighty years old, even after a lifetime of study, but I will be repeating the same simple stories I learned as a boy. That's the power of fables and parables: the understanding is immediate. The parables use symbols within our reach. In fact, the spread of the church was realized by the simplicity of the parables, because Christians could easily memorize them and pass them on. But with the parables we can also draw relationships to our own lives. Like the "Sower of Grain" parable that starts: "Once there was a man who went out to sow grain, and as he scattered the seed in the field, some of it fell along the path and soon the birds came and ate it up." From the first line we can see the pictures in our mind. We have seen these things ourselves.'

Renee asked, 'But isn't there endless confusion about the parables?'

'Oh yes, but mostly only among adults, like myself.' He smiled. 'But like you said, Renee, and I agree, looking too deep tends to generate more confusion than is necessary when the message can be understood by children who have heard the words for the very first time. It's only when we become adults that we make things difficult. Funny that we stumbled on to this topic. Only yesterday I was talking to another person about miracles and parables. Let's see, how did he put it? Referring to the Wedding Feast at Cana, this fellow said to me, "Why did Jesus keep the kegger going?" In other words, how was it appropriate for Jesus to increase the amount of wine at the wedding feast when they were already drunk. He argued that the addition of more wine would only increase the amount of sin and Jesus might have been better off to "uninvent" alcohol. I told him that his confusion was justified. I've read various opinions on that story. Jesus did that miracle at the beginning of his ministry to reveal his glory, and his disciples began to believe in him. But I think there is another lesson in it. If you recall Jesus' personal life, he did not shy away from the realities of the world; he did not label the people at the party evil, nor did he hole up in some monastery and meditate. No, he participated; he was in the game, playing every quarter and position. He was at all the best parties, with the beggars, the swindlers, the fools. He was out in the world. But he did not judge. It sounds simple. Ha! Simple, but nearly impossible in practice. It is a rare day that I don't fail by noon. The only people whom Jesus did judge were the Pharisees – who themselves judged everyone, labelled everyone, and told everyone how bad they were. Happiness was the enemy of the Pharisees and

Jesus was its protector. Weddings are happy gatherings, and wine is a wedding staple. The joining together of people in celebration is not something to be upset about, like some folks are these days. We should appreciate any gathering that celebrates life in a positive way. That, as I see it, is the "why" to the wine at the wedding.'

'Who was asking you about that particular miracle?'

'I shouldn't tell you that.'

Ray said, 'It sounds like something Tommy Blanks would say. I've heard him talk about that parable at least twenty times. I think he is still looking for an excuse to party.'

Father Dimer shrugged his shoulders but smiled.

'I have a good one for you to read, Father: *Elbow Room*,' said Renee. 'I'll stop by to drop it off some time this week.' Renee changed her voice to a Southern accent. 'It's all about the South, by a gentleman named McPherson. He was from Savannah, Georgia. You know the South, Father? It's that hot place so far away that always seems so full of trouble. Excuse me, Father, did I just pass judgment? Why, I've never even been past the Mason–Dixon line. Just thinking about that heat makes me feel faint.'

'Trouble in the South!' Father Dimer laughed. 'Great, I can't wait. Thank you, Miss Scarlett.'

Ray wondered if Renee felt at all hypocritical standing in front of the priest after taking the pill. Did she have any remorse? Probably not. She was like that. He couldn't think of the word for it, but 'progressive' was not the label he wanted. His initial anger at seeing the pills had subsided, but he wondered how long she had been taking them. She knew that getting his forgiveness was easier than getting his permission.

Meanwhile, the boys and John worked on constructing the Nativity, but every time they placed a sheep or a Wise Man somewhere, John scratched his head.

'Oh, I don't know about that, I don't think . . . no . . . now, boys.'

Soon all of the pieces were in the right places, but John continued to fuss. He considered starting again because the boys had not followed the proper sequence. He asked Ethan to move the Wise Men to the other side. Jacob had placed five of the sheep statues directly around the baby Jesus, including the hungry-looking one. John threw his hands up behind his neck and said, 'Jacob, what have you done?'

Jacob said, 'I thought Jesus might want some friends.'

'Good night! Not the hungry sheep!' John stepped forward and knocked over Melchior, but Ethan reached out his foot and caught the statue before it struck the floor. John did not pause: he made a beeline for the hungry sheep and plucked the statue from the herd surrounding the baby Jesus.

He scolded the sheep. 'You are not that hungry, now there, Mr Sheep.'

Jacob said, 'How do you know if he's hungry or not?'

'Well, look at him, now there,' John scoffed. 'With his mouth open and teeth all sticking out. This feller is ready for a meal.'

'I thought he was singing.'

'Singing!' John scoffed again. 'A sheep can't sing. Little

boy, you must not know very many sheep, but let me assure you that I wouldn't want to hear the music they would make.'

'I think I can hear him,' Jacob said. 'He's singing a song from the radio.'

'The radio!' John leaned backward and then forward.

'Yes. Listen closely. It's an Elvis song, isn't it?'

'Elvis!'

'Shh! Listen! I can hear it really good. The sheep is singing that one song.'

'What song?'

'That one.'

'Which one?'

'"Devil in Disguise."' Jacob started to sing and mimic Elvis by shaking a leg. '*You're the devil in disguise, oh yes you are, devil in disguise, ooh-oo-oo . . .*'

John shifted the hungry sheep under his right arm and with his left hand covered Jacob's mouth. John said, 'Go away, little boy, now there, you are a bad seed!'

'Seed!' Jacob squeaked. 'I am a seed! And you're not a seed at all. You go away!'

'You go away!' John whispered harshly.

'You dry up.'

Flustered, John said, 'Oh, you are a little Damien child, here now there. I should give you a good one . . . now there, I should give you one . . . or two, even . . .'

Jacob started an auctioneer chant: 'What do you want to give me for it, here now there, I got one, I'll take two for it, now three, got four over there, got a bid from the hungry sheep, take five from Ethan in the back there, Wise Man – thank you, six-fifty now seven . . .'

Ray overheard the commotion and said to Father Dimer, 'Excuse me, I'm going to put the brakes on Jacob.'

Jacob continued auctioneering with his back turned to his approaching father. 'I have eight dollars here now, there nine, now nine, there nine, throw me a bone, now nine-and-a-half from the Virgin Mary, thank you, Virgin, now the hungry sheep, now ten, now eleven to the Elvis sheep, thank you very much—'

Ray seized the back of Jacob's neck with a powerful grip, reducing the auction to a wheeze. 'Sold! To the hungry sheep for twelve doll—' Ray squeezed harder and ended the bidding altogether.

His face beet-red, John said, 'He's a bad boy, that one. He put the hungry sheep by Jesus!'

Not sure who made less sense, Ray said, 'He is being a bad boy. Aren't you, Jacob? I think he'll be quiet until we get home. Won't you, Jacob?'

Jacob thought of saying something funny about the next item up for bid being a spanking, but kept quiet when the grip on his neck tightened even more, and instead nodded with conviction until he could breathe again.

Ray felt he had already let Jacob act up one too many times. Both the morning nudity and the herbicide meddling warranted a spanking, and with this, Jacob had a hat-trick for the day. Ray escorted him back to the altar.

Father Dimer asked what Jacob had been doing, and when Ray explained the mock auction, Father chuckled and gave Jacob a speech on the importance of the manger scene. Trying to get bids from the holy family was disrespectful. He told Jacob that in a year's time he could be an altar boy like

Ethan, but only if he could behave. Meanwhile, Ethan helped John restore order to the manger.

Father Dimer instructed Jacob to take a pew. The boy kneeled with his eyes closed and his hands folded in prayer.

Ray apologized: 'Just our daily affirmation that he's a naughty boy. I think all of the intelligence ended up in Ethan.'

Father Dimer asked, 'Was his auctioneering any good?'

The comment surprised Ray. 'Actually, now that you mention it, he was doing pretty well.'

Father Dimer said, 'It's not always easy to see the unique talents in kids, but it's always in there somewhere, Ray.'

'His teachers have all gone insane at school.' Renee pushed her hair over her ear. 'Honestly, I don't even know how to handle him sometimes.'

'Oh, that one will grow up and do something well,' Father Dimer said. 'He's got the spark.' Father Dimer noticed the clock in the rear of the church. 'Oh, you better get going. Get ready for tonight. Don't try to drive if it gets too bad. Ray.'

'What?'

'Did you hear me, Ray?'

'Of course I did.'

'Ray. If the roads are bad . . .'

'Yep. Yep, okay.'

Ray nodded but he intended to make the midnight Mass. Renee turned around and saw Jacob with his chin on the back of the pew in front, praying. She nudged Ray. Both parents doubted he was in prayer, and they were correct: he was thinking about gambling turtles.

The family said their goodbyes to the priest and waved to John, who gave everyone a smile but tried to avoid the eyes of the evil child. He held the hungry sheep in his arms, still trying to decide where to place the statue.

As the Maraks exited the church, John looked down at the hungry sheep with concern. Like an inspector, he turned the sheep from side to side to examine the different aspects, and, after deliberation, mumbled, 'Now there, call me a monkey's uncle. Maybe this dog-gone sheep *is* singing.'

9

Josh Werther was fuming. He did not say a word to Kathy until they arrived back at the bank. She followed behind him, asking several times why he had become so upset at the Legion.

'What's wrong, Josh?'

He ground his teeth and shook his head while marching up to a side entrance of the bank.

'What is the matter?'

He fumbled with his keys, and then flung open the side door and walked swiftly towards his office. He grabbed his coat to leave for the day and started to lock his desk drawers.

'Oh, come on,' she said in disbelief, fuelling his ire. Kathy leaned against his doorway, no longer concerned about the tear in her skirt. With her arms folded, she watched Josh complete his spasmodic search.

She said, 'What kind of man throws a tantrum at a little flirting under the table?' She leered at him as he dropped his keys. When he straightened up, his face was flushed with blood and the smart look on Kathy's face drove him over an edge. She tapped her fingers on her folded arms until Josh yanked her into his office and shut the door, quietly but firmly. Her smirk turned into a grimace as Josh pushed her towards the chair across from his desk.

'Sit down.'

'Pardon me?' Kathy asked. 'You must have just hit your head on something, because you don't tell me what to—'

Josh turned to her, with his cheeks fully blossomed. 'Quiet, you!'

'Oh, you are nuts.' She laughed in disbelief. 'You are shit-nuts if you think—'

Josh cut her off by pointing his index finger at her nose. 'What were you thinking? I want to know. *Were* you even thinking?'

'I was thinking . . . thinking that you were *sane*.' Then she poked at him again with the word 'Crazy'.

'Enough of your mouth. Listen up. Half of my clientele was at the Legion, and if any of them saw you feeling up my leg under the table, by tomorrow everyone in the whole town of Immaculate will know about it.'

She crinkled her forehead and squinted. 'So?'

'So?' he mocked. 'So do you know that half the town already hates me for foreclosing on six farms this year? Do you know that certain people would rather see me hung in the street than have a bank teller hang on me? I already have a reputation. They think I'm a wolf, when all I am is someone whose job requires some math. And next year is going to be worse than this year, and the year after that worse still, but of course that doesn't matter to you. Every farm in the area might go under. Some bankers are already getting death threats, and, frankly, I don't want that kind of attention. Understand? Do you know what the word *crisis* means?'

'Dear God, two syllables! I have no idea.'

'Plus I hate Christmas. Every year I hate the season, and

I just try to get through it so that I can get back to life, in this God-awful town where I am so hated.'

'I understand, Josh.' Kathy covered her eyes while stifling her urge to laugh and then let her hand slide down her face and neck until her hand rested over her heart. 'Yes, I see it now. The hardships you've suffered, Josh. It's . . . it's nothing short of a modern tragedy. I see it now, this burden you bear, this *millstone* around your neck! And how could I be so blind, so callous, as to overlook a living martyr? Who would ever think the economy would impact you, when you've chosen banking as a career? I'm . . . I am truly stunned. And you don't believe in Santa Claus? Join me in prayer, Josh. What will become of society when there is nothing to believe in? My dear Atlas Werther, is nothing sacred any more?' Her satirical tone changed. 'You're a neurotic child, Josh!'

'And I think if you need sex that bad,' said Josh, 'maybe you should go find a post to rub up on like a cat in heat does.'

Kathy's hand shot out and rapped his cheek. She pointed her finger like a gun under his chin, and said with gritted teeth to him, 'You call me a tramp, I slap you out of this window. Then the town will have something to mock you about. What kind of a man shrinks when a woman touches him? To think I liked you, you miserable jerk. No wonder you're single. If you want to make remarks about me, you can forget about it. It's not going to happen. I watched my dad rule my mom for twenty long years, and I promised myself that any man who tried that shit on me would earn his stripes. So if you want to get started, say something else. Go ahead. I'll donkey-slap the shit out of you.'

'My God, you are a first-class bi—'

She slapped the word out of his mouth. Josh yanked her by the blouse towards him and held her back a foot from his face to look at the reaction in her eyes. She slapped him again, and he kissed her. She jabbed at his ribs, but he kept kissing her, and she threw her arms around his neck and kissed back. They came to an understanding. Josh cleared his desk of twelve years of trinkets with one swipe of his hand. They kissed and groped at each other almost violently.

Josh said, 'I could kill you right now.'

'Try it, you pansy!' She bit his lower lip.

Josh noticed that the drapes to his office were wide open. He walked Kathy backwards towards the window and swatted at the drapes to close them. Leaning backward, Kathy pulled him towards her, directing the action towards the floor. Josh grabbed the drapes just as Kathy let her weight fall backward, and as she fell Josh tumbled with her and the drapes tore through the curtain rings. They kissed underneath the drapes, sighed loudly, and forgot about Helen, who was still in the building working the teller stand.

The skirt tore some more and Kathy started to remove it.

Josh whispered, 'What are you doing?'

'What do you think I'm doing?'

'You can't do that.'

'What?' Kathy stopped moving.

'If you take your skirt off we're going to have sex.'

'That is the idea. Are you saying you don't want to have sex?'

'Of course I do.' He untucked her shirt and slid his hands underneath. 'Which is why you can't take your skirt off.'

Their hips moved in a harmonic grind, and they continued to kiss while they conversed.

Kathy said, 'You want to have sex, but you want me to keep my clothes on.'

'Exactly. That way we won't have sex.'

'But then we'll wish we had, and want it the rest of the day.'

'Oh, no question. Without a doubt.'

Kathy stopped kissing him and seized his head in her hands. 'I don't get it. Are you missing a vitamin in your diet or something?'

'You don't get it? Aren't you a Catholic?'

'Whatever. How about I leave the skirt on?'

'Oh, that would be perfect!'

He tore her skirt further and abandoned his waning self-control. Kathy yanked his shirt collar hard enough that the top three buttons popped out and bounced on the floor. Josh twisted a handful of Kathy's hair. He turned her head and put his mouth on her neck. Her lips opened wide, her neck tilted back and she sighed.

The sigh was so loud that it caught Helen's attention at the teller stand. She paused her counting of ten-dollar bills, listened for a moment, but hearing nothing more, licked her thumb and resumed the count.

Josh kicked off his pants while lifting Kathy's skirt. He jerked Kathy back and forth, bumping her head against the wall.

'Careful, you idiot.'

He said, 'Consider it payback. You're lucky that's all I do.'

'If that's all you do, I'll do it myself.'

Moving her legs, she made room for Josh and he found his way. Their hands wandered. She gasped and wrapped her legs around his back. He looked into her face, waiting for her to open her eyes and look back. The familiar smile excited him again, and they began moving in sync, his knees chafing on the carpet. Whenever he manoeuvred for a better position, his elbow knocked against the office door. Helen looked up again from her counting. 'This old building . . . just gonna cave in on itself one of these days,' she said, and resumed counting.

The violation of bank policy continued for another ten minutes, until Kathy's blue eyeliner was smeared into a gradient around one of her green marquise-cut eyes. Josh had a light sweat on his skin, which was pale next to Kathy's. Rolling on to his back, Josh sighed and ran his hand through his hair.

He asked, 'Is this when you tell me you have a boyfriend? Bill or George, or Sue?'

'I don't have a boyfriend.' She rolled her eyes. 'I've been waiting on you but you're so dense, I swear. For God's sake, I thought I was going to have to put on a sandwich board. Were you always a little slow?'

Josh leaned over her. 'Well, it's not like I come to work looking for women. It has been a stressful year . . .'

'Yeah, yeah. The hard-luck story.'

'But you are right about one thing. I am neurotic.' Josh laughed. 'I've felt so stressed that I didn't notice the flirting. And that's not like me. Now that I think about it, I have crossed paths with you a lot lately.'

Kathy smiled, 'I was starting to think you were gay.'

'Gay!'

'Well, you know. I read a lot of magazines. You fit the profile pretty well.'

'What kind of magazines would talk about something like that? What profile? You're kidding me, right?' Josh was in disbelief. 'I've never met a gay person in my life. They don't even exist in Immaculate – or Minnesota.'

'That's what you think.' Kathy laughed. 'You need to go to Minneapolis more often. And they always kind of remind me of you. A little too handsome for their own good, in good shape, nice hair, nice clothes. Single. Probably all bankers.'

'Did I seem gay just now? I mean, really.'

'Do you want me to answer that?'

'Honestly, that's ridiculous.'

'I'm kidding. But you do have feminine qualities. Maybe you just haven't discovered yourself yet.'

'Oh, wow, thanks. And you call me crazy? Man, oh man.'

'See, there you go, talking about it: "Man – *oh* man!"'

'Funny.' With his finger, he drew the word on her stomach and underlined it. 'You're funny.'

'I try not to be boring.'

'Insane people are never dull.' He looked down at her body and added, 'But that's okay. Wild is good. At your age it's best to be crazy.' He leaned in closer to kiss her.

Kathy said, 'Have you ever heard the saying, "If you're not a rebel at twenty you're dead, and if you're still a rebel at thirty, you're an idiot"?'

'I don't think so.'

'Well, I'm on that plan.'

'Sounds reasonable. And what exactly does the plan entail?'

'Nothing. And everything.' She paused. 'It means I'm going to get out of Immaculate and try some things, see some places, get around until I'm about twenty-six or twenty-seven, then start a career somewhere and make a life. I don't know. I would like to be in a movie some day, even as an extra. Wouldn't you like to get out of Immaculate?'

'And go where?'

'I don't know. That's the whole point: not knowing. Somewhere. Anywhere.'

He smiled at her, but then he thought about his commitments and his smile dissolved. 'I'd like to leave, but I don't think I can.'

'Why not? Why stay? You said yourself that everyone in Immaculate despises you.'

Josh shrugged. 'Well, not *everyone*.'

In the lobby, Helen closed her drawer and started to turn the lights off. She went to the corridor where Josh's office was located and flipped the switch. She turned to walk away, then stopped and turned around to flip the light on once again. She walked down the hall and peered into Josh's office, but saw no one at his desk. However, the usually neat desk was in terrible disarray. She looked closer and noticed that his jacket was thrown on the desk. Clucking her tongue, she said 'What a mess!' before walking back down the hall and flipping off the light again.

Josh and Kathy clung to each other and bit their lower lips. They did not breathe until the footsteps moved away, and they decided to remain quiet in the office until the bank was officially closed. To kill time they did what any rational new couple would do.

Later, the two of them, quite dishevelled, tiptoed down the hallway. Kathy's mussed hair formed a wispy jump in the front and one of her earrings was missing. Josh moved cautiously into the parking lot and popped the hood of his car so Kathy could give him a jumpstart. The temperature had started to drop and he felt the cold leap into his fingers when he touched the metal. Once the car was started, they made plans to attend midnight Mass together, despite Father Dimer's warning. Kissing each other goodbye, they went separate ways.

Josh no longer cared if his image would be tarnished. He felt rejuvenated. A single snowflake landed on his windshield and he considered skipping church. A quiet night at home sounded more appealing than ramming through snowdrifts. But although he was considered *un*-Immaculate, he never missed a midnight Mass, and even while he entertained the notion he knew that absence was really not an option.

On his doorstep, Josh checked his mail and found a single letter, which looked like a late Christmas card. He tore the envelope open, finding inside a single piece of paper with nothing on it. He flipped the card over and saw handwriting and a short cryptic message:

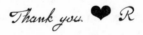

His heart surged when he recognized the handwriting. He turned the card in his hands several times, confused but grate-

ful for the words, any words. He entered his house triumphantly, sat in his armchair and held the note in both
hands while he revisited the memory that had consumed most
of his adult life.

10

The air from the north began to descend on Minnesota, passing over Manitoba without dropping its payload, but dressing the land in a bitterly cold wind. In Immaculate, the temperature dropped, causing a stir of activity. Traffic increased by the hour, as people made last-minute stops for supplies and to impart Christmas greetings. Cars full of grandkids arrived, hoping to reach Grandpa and Grandma's house before the drifts covered the roads: these included Ben Masterson's sons and their children, who settled in for the night with no intention of risking the drive to midnight Mass. On the main intersection cars were backed up three deep, and, for once, not because of a tractor making a wide turn.

An aerial observer passing over each farm would have seen activity everywhere: farmers drove three-wheelers to herd cattle into barns or chased steers on foot into warmer lodging; feeder wagons kicked out silage into concrete bunkers for cows that would have to eat quickly before being shooed under a roof; tractors and trucks pulled extra straw towards sheds where calves and bulls were penned; using rubber nipples and warm powdered milk, wives and children jogged from calf hutch to calf hutch and lured the young Holsteins out of their shelters into the warmth of the barn; cats with fluffy coats were flushed out of garages, and dogs were turned away from houses (cats and dogs set aside their differences and shared body heat in the doghouses); additional firewood was cast down chutes into the basements for wood stoves; barn lights and udder-pumps were switched on earlier than usual, surprising the cows that were accustomed to rigid milking schedules; wives double-checked the storm windows and gazed down with pity at flowerbeds buried in snow; following their parents' orders, children wore full facemasks and snowsuits; men removed iron lids covering cisterns and looked inside to assure themselves the water was flowing properly; stray flashlights and lanterns were gathered and brought inside to be fitted with new batteries; concrete blocks were butted against barn and shed doors to keep the wind out, while, inside, hay and straw bales were stacked up against draughts; pliers were used to twist off wire loops intended to secure to the body of buildings sheets of damaged and loose tin; extension cords were plugged into engine-block heaters; fingers, toes, ears and noses turned red in the growing breeze. People shuttled back and forth under a sky that paled into a sterner shade of grey, and the sun dimmed when the first clouds moved in like scouts, in twos and threes, followed by the massive front, and as the shadows grew long, night escorted the storm into Immaculate.

Jacob slept for nearly three hours. He awoke to a flapping sound that seemed to be right over his head. He lay still and stiff, scared to open his eyes. The flapping waxed and waned and seemed to make a circular path over his bed.

While he lay immobilized, his parents had a moment alone in the kitchen. Ethan had also fallen asleep. Having made preparations for the storm, Ray came into the house ready to discuss the subject of birth control, boosted by his belief that he held the moral high ground. Pulling his cap from his head, he sat down at the kitchen table and fidgeted with a placemat. In more than ten years of marriage, Ray could hardly be said to have won an argument, mostly because his position was never as well planned as Renee's, who knew how to steer the argument: when to stand fast and, as a last resort, when to cry. Not that Renee sought to be shrewd; she merely knew how to argue better than her laconic husband.

Continuing to fiddle with the placemat, Ray spoke without looking at Renee. 'So were you going to tell me about the birth control or just let me think you'd gone barren after all these years?'

Renee sensed a placid religious condescension that raised the hairs on the back of her neck. In front of the open cupboard where she had been putting dishes away, she stopped moving and set the bowls in her hand down on the counter-top. Before responding she reminded herself of her rule of arguing – *talk slowly, think quickly*. She turned only halfway towards Ray so that he could see her profile and ponytail. She pushed a few stray hairs back with one hand and put the other on her hip. 'Ethan and Jacob – those two boys are a handful already. I want to give the best to them. Don't you agree, Ray?' She turned her dark eyes on him. The stray hairs fell back down around her face.

He looked at her with a serious expression. Ray already felt that tackling the subject had been a terrible mistake. He remembered why he tended to avoid confrontation. 'Of course I want the best for 'em. I don't think birth control has anything to do with providing for them.'

Staring out the window, Renee seemed to be speaking to the statue of Mary in the yard. 'Some day I'd like to see Ethan and Jacob graduate from college. Some day I'd like to be able to go visit them wherever they are living. If they decide to leave Immaculate, I mean, if they want to, that's great. If they want to stay in Immaculate, I will be just as happy, but I intend to leave no avenue blocked for those boys when it comes to opportunities in this world. You and I, our genera-tion, we didn't even know what was beyond Immaculate when we were eighteen. I still don't.'

Ray tried a hometown cliché. 'Now, honey, good things grow in Immaculate. Those boys will do fine, and they will have chances we didn't. Of course they will. But how will going against the Church make it any better for them? If any-thing, our sins will make it worse for our boys.'

Her eyes sharpened. 'That's an old lie that kept wives on

their backs with their ankles in the air. If women weren't pregnant they were getting pregnant or recovering. And I for one am not going to manufacture children like some . . . *machine*. I will not. Church doctrine or not, I'll say the same thing to Father Dimer if you feel the need to take it up with him.'

Ray straightened in his chair and put his hat back on his head, then answered sternly, 'That's all well and good, but I hate to tell you that you do not decide and I do not decide. Do you think after two thousand years the Church is going to change the rules? Are you wiser than all of those who came before and decided that we are better off in the eyes of God by making up our own way? You cannot take those pills. It is not the right thing to do. And you know as well as I do the rule that we live by in this house. What have we always said to each other? The right decision is usually the harder decision.'

Renee turned towards the cupboard and rolled her eyes so that Ray would not see. She said softly, 'Well now, that motto can be applied two different ways. How about you quitting smoking then, Ray?' She turned again to face him while she parsed the teeming thoughts in her head. She continued with soft authority. 'And what decision is the correct one in this case, Ray? There is such a thing as hardship for the sake of hardship. A hard decision is to have six kids and work like a dog from sunup to sundown, fill up a pew and look and smell like shit twenty-four hours a day. Maybe a harder decision is to raise two kids properly, and fully, and to have time to talk to them, to get to know them, to help them with homework, and to follow them in their journey through life. With more kids, it's less time for each. I don't want to be a warm tit and that's it.'

Ray stamped his hand flat on the table. 'Renee, you have a sacrilegious way of arguing. That's out of line. You may not like the way things are but that is the way things are. We aren't above it. That is the way family is. It has to be. You have a big family and you work hard and the Lord provides.'

'This is not 1950, Ray.'

Renee eased off to keep Ray civilized. She respected his ability to lose an argument more tactfully than he could start one. She knew enough to let him speak his mind without letting him make a fool of himself in the process. She understood the physical strength of Ray and the emotional strength inside him. Ray could bear a world of weight, but one too many sharp words from Renee and she could make him brittle and conversation ground to a halt. Renee had once called him 'stupid' and Ray had raised his hand as if he was going to hit her, but he withdrew his arm and left the room. Afterwards Ray clammed up for months, saying little more than obligatory greetings. Ray needed to reach the right conclusion by himself – her conclusion. He was the driver and she the navigator. She allowed him the illusion of power. Renee appreciated that Ray withheld the threat of physical violence in arguments. She knew women in Immaculate who shared beds with men who didn't.

'We do work hard,' Renee said. 'We are blessed. We know how to last in hard times, even if in the next year we go bankrupt and the barn blows down, or Tippy kicks the bucket – whatever. Do you think I am not on your side, when I've wore an apron as many days as you have worn overalls? Family planning is not an attempt to block God or your good intentions. I have the right to take these pills, and we are better off for it. This is not to cuckold or overrule you. It's to love you and our children *better*.' She paused and approached Ray in his chair. He sat on the front edge of the chair, leaving her room to swing a leg and slide down behind him until her blue jeans touched his. She spoke softly into his ear: 'And, Ray, I will always love you. You're a good man.'

Ray tried not to smile but failed. He wondered what the word cuckold meant.

'You've never even worn an apron.' He blushed.

'Have too.' She touched his ear with her lips. 'It's an invisible apron. Aren't you my good man and my boys' daddy?'

He beamed at the praise, unable to stay angry at his beautiful wife. Renee blew in his ear and he was toppled.

'Quit it.' He winced and laughed.

'Make me.'

'Be careful. I'll make you into a woman.'

'Oh, I dare you.'

Ray said, 'I'll make you into a *cockold*.' He turned in his chair and with one arm reached around Renee's waist and stood up, carrying her towards their bedroom, which sat next to the kitchen. Renee squealed in protest and Ray declared, 'I'll show you my point in more direct terms. I'll make you speak in tongues. I'll make a believer out of you.'

'Promise? Can I get a witness?'

'Not where I'm taking you.'

The bedroom door slammed shut and they started to tug at each other's faded blue jeans. Renee loosed her long hair from the ponytail and leaned against him, asking for her lips to be met. Ray squeezed her tight and looked hard at her eyes. He said, 'I will love you for ever, even if you drive me nuts.' She smiled and closed her eyes. She untucked her shirt and he pushed down her jeans. But just as the Levi's hit the floor in a soft thump, a set of wild footsteps trampled down the stairs, through the kitchen, and towards the bedroom.

Jacob flung his parents' bedroom door open and tumbled into the room, yelling, 'Sparrows! Sparrows! Jesus, there's sparrows!'

He ran up over his parents' bed and ran twice around their embrace, all the while yelling, 'Sparrows! Sparrows!' He circled his mother and father a third time, and finally clung to his mother's exposed leg. She was grateful to still have underwear on.

Ray said, 'What sparrows?'

'In my room! There's a sparrow in my room!' He squealed and crawled under the covers of his parents' bed.

Ray and Renee exchanged dubious looks.

Roused from his sleep, Ethan came to the bedroom doorway to see what the commotion was about, but seeing his mother and father in their unbuttoned state, he ducked back into the kitchen and sat on a chair to listen.

Ray buttoned his jeans and asked Jacob again, 'There is a sparrow in your room? Right now? Are you telling the truth?'

Jacob peeked out from under the blanket. 'It's huge!'

Ray marched out of the bedroom to give Renee some privacy. Tagging along, Jacob whimpered and giggled behind Ray as he climbed the stairs. Both boys followed closely as they reached Jacob's bedroom door. Ray put his hand on the doorknob. Jacob squealed with delighted fear.

Ray asked, 'Now, Jacob. What is in this room? What did you see, so that I am prepared?'

Jacob's big eyes darted back and forth. He whispered, 'A sparrow.' He gritted his teeth in fear. 'Flying in circles . . . like it was on a string!'

Ray opened the door and flipped on the light switch. The two boys peeked underneath Ray's outstretched arm. The room was silent.

'He must have landed on something.' Jacob looked up and whispered, 'Probably making a nest.'

Satisfied that it was a hoax, Ray entered the room, leaving the door open behind him.

'Let me tell you a story about the boy who cried wolf—' But as soon as Ray spoke, Jacob's wolf flew up out a corner. Jacob screamed and dived under the covers of his bed. The beating of the wings was too fast for any sparrow. Ethan yelled, 'It's a bat!'

Jacob peered out from under the covers. 'Dracula!'

Ray pulled a pillow out from under Jacob's head. Ethan grabbed another and together they assailed the bat. With almost supernatural agility, the bat swerved and avoided the flailing pillows and flew into the hallway. The two hunters gave chase and continued to swing, while Jacob, leaping out of bed, jumped up and down like a cheerleader. The bat darted into the open door of Ethan's bedroom and Ethan knocked his lamp over with an errant swing. With the next swing he hit Jacob in the head and knocked him to the floor, causing Ethan to pause and laugh for a moment. But his laugh became a gasp when the bat nearly struck his chest, before turning sharply and climbing up and over Ethan's head.

Ray swung the pillow in wide and heavy blows, grunting and heaving, grimacing and smiling throughout the chase. The bat eluded the pillows time and again, until finally Ray connected, and the bat launched into a corner of Ethan's room, striking the wall and dropping to the floor behind an old rocking horse and a toybox. Pillows at the ready, Ray and Ethan advanced with caution. Together they peered over the dusty rocking horse. The darkness of the corner hid the fallen bat, until it suddenly shot up again, diving between them. They swung their pillows into each other and the chase resumed. Renee, reassembled, arrived at the bedroom doorway and the bat careened over her shoulder, causing her to scream and duck. The hunters barrelled past into the hallway. Jacob ran up and down, shouting invectives at the bat and blocking the pathway. At one end of the hallway, near the staircase, Ray waited with his pillow raised. The exhausted bat, wobbling like a knuckleball, flew into Ray's zone and, with a chopping motion, he knocked the bat down the staircase to the bottom of the steps. And that was the bat's demise.

'Whew!' Ray sighed. 'How's that for exciting! Ethan, grab a washcloth for me.'

Thinking of her limited supply, Renee protested. 'Not a washcloth! Hold on.' She ran down the stairs, leaped over the bat and went into the kitchen for a pair of tongs. She handed the tongs to Ray, who picked up the bat and examined it.

He held it up for display. 'Looks like we have our Christmas bird!'

Triumphantly, the boys and Ray marched outside and placed the dying bat in the snowy yard. Ray could see that the bat was still breathing. 'One of you two go and get something to put this brave little guy out of his misery. If I had my boots on, I'd just step on him.'

Ethan said, 'Almost hate to see him die after all that.'

The hunters became fascinated with the valiant bat, and with a frozen twig Ethan pointed at his little teeth, thin rubbery wings, sharp ears, and almost – but not quite – cute nose and eyes.

Ethan said, 'Bats are mammals.'

'What do you mean?' asked Ray.

'We're related to them. We're both mammals.'

'You don't say. How can that be?'

'I don't know. But my teacher said so.'

Jacob ran inside the house to retrieve an execution weapon. He had no idea how to properly finish off a bat, but after seeing how difficult it had been to knock the bat down, he imagined it would not die easily. He grabbed a dirty skillet from the kitchen sink, but Renee swatted his hand and separated him from it and she shooed him away. Jacob returned to the mudroom and frowned at his father's size fifteen boot. It was not dramatic enough. With his hands on his hips, he looked around the room and noticed the gun rack.

In the yard, Ray and Ethan were still doubled over, side by side, prodding the bat, when the barrel of a twenty-gauge shotgun slid between them.

Ray whirled around and violently snatched the shotgun from Jacob, knocking him to the ground with the back of his hand, much harder than he had intended. But he didn't apologize. He looked at Jacob's stunned face and his own face reddened as he checked that the safety switch was secure and ejected the shells.

'What the hell is wrong with you?' Ray yelled down at his son. 'How fucking stupid are you, kid?'

Punch-drunk and ashamed, Jacob lowered his head and in silence cried on his chest.

'Yeah, you've been quite the idiot today. Go ahead and cry. All day it's been one thing after another. I'd swear you are trying to kill us. How many times have I told you not to touch the guns? You could have killed someone. It doesn't take much of a brain to realize that a shotgun is just a little too much to kill a bat. Good God Almighty, Jacob, I think your head is filled with straw.'

The words came too easily to Ray. He had heard the same comments from his father – words that he hated and never forgot but couldn't help unloading. This was an argument he could win. He stormed into the house and said to no one in particular, 'Can't keep a gun in here any more.' A clatter came from the mudroom when he slammed the gun into the rack. A trembling began in his forearms and he squeezed the stock and barrel in his fists.

Hearing Ray's tone, Renee poked her head out from the kitchen. 'What happened?'

'I think you're right, Ren,' said Ray. 'You better take the birth control. Double up on the dosage if you have to, because one more kid like that around here will kill us all.'

Renee went quietly to the window of the mudroom and saw Jacob weeping in the snow. With her hand over her mouth she demanded details from Ray, gasping during his account of what had happened. She ran outside in her socks to console Jacob and explain why Dad was upset.

The snow began to fall. The cold northern wind bore down on a warm southern air mass. Fat flakes wafted down to the earth creating a primer for the many inches to follow.

For five minutes Ethan prodded and inspected the bat and would have continued to do so for much longer had Ray not emerged from the house with his work boots on, bristling with intensity in his words and his expression. He said to Ethan, 'Time for chores. You squish that thing yet?' Ethan lied, then stood up and rushed inside to get changed for chores. The bat died slowly in the cold snow because Ethan could not bring himself to snuff the beast after such a noble flight.

When Ray passed Jacob and Renee in the snow, Jacob bowed his head. Renee coaxed Jacob to smile by using kind words and encouraging him to do his chores and show his father what a good boy he really was. For a moment, Jacob believed that he would indeed work hard at his chores, and good intentions lifted him to his feet.

But as Jacob's tears dried into dirty streaks on his cheeks, he dawdled at the feed-cart with his feet planted in front of the cow named Tanya. He was required to pour out two scoops of feed, but his feet could not move until he had completed his daily ritual of saying Grace for the cows.

'Please bow your heads for the blessing, ladies.'

Flanking Tanya were two other cows, and all three looked at the boy with moist eyes, waiting for the scoop to pour out their feed. While he preached, the cows picked their noses with their tongues and rubbed their necks against the metal of the stall.

'Remember, cows: your response is the switch of the tail, the chewing of the cud, followed by the belch, and a short moo.'

Meanwhile Ethan worked his way down the other aisle, scooping and dumping out feed while pushing the cart ahead at a constant speed, exactly as Ray had taught him.

'We have gathered here today to, yes, once again, to swallow seeds in big mouthfuls. But before we do, remember that we all came from seeds, including me and all of you, Tanya, Betsy and Lulu. There was a time when you, Tanya, were just an oat. I remember you then, so small and brown, not noticed by anyone but the squirrels. And here you stand today so large, quite a milker you are (so I've heard). You came from the pasture where your mother planted that oat in a cowpie and you grew into a big, fat cow. And now you have swallowed oats yourself and planted them in cowpies. But you seem to forget. Your long tongue sucks up seeds like a vacuum. I have watched you, Tanya, gobbling without a care. That is why I give you just a little seed today to start with, so that you will remember that everything comes from seeds. We are happy seeds; we plant the seeds and pick the fruit so that the seeds are also pleased. I've seen you, Tanya, mooing for seeds at night, crying out as if praying to the Holy Seed itself – and it is not pretty. You remember the seed only when you are hungry. But I say to you now, Tanya, only moo once, and you will receive.' Jacob paused for a breath, and for drama, before continuing his homily. 'Not so long ago, things were much different. Much, much, much. For a long time there was only the giant and a turtle and no seeds.'

Ethan finished his aisle and began working Jacob's. He approached his brother from the opposite end of the barn, eyeing both Jacob and his work. One of the few of Jacob's seed stories that did not irritate Ethan was about the origin of seeds, so he increased his speed to get to the end of the aisle in order to hear the story.

'The giant was in charge of everything and decided that he didn't like sharing the land with the turtle. The giant was bossy and thought he could do whatever he wanted, so he locked the turtle in a cave and rolled a rock in front of it. The turtle felt around with his feet in the dark cave and felt lots of bugs and crawly things around him. He got so scared he started to imagine a nice place, with lots of green and yellow things. The turtle hollowed out bits of rock, made little shells and then crammed things into the pockets and he named each little package something different. The giant loved to look in at the turtle and laugh, every day he did this, and as the giant rolled the stone away from the front of the cave, the turtle threw his tiny packages over the giant's shoulder, outside into the world. He hoped his little packages would turn into the things he imagined, out in the world where he couldn't be.

'That was how you cows came to be here today. The turtle's seeds grew more seeds. Now seeds grow trees that grow nests that grow eggs that grow birds. There are dinosaur seeds, plain seeds, watermelon seeds, crazy seeds, dog seeds, nut seeds, building seeds, tractor seeds, cat seeds, people seeds, table seeds and birdseed.'

Ethan arrived at the end of Jacob's speech and added, 'And they all lived happily ever after.' He poured out grain for Tanya, who immediately bowed her head and extended her tongue and slurped the grain.

'Amen,' Jacob said. 'You may eat the bride.'

'Look at Tanya,' Ethan said, tossing extra grain to her. 'She says, "Too much talking. Finally some seeds to eat."'

'She doesn't say that,' Jacob argued. 'Tanya says she wants to hear the story of the Christmas Seed and the Christmas Fairy, don't you, Tanya?'

Ethan said, 'I don't think I've heard that one,' and then added, 'Not that I would want to.'

12

While the boys and Ray worked in the barn, Renee wrapped Christmas presents in the living room, keeping a blanket nearby to hide the gifts in case Jacob came hurtling into the house like a comet. Bits of glitter were stuck to her cheeks, making her sparkle. As she cut the green and red wrapping, she recalled her grandfather's stories, stories that had been told and reformed many times over the course of a century. The old, wistful drunkard came alive on Christmas Eve for an hour, as if he had waited the entire year to dust the old stories off. It was her favourite night of the year. When Renee was a child her family had said the rosary prior to story hour. By the time she had finished the Fifth Glorious Mystery and chanted the two hundredth Hail Mary, she needed a great performance from her grandfather.

It took a pitched battle with Ray to end the tradition of saying the rosary. She believed that nothing ruined Christmas like excessive prayer. Her grandfather, a Navy veteran, always began the night with a story he called 'The Tale of Captain Morgan and Father Drowning', which was hardly a Christmas story but was full of icebreaking ships and the false origins of Immaculate. It involved a Viking vessel guided by an Irish priest who mistook a moose for a mermaid after one too many afternoons of sailing in circles on Lake Agassiz while trying to find a passage to the Mississippi river. She smiled and tried to remember the detailed anachronisms, but the phone rang and interrupted her. She placed a last piece of tape on the present she was wrapping, and then covered the gifts with the blanket before getting up from her knees to answer the phone.

On the fourth ring she picked up the phone but the other end of the line was silent. She said twice, 'Hello?'

There was no response. Ray picked up the phone in the barn and Renee heard the blare of the milking pump in the background.

'Is it for me?' asked Ray.

'No. I think it must be a wrong number. There's no one there.'

'Well, at least the phones are still working. See you in an hour.' He hung up the phone.

Renee started to hang up but stopped when she heard a voice on the other end. She put the receiver back up to her ear and said, 'Pardon me?'

The muffled voice on the other end said, 'You're welcome.'

'I'm welcome?' Renee laughed. 'Great! Who is this?'

'Just wanted to . . . wish you a merry Christmas. And . . . you're welcome, Ren.'

There was a click followed by a dial tone. She froze, with the phone buzzing in her hand. She slowly set the receiver on the wall hook, then bit her nails and wondered why on earth he would ever call her house. The glitter on her cheeks kept sparkling as her face filled with colour.

Renee left the kitchen and went to the living room, but she was too agitated to continue wrapping gifts. Her thoughts of stories and Christmas were supplanted by a racing uneasiness, as she felt angry at him for his failure to remain within his space. She suddenly despised him as a coward. Part of her wanted to call Ray in from the barn and tell him, but that would be a disaster. Perhaps the time had come. She felt sick to her stomach as she paced back and forth in the living room, hands on her head, hands on her hips, hands on her head, pondering why she had sent the note to him to thank him, all because of a few payments. She went to call him back and when she placed her finger on the dial she realized that she knew his phone number by heart, as if she had never forgotten it. She slammed the phone down in disgust and put her hands against the wall above the phone. She loathed him; she wanted an apology for the invasion across the agreed-upon boundary. As if she needed to be reminded of the past – but then it was too late and her mind was walking in time, into a memory she had stifled many years ago. Why hadn't it died like it should have? From starvation, privation, disaffection; why hadn't it died like all other things had died? But it was too late. Leaning against the wall in her kitchen, she walked into the poem of her life.

Against her will, Renee was there again, in the summer of graduation, 1968, at the Immaculate baseball field under the lights, watching a game with her girlfriends. Renee and her friends intended the summer to be one continuous party before they went off to university, or back to the farms, or to the Tonnamowoc Cosmetology School. Her boyfriend of four years, Ray Marak, was at the plate, batting fourth, in the cleanup slot. He would get a base hit, or a double or a home run. Renee barely paid attention to the games. She didn't need to watch to know Ray was the star. Batting after Ray was Josh Werther, who stood outside the dugout in the on-deck circle.

In the bleachers, Renee felt a nudge from her red-headed classmate, Sandy O'Meara, who said, 'Look at Josh in those pants.'

Renee scrunched her forehead. 'That scrawny thing?'

Josh swung the bat around his head and paused in his warm-up to wink at Sandy, then he bent over at the waist and stretched out, clearly aiming his body at a section of the bleachers. Sandy appraised him in no uncertain terms. Renee rolled her eyes and said, 'Yeah, he's all right, but . . . he's such a wimp. He's almost feminine.'

'Wimp?' said Sandy in disbelief. 'Well, that's not what I was calling him last night on my parents' sofa.'

'Oh my God!' gasped Renee. 'You did not!'

'I did. And I'm going to do it again tonight, I'll tell you that right now, Ren.'

'Oh my God, you had sex with him? Are you serious? You tramp! I want details.'

The ping of the bat connecting with the ball brought a cheer from the small crowd as Ray hit a line drive into a gap and rounded first base for a double. He slid into second base and got up to dust his uniform off. For a moment, Renee hoped he would look up at her and wink or wave, but he only looked at the third-base coach and waited for a sign. Strong, sure-footed, macho without trying – he was a man's man, even at age eighteen.

The game ended in an Immaculate victory. Ray packed up

his cleats and quietly left the dugout, acknowledging a few congratulations on the way. But his teammates noticed something different about Ray that night. Usually he smiled a lot and seemed to take an interest in everything happening around him, but he didn't smile once that night. Nobody bothered to ask if anything was wrong. The truth would only be told to Renee that night.

Renee and her girlfriends waited for their boyfriends or potential boyfriends outside of the dugout. In her short shorts and tight T-shirt, Renee greeted Ray with a kiss and a 'Great game', a standard greeting between the two of them after years of varsity sports. The other players glanced at Renee even while they kissed their own girlfriends. She had the team's attention. As she and Ray left the field, Renee turned and walked backwards and said to her friends, 'So we'll see you at the quarry?'

As she said it, she noticed Sandy with Josh Werther. They kissed each other long after everyone else had stopped pecking. It was not subtle kissing but passionate public necking.

Hearing Renee, Josh paused and responded confidently, 'I'll see you there.'

Renee scoffed with condescension but Josh surprised her by blowing her a kiss. The redhead laughed and pulled his face back towards hers.

Renee's own face reddened and she grabbed Ray's arm and hugged him, making it clear to Werther that she was not interested in his flirting.

That night, everything changed. Down a dirty road, Ray drove his father's Ford truck into the valley to a quarry party. It was Minnesota August, humid and beginning to feel like the end of a season. The air smelled like the last fresh cut of alfalfa, the radio played 'Light My Fire' by The Doors. The summer was already overripe. In four weeks Renee would be off to the University of Minnesota. She rode in the cab's middle seat, beside Ray, and they shared a can of Miller beer.

Then he handed her a letter. She playfully asked if it was a love letter, but Ray said nothing and she could not see his eyes in the dark truck cab. She pulled the letter from the envelope with excitement and struck her cigarette lighter to read the words. Her expression slowly turned from a smile into a frown.

'I leave for boot camp in three days,' said Ray sadly. 'I wanted the summer to last as long as possible before I told you.'

Stunned, she let the lighter go out and leaned back in the bench seat, remembering other boys from Immaculate who had left and come back from Vietnam – or hadn't come back.

They went to the party and drank from the keg with everyone else, but sat on a log by the bonfire without making much conversation. The joy of the other partygoers glanced off them while they tried to absorb the situation. She quietly smoked cigarettes and sipped on a beer. On the other side of the fire sat Sandy and Josh Werther, petting each other as if Josh was the one going to war instead of getting a deferment and going to college.

Ray said very few words that night, other than, 'I'll write you every day, Renee.' She fought back tears and held fast to his arm, trying to be strong, but at the same time angry at him for this misfortune over which neither of them had any control. She thought of fleeing to Canada that night – the border was only a hundred miles away, but she knew that Ray would never agree to dodge the draft. It was a heart-breaking night and a night of tears and lacklustre sex. They yearned for what was done to be undone. The three days passed quickly and Ray boarded a bus to Fort Bliss, Texas.

As promised, he wrote every day. At first the letters were trite, unaccustomed as he was to writing. She could tell that the drill sergeants were hardening him. He told her that he read the New Testament each night in his bunk and tried to get along with people, to lay low. He never volunteered for anything but his size seemed to volunteer for him. A few fistfights occurred: he was a big target for little Napoleons in the barracks. But he tried to keep something inside him that the sergeants couldn't access, and he developed a knack for the love letter, writing better than he ever imagined he was capable, or would ever admit later on. From his bunk he wrote words that Renee drank into her soul, deep into her heart. Ray even dabbled in sonnets in his attempt to make love to her through the US Mail. As the letters shortened they became more meaningful. It reached a point where Renee had a wild yearning some nights while she lay in her dorm room, reading Ray's poems time and again:

'I can pull down the space between us and I can see
    you, girl.
I roll in my sleep and reach out across this bunk,
In the breeze at night I can feel you, and I fall out,
I let go and panic until you catch me.'

Renee found her quiet room a den of venial sin on lonely

nights. At school she had had no interest in other men despite many approaches. She stayed busy, studying by day, writing by night, supplementing her literature classes with a stream of mail between her and Ray. The depth of her emotions could not be understood by her freshman friends, who came to see Renee as a homesick case not suited to college. The anti-war sentiment pervasive on campus made Renee's soldier-boy an unappealing and sometimes provocative topic. The absence of the object of her love altered her.

The never-ending stream of steamy letters from Ray could not last. He moved from Fort Bliss to Fort Polk and soon afterward to war. Still he spent what time he had writing in the dark jungle. He was scribbling, but more than that, he was showing his commitment. Ray stayed up later than anyone else in his platoon, determined to seal an envelope addressed to Renee every day, even if he couldn't get to a US Army post office, particularly during his ordered crossovers into the confidential Laotian front. So the letters were sent in irregular bunches, instead of once a day, making the wait for Renee harder, and the reading less ritualistic. Sometimes the letters were senseless.

Renee's excitement over the mail abated when news of her mother's emphysema arrived. She suffered silently through the stages of bereavement. Ray's absence, which had once made love stronger, now only compounded her misery. The object of her affection was dislocated: too distant to feel real, separate from her daily life. She stewed in her misfortune, taking care of her mother twelve hours a day, seven days a week, for nearly nine months. Her father took the other twelve hours of the day, but he also took up drinking. Her brothers returned only on the occasional weekend. Death slowly installed itself until her mother said that she could smell herself rotting. All Renee could do was hold her hand and read, as the once beautiful woman flitted in and out of consciousness.

In some ways that year, during which she learned so much about life and read half the canon of classical literature, was a greater education than four years at the university would have been. But she missed out on certain things, and the cumulative weight of Ray's absence, her mother's passing and her father's alcohol-fuelled breakdown turned her into a rock of self-control. For Renee, love started to fade.

The opposite happened to Ray. Renee was his only reminder of civility, his only symbol of hope and home. With his natural aptitude as an infantryman and his inability to say 'no', Ray became the soldier to whom unwanted tasks were assigned. His bravery and strength and his ability to keep his mind together quickly made him a sergeant, but the experience of war stripped him of his faith in God for a period of time. Faith flipped upside down and hell was no longer a mere concept but a location. Meanwhile he imagined the comfort of Renee's life in Immaculate.

After the funeral, Renee took on her mother's role on the farm. She tried to stir her father back to life, and without her the farm would have gone bankrupt. The loss of his best friend after thirty-five years of marriage knocked the wind out of Ben Masterson. In grieving he leaned too hard on Renee, using her as a crutch and pouring out his emotions when drunk. She needed an escape. She felt herself becoming prematurely old.

A few girlfriends began calling on Renee to go out in Tonnamowoc. At first she went to the dance halls only with reluctance, but after a few nights of getting blind drunk and experiencing genuine laughter with other nineteen-year-olds, she returned to being an ordinary kid, at least on Thursday, Friday and Saturday nights. Even on the roughest mornings, Renee managed to get out of bed and milk the cows, while her father lay paralysed in his room, hung over from depression as much as from Wild Turkey.

Men in Tonnamowoc started to notice Renee and soon she had many offers for dances and dates. On any given night at the Tonnamowoc Hop-Haus at least a dozen men asked Renee to dance a polka or a swing. After an initial period of shyness she considered herself a rather good dancer, despite never having been taught any proper steps. Men approached her with pickup lines they had practised all week in their mirrors. Renee obliged them all with a spin on the dance floor but curtly left them standing alone at the end of the song to return to her friends, who watched her with envy and admiration from a corner table.

One night at the Hop-Haus, Renee and her friends sat at their usual table in the corner, laughing and doing shots of Phillips schnapps to celebrate a bachelorette party for Anne Moran, a mousy classmate of Renee's. Before the women sat down, they could see the bar filled with the same young men, old bachelors, and married men *sans* wedding bands standing with their backs to the bar. The light of Schmidt's and Pabst Beer neon signs reflected reds and blues off of the boys' fresh-shaved faces. A barmaid showing cleavage handed out beers with a smile and collected cash while her frumpy barback stocked the iceboxes silently behind her. One man and two women leaned on pool cues watching a shooter who parked a burning cigarette over his ear, like a carpenter's pencil, and then shot a combo into a side pocket. An old pinball machine was the territory of a Tonnamowoc crew from a private school, marked off from the rest of the customers by their new clothes and new haircuts. One wall held a row of booths, with four people crammed in on every bench and two drinks on the table for each person, to prepare their feet for the dance floor.

Renee, who was the maid-of-honour, had consumed four shots and was warmed up enough to propose a toast for the bride-to-be. Feeling garrulous, she said, 'Have you ever noticed how we always end up in the corner of this place? We somehow manage to do that in every bar we go to. Do we just gravitate towards the corner like magnets? Makes you wonder what would happen to us if we ever went to a place with a round bar. We'd probably just keep walking in circles all night, like we were in that one of ring of hell. Well, anyway, let's make a toast to Anne. Here's to the beginning of the end!' Renee nudged the bride with her elbow and the shot glasses clinked. The bride was about to drink her shot when Renee stopped her, pulling the glass away from her open mouth.

'Just wait now, love, I'm not finished yet. Before you marry this man, we want to thank you for being first, being a guinea pig for the rest of us. We will all be riding in the back seat as you pop your connubial cherry. And in the years to come we will come crying to your doorstep for advice: "Oh Anne, what's the recipe for tuna casserole? Oh Anne, what's the best laundry detergent for grass stains? Oh Anne, will I have puppies if I do it doggy style?"' The table erupted with laughter. 'You will be taking the plunge for all of us and we, of course, are jealous of you and hate you. But remember, no matter how bad it gets, you know what they say: only the first twenty-five years of marriage are the hardest!'

A man walked up behind Renee as she drank the shot. The laughter continued to roll around the table without anyone acknowledging the person standing behind Renee.

'I love you, Anne,' said Renee. 'And by the way, I intend to be the next one getting married.'

One of the other girls said to the man behind Renee, 'Oh my God. I didn't even recognize you at first.'

Renee turned around and by accident looked squarely into the eyes of Josh Werther. He stared back as he said, 'I just got back into town.'

Renee pushed her hair back over her ear. 'From where?'

'From school. In Duluth.'

Anne said, 'Ooh, Joe College.'

'Don't hold it against me,' Josh said, still focusing on Renee. 'Any chance my old classmate will dance with me?'

'I don't think so.'

'Oh, Renee,' Anne prodded, 'give the preppy one dance.'

'Well, maybe I'm shy,' said Renee. 'And I've got a dance partner.'

Josh turned his head away for a moment from Renee. 'Is your partner here?'

'I don't think he'll mind,' said Anne. 'Kind of hard to dance with someone who is three thousand miles away.'

Suddenly Josh realized that Renee had never stopped dating Ray. 'Oh, still with Ray, huh? He's doing okay, then?'

'As far as I know. The mail I get is postmarked a week or two in the past. But yeah, he's okay.' She shuddered. 'He'd better be okay.'

'Well, let me ask you to dance on his behalf.'

Renee looked at Anne and the other girls, who offered only encouraging looks. She mouthed 'No' to the girls, but they didn't relent.

'Just one dance,' Josh said.

Defeated, Renee walked to the dance floor without waiting for Josh, who smiled back at Renee's friends and thanked them. After a year in college, his body had filled out. No longer scrawny, he was strictly attractive. He exuded confidence without being abrasive. Renee's friends hoped that he would soon be rejected by her, so that they might have a dance, and a chance. He straightened his collar and followed Renee to the dance floor, admiring her from her bell-bottoms to the long blonde hair lapping at her shoulders. Josh dodged a couple doing a polka and then snatched Renee's hand to draw her towards him. She acted surprised by his grasp, but she began dancing right away to avoid getting run into by the next couple careening in their direction. They made several loops around the wide dance floor, keeping up with the music. Renee marvelled at Josh's dancing and she was glad to have finally found a dancer as talented as she was. Before the song ended, Josh steered her to the edge of the dance floor.

'Why did you stop?' asked Renee.

Josh stammered, 'I'm not sure how to tell you this, but ah . . .'

'What?'

'Renee, you're a terrible dancer—'

'That's a hell of thing to say!'

Josh held up his hand to calm her before she could run away. 'But wait! But . . . you could be the best dancer here, Renee. When the next song starts, follow my lead. I'll count and narrate. Step, close, step and hop. And I promise . . . you will be a natural by the end of the next dance.'

Renee blushed with numb embarrassment and looked at him. A new song began. Before Renee could argue they were navigating the dance floor with Josh saying 'step-close-step-hop' to the rhythm of the music. Renee tried to look down at her feet but Josh ordered her to look at his eyes instead. Within a minute she felt comfortable and found the steps easy to make with the constant counting of Josh: 'Step, close, step, and hop; step, close, step, and hop . . .' By the end of the song Renee smiled and felt a little embarrassed to realize that she had never really danced a polka before. She wondered how foolish she had looked prior to Josh's tutoring.

They danced to another song, and another, until the band switched to swing music and Josh taught her the basics of swing. They danced all the songs until the band took a break from their first set. During the break the music switched from live music to records – Chuck Berry and Chubby Checker – which Renee found easier to dance to without Josh's guidance. She had nearly forgotten about the bachelorette party until she saw her friends dancing beside her, with men who had discovered the corner table.

Josh felt envious eyes on him. Wherever he and Renee danced, men who had tried to woo her and failed watched and wondered what the new guy had said or done to keep her dancing. Dancing let Renee forget more than alcohol did. That night she felt the best she had in months. She said nothing as she danced, and Josh said nothing back. He kept her in constant movement. For Renee, it was a rare night of happiness after a long spell of twisting sorrow. And Ray really was three thousand miles away from her.

The band returned to perform the second and final set. Josh and Renee continued dancing. Soon she knew the lindy hop and the jitterbug in addition to the swing and the polka. As the night wore on, the couple pressed closer to each other. Some of the men assumed Josh was the soldier she had claimed to be waiting for and turned their efforts to other girls.

The band finished with several fast polkas and then records began to play again. A few final slow songs gave the couple a last chance on the dance floor before the lights came on.

'Wise men say, only fools rush in . . .'

Josh pulled Renee in close, only then realizing how moist the two of them were from perspiration. Still smiling, she put her arm around his waist and pressed her cheek against his shoulder. Josh's heart raced against hers. He became terribly nervous. Renee was easily the most beautiful flower to ever come out of the Immaculate mud. He urged the song to last for a week so that he did not have to risk putting his foot in his mouth. In college he had had a knack for getting to know women but it usually involved a lot of talking. But this feeling with Renee – the nature of the entire evening – had caught him completely by surprise. This feeling differed from his usual desires: it was not at all the lust that he and the other Immaculate boys had suffered from in high school.

A second slow song started, but Renee pulled back from Josh to say something.

'I forgot about my girlfriends. I should go see what they are up to.'

'Is our one song finally over?'

'That was a very, very, very long song.' She held Josh's forearms and leaned in, making him think she might be coming in for a kiss, but she laughed and let go of his arms.

'Come back to the table with me,' she said. 'Let's see if they can still stand.'

Quiet as an altar boy, Josh followed. At the table the girls were intoxicated, truly, enough that they barely noticed the return of Renee.

The bride said to Renee, 'These sluts are all over me,' causing the other girls to gasp and snort humorous replies.

'Okay,' Renee said, acting motherly. 'I leave for a few minutes and you've all become sluts? And why wasn't I invited? Give me the keys, Anne.'

Anne slid the keys across the table to Renee. One of the other bridesmaids nudged Anne and she fell from her chair on to the floor. Renee said, 'Okay, you know it's time to go when the floozies are falling off the barstools.' The girls huddled together and moved towards the door en masse, with Josh straggling behind, earning jealous glares from the men leaning against the bar.

In the parking lot, the girls climbed into a station wagon, giggling and screaming. With great care, Renee helped Anne into the passenger seat, picking up one foot at a time and setting it down gently. Renee shut the door and went to the rear of the car where Josh stood waiting for her. The lights in the parking lot lit up half of his face. Renee stopped a few feet from him. He took a step forward and kissed her on the cheek. She shied away but then turned her face to him and put her arms around his neck, and there they stood holding a kiss for ten seconds. It was the kiss of melting. It was the chemical kiss; that kiss that releases the mind's rarest concoction called *bliss*. It was the electrical kiss that stays buzzing on the lips for three days. Josh waited in that eternal moment, tasting and savouring that kiss, which became the addiction of his life, his poison and his antidote.

Renee pulled back from the kiss and with a final look at Josh she got into the car and drove off. Josh breathed heavily, feeling like an infant set afloat on an ocean.

13

In the parlour, Ray was milking cows and listening to the radio. From a tin-can speaker, a WCCO disc jockey said, 'Porkbellies down three cents, corn futures dropped a cent, and soybeans had a slow trading day, showing little movement. Now back to the music. Here's one from Dean Martin.'

His anger over the incident with the bat subsided while he worked. To the cow in front of him, Ray said, 'What else is new? Thank you very much, Ronald Reagan. Isn't that right, Tanya?'

With bovine malaise, Tanya looked down at Ray on the parlour floor. Ray danced a few jerky steps to Dean Martin before he hung up the milker and dipped Tanya's udder with sanitizer. In a tight black Hanes T-shirt and canvas overalls, Ray's arms and neck bulged with every movement. His tall and lean frame moved mechanically from cow to cow, repeating motions performed a hundred thousand times before.

He sang the song out loud to the cows: '*And since we've got no place to go, let it snow, let it snow, let it snow!* Dance with me, Tanya!'

Tanya emitted a disinterested moo.

The inventory of the Marak farm included forty cows, twenty steers, twelve calves, fourteen heifers, one bull, one dog and about a dozen cats. Ray called each cow by her given name as he dumped protein mix into the feeders: Tanya,

Loretta, Dolly, Tammy, Louise, Barbara, Dorothy, Betsy, Lulu . . . names borrowed from country music starlets.

'Merry Christmas, my beautiful ladies! No man should have this many girlfriends, ain't that right?'

As a Christmas present, he gave each cow an extra scoop of grain and an extra scoop of protein mix, though the cows did not seem to notice as they licked it up with their long tongues. Despite a trying year, the Christmas spirit filled Ray. He did not follow politics in any detail. He did not care to know any more about economics than the prices of corn, milk and soybeans. Some men in town talked about a Soviet embargo, a war in Afghanistan regarding God-knows-what, a Beirut car bomb, nuclear negotiations in Geneva, martial law in the eastern bloc. Ray's need to know the motives of government had died in Vietnam. His understanding would accomplish nothing to improve the situation between the American, Soviet and European governments. Vietnam had taught him that political minds, be they Communist or any other brand, voluntarily courted annihilation, and the only guarantees a soldier could ask for were three squares a day and a little Memorial Day flag stuck into a burial plot. He appreciated mercy more than politics and believed that if the Soviet people were starving, the Christian thing to do was sell the food to them, even if they were a bunch of godless heathens.

'Enjoy, ladies.'

Ray's cows stayed calm because he treated them well. He played oldies while he milked, but the rest of the day the cows heard soothing elevator music. Still, not every cow fell into line, and the occasional nonconformist required coercion. As readily as any farmer in the township, Ray used the prod and the kicker and he kept a solid stick handy for leveraging stubborn heifers.

The hired man, Joke, strolled in through the front door.

'What are you doing here?' asked Ray. 'I told you to take the night off.'

'Nothing to do at home.'

'Sure there is. It's Christmas Eve. There are lots of things to do.'

The four cows on the left side of the parlour had finished milking. Joke opened the front gate and let Sasha, Tanya, Sherry and Belle walk out single-file into the barn. He let four new cows into the parlour – Carlene, Joanne, Lois and June – and scooped feed for each of them.

Ray said, 'Now don't be stingy with that feed today, Scrooge.'

'Scrooge?' Joke scoffed. 'Let's talk about my wages.' His voice sounded weak.

'Oh? Well, fine then,' Ray joked. 'You can have some extra protein today, too.'

Ray was embarrassed by Joke's comment. He wanted to pay him more but every dollar for the next year was budgeted, down to the last penny. Ethan was old enough to do most of the work Joke did, and sooner or later, Ray would have to start phasing out Joke's role. He reasoned that Joke needed to take over his father's farm, which had more acres and cows anyway, and somehow Joke had to learn to work with his father, Bill – miserable as the man was, sober or not. Although he tried to stay out of his neighbours' business, stories of Ray's occasional 'moral corrections' of straying individuals were not uncommon around Immaculate. He sometimes had difficulty staying on his island.

He said, 'Seriously, you're not supposed to be here. Go on home.'

Joke said nothing in reply and kept his back towards Ray.

Ray noticed Joke had his Minnesota Twins cap pulled down over his eyes. 'Something wrong? Did you just learn that Santa Claus isn't real?'

'He's not?' Joke's nose sounded stuffy. 'You mean that wasn't him at the grocery store today?'

'No. I'm sorry to be the one to break it to you, but that's just fat old Joe McKinney who dresses up so that kids will sit on his lap.' Ray laughed, but then felt guilty about mocking the venerable town Santa.

'That will be your job some day.' Joke spoke quietly. He tried to laugh, but it didn't take. He added, 'You are starting to get a little pudgy.'

'That's a good idea.' Ray smiled and moved closer. 'And you can be my elf.'

Joke asked, 'You need anything done?'

'No. Go home, bud.'

'Ah, that's okay. Don't feel like it.'

'Go on strike. You work too hard for a guy your age.'

Ray tried to peek at his hired man's face, but the cap covered his eyes and nose. The voice sounded like pain. Some facts about Joke's home life were known to Ray, but no details. Joke walked down the steel steps to the parlour floor and checked a couple of milkers. Ray waited for him to move closer and Joke pulled his Minnesota Twins hat as low as possible on his head.

Ray sighed. 'Look at me, Joke.'

Joke didn't turn. He fiddled with a hose connected to the cow he was facing. Ray walked to Joke, dwarfing the young man, and repeated the command.

'Just look at me. Just for a minute, then you can look away again.'

Feeling Ray's shadow fall on him and hearing the seriousness of his voice forced Joke to turn to Ray and show his face. Ray pushed up the baseball hat, exposing a crooked nose and two fresh shiners, one on each eye, with a gash arched over the left eye outlining the bruise. Ray gently pushed the hat back down.

His stomach squirming, he maintained a calm tone with his voice. 'It doesn't look that bad. How's your nose?'

'It's fine.' Joke tried to laugh. 'I got a few punches in.'

'It's broken, you know. I won't ask you to explain it, but why don't you go ahead and tell me what happened anyway.' Ray folded his arms, and the veins in his forearms bulged.

Although Joke hadn't intended to admit anything, Ray's sternness changed his mind. He was still riled from the fight and stuttered a bit as he told Ray about it. A blank expression stayed on Ray's face throughout. Joke's father, Bill, had become angry over his lukewarm Christmas Eve supper and called Joke's mother a few unforgivable names. Joke responded with similar words on his mother's behalf, and out the door they tumbled, as they had done several times before. Joke got the worse end, as usual.

Ray listened until Joke had finished. 'It won't be long now and you'll be running that place, Joke. Or you can always move out. Hang in there. Always hang on to your sense even when nothing makes sense. Especially when nothing makes sense.'

Joke nodded and tried to smile, but his eyelids welled up with tears.

Ray said, 'Oh, shit.' Ray pulled Joke into a bear hug that the boy could not escape. He felt tears falling on to his shoulder. For a minute he did not say anything and just let the boy shudder.

'You bring out the best in me, kid. Don't tell anyone we were hugging in the damn parlour, now, you hear? If Hank Murphy got a hold of that news . . . ho-ly hell would we hear it, eh?' A muffled laugh came from Joke. Ray went on, 'The last thing I need is a reputation for being a man-hugger. My wife already thinks I tell the cattle I love them too much, so I'm already a suspect. Then on top of that, the boys caught me undressing Renee today, so they'll probably grow up and tell stories, too.' Ray laughed and grabbed Joke by the shoulders and held him at arm's length. Ray said, 'You'll be all right, Joachim. You're a Goddamn good man. And don't you ever forget I told you that.'

In Immaculate the ultimate compliment was to be called 'a good man'. Ray meant it, and Joke knew that he meant it. Hearing the words from Ray Marak, the biggest man in Immaculate, brought some of the salvageable pieces of Joke back together. He straightened up and pulled his hat up.

Ray said, 'You can help me milk if you want to, but then you go home tonight and sleep, because your mom needs you. Your dad will earn his regret, because God has his ways of turning tables. There is only one way for you to face this situation and that is to shake it off. It's like riding a horse. You fall off and don't want to get back on, but you have to. Evil can be endured, Joke. Don't let this settle into your head and get its roots on you. I've lost fights, and I tell you . . .'

Joke laughed in disbelief, 'Like you ever lost a fight, Ray . . .' He looked up, but stopped laughing when he noticed Ray's hideous scars.

'Oh,' Ray said seriously, 'I've lost fights.' He paused for a moment. 'I'm as breakable as you are, Joke. And, truth be told, I've never won a single fight with Renee. I even lost one today.' He smiled for a moment before his expression went flat again. 'But I've lost fights with fists, hell yes – I lost that kind of fight, too. I know that feeling, Joke, like . . . like you are ready to split in half with rage. You get insane after a fight because you overthink. You think, "That's what I should have done. I'll do it next time. I'll do it now. I'll kill the fucker that took a piece out of me." That's how it feels, right? Isn't that how it feels right now?'

Joke raised his voice and cried out, 'Some day I'm gonna fuckin' kill him!' Joke no longer caring if Ray saw his tears.

'That's right, Joke. You wouldn't be a man if you didn't want to hurt him. You want to kill him, right you are, you've been here before, I knew it. That's a hurt that's never gonna stop, Joke, but it's a hurt that you can control. Pride is gonna eat at you all week, Joke, all month. Ten years from now, out of the blue, you will feel it sopping you up one day. That's the hurt that never stops. Pride. Pride makes you ready to cash it all in for one moment of revenge. But know this, Joke, that the Devil got into hell for his pride, and so would I if I tried to satisfy it every time it hurt. We all would if we tried to keep pride happy. But do you know what happens after a fight? If you can make it through the night? Do you know what happens?'

'What?'

'Do you know what happens?'

He shouted. 'What!'

'Nothing. Nothing happens, Joke. It's over. All you can do is stand around and look stupid for a few days while the bruises heal. And it's never the last time, Joke. The auger will keep on turning on you, and it will come back to cut you again, and you better be ready so you can pull yourself out in time. With you or without you, the auger of life turns, just like the world. That's why you can't wallow long, Joke. On days like this, you keep moving away from what hurts. What you do today, Joke, is decide that the only person who can ruin yourself is you. You take God,' Ray held out his hand, 'and you make a fist around God, and you put and keep him *here*.' Two times Ray smote his chest.

The loud thumps caused Joke to flinch.

Ray held out his fist once again and showed it to Joke. 'And even if they slice you up and leave you for dead, you never let any motherfucker pry your fingers away from that.'

Looking at Ray's huge fist, Joke wondered if God really was inside the man's hand. Stories about Ray Marak's actions in Vietnam circulated in Immaculate, but no one knew the facts. Because Ray never spoke of it, everyone suspected the worst. Judging by Ray's fist alone, Joke believed that the rumours probably had some truth in them. Joke learned more in a minute from Ray than he had ever learned from his own father. For a moment, his tears lulled, but a new wave of sad anger welled up in his diaphragm. He put his palms over his eyes, gritted his teeth, and cried. A large pair of hands reeled him into a hard embrace, and they said nothing more about the fight.

Ethan and Jacob entered the parlour to report that the stalls were clean and the feed was down. Jacob stopped to pet one of the cows on the nose.

Ray let go of Joke and said, 'You boys can go on inside and get ready for church.'

'Father Dimer said we should stay home, didn't he?' asked Ethan.

'We'll see how the roads are at nine. I think we'll be able to make it. That is, if Hank and Blanks can even get through.'

14

Hank Murphy spoke into the CB radio to the other drivers: 'What's pink and wet and you have to eat a lot of it to get your fill? Over.'

Blanks responded, 'That's easy.'

'Wrong, over.'

'How can I be wrong? I haven't even guessed yet.'

'The answer is watermelon, over.'

'That's what I was going to say, over.'

'Yeah, you bet.'

'Roger that.'

Ben Masterson said into his CB, 'Sick, sick minds. It's coming down heavy now on my side of town. Over.'

Blanks answered, 'We are definitely underway. Highway 12 is starting to pile up. Blowing more by the minute, too. I was thinking, this summer we should plant some trees on that sharp turn by Broan's farm. It piles up really fast. Over.'

'You do that, Johnny Appleseed,' said Hank. 'In fact, write up a memo about your plan and have it on my desk in the morning. Over.'

'Maybe I will.'

'Then submit a revised version to the township, write up a work order, draft a report that evaluates the pros and cons, lobby your state congressman for the rights to dig in that ragged ditch where pheasants hatch their precious eggs, then we'll get our hopes up before getting stonewalled by some bureaucrat. Over.'

Blanks said, 'Your outlook on things inspires us all, Hank.'

The other drivers listened to the Hank and Blanks Radio Show, interjecting only to pass on relevant facts about the surface of the road they were on. The banter would keep the drivers awake, especially in the small hours past midnight. Somehow Hank and Blanks never ran out of stories. When the other drivers weren't shaking their heads in disbelief or disgust, they laughed outright at the men's audacity.

Hank turned on his wipers for a moment to break the monotony of the falling snow. The wipers squeaked and moved in rhythm with the falling snowflakes. The voodoo swirl of the snow hypnotized him but he kept the wheel straight and kept on talking. Hank did not want the drivers tuning in to slow Christmas songs on the radio.

'Hey, Blanks, do you remember that December of . . . I think it was 1970, one of the worst blizzards I can remember. We should have been in the plough business then. Night a lot like tonight. It was a Saturday and I was nursing a hangover with a late afternoon Bloody Mary. You wanted to go to St Paul to party that night because we had tickets to the Vikings and Packers game the next day. I said no way, but then you came up with the motivation I needed. Remember what you said, Blanks?'

'I do remember,' Blanks said. 'I knew that you were going to sack out on the couch so I said, "Tonight is the night I'm going to find Jesus, and when I do I'm going to buy that man a beer."'

'That was it.'

Hank felt at home gabbing into the CB, like a radio disc jockey without a censor. 'So with that nugget of inspiration we went out into the blizzard and we made it to St Paul through blinding snow in an absolute piece-of-shit Dodge. Blanks had recently wrecked his Toyota pickup, which was another matter – another *faecal* matter. Thanks to St Christopher we made it safely to a sauce house. That was when we started ordering double whiskeys and were later asked to vacate the establishment. We ended up going back to a woman's house, one who had just moved to St Paul from – God knows where – I want to say Japan. Over?'

'She was from Iowa.'

'Right! Iowa. Josh Werther came with us that night. Of course, Werther was dating this Iowegian. Oh, I remember now – he met her at college. Well, he was upstairs screwing half the night, so Blanks and I drank every last thing in the house short of the hair spray and mouthwash. Blanks ran around naked most of the night for some reason. It was truly disgusting, over.'

'That's a lie, over.'

Hank's words phased in through the static, '. . . reminded me of my nephew, who's a toddler. Blanks could only be considered well-endowed if he was a rodent. A few other girls were at the house and they got involved in Blanks's little game of nudity, but if I remember right there was no steamy sex. Blanks's feet spend more time in his mouth than in shoes. We drank until the sun came up and the game started at noon. I woke up to the sound of a second heartbeat in my head. What an awful morning. I thought I was going to die, so I started to drink immediately. Werther would not get out of bed. Seems the poor guy fell in love overnight! She was much older, like forty, I think. Ooh la la, very sexy, though. We ditched him, left him at the house, but he showed up at the stadium later, furious with us for leaving him. He was in a real mood that whole weekend. He was almost reckless for once. That was the beginning of the most expensive weekend of my life. Haven't I told this story before? Over.'

One of the other drivers chimed in, 'I swear you've told it fifty times, but last time you said it was the Chicago Bears. Over.'

'No,' Blanks argued, 'it was definitely the Packers.'

'Roger that,' Hank continued. 'The game ended with the Vikings losing. Like I cared. After the game we discovered a dirty hole-in-the-wall in Minneapolis which had some very shady characters. In fact, one guy had a great nickname. Remember his nickname, Blanks?'

'Thirty-eight.'

'That was his name: Thirty-eight. I say again: Thirty-eight. Who is going to mess with a guy named Thirty-eight? I spent a hundred and forty dollars on lap dances and Blanks disappeared into the back lounge for quite a while. To this day he hasn't told me what went on in there. What went on in there, Blanks?'

Blanks said, 'We discussed the bean market.'

'The only thing you discussed was the market rate of getting her ankles up in the air so you could snap her bean. That's one of the Glorious Mysteries of Blanks, and we may never know what happened there until his nose starts to fall off. Anyway, by three o'clock in the morning we were getting hungry. We sat down for a nice dinner at an all-night slum in some drippy icicle alley. We met some black girls from North Minneapolis. They thought we were pretty fun. But that's when the argument started. Blanks and I were both living with our parents and working as rendering truck drivers, picking up exploded roadkill and bloated cattle. We constantly smelled terrible, south of cheese. Hands down, the worst job on the planet. Needless to say, we hadn't exactly set the world on fire after we dropped out of high school. My Pontiac was up on blocks, so what did I have to live for any more? Blanks and I started accusing each other of being a mama's boy, and . . . what else did you call me?'

Blanks cleared his throat, 'A leech on the balls of progress, over.'

'And you *still* use that line to this day. For originality, you are a zero, Blanks. You've been hammering at the same things for twenty years.'

'Including your mom.'

'Well, that's better. Anyway, during the argument an idea touched me like it was from God's mouth to mine. Does God have a mouth, over?'

Shelly said, 'He has a hand, over.'

'Oh? A hand? It must be enormous. Then it was his hand that moved my lips. The winter had been really cold and I had been dreaming of moving to Hawaii for a long time – days, even. Next thing I know, Blanks said yes and we were cruising back to the Minneapolis airport, driving one hundred miles an hour. The other cars seemed like they were standing still, and the music was blasting. Josh Werther was asleep through it all so I punched him in the stomach so that he could appreciate what was happening. We made him promise not to tell anyone about our idea. In the Minneapolis airport we said goodbye and hugged each other like idiots, saying, "It was nice knowing you, Werther" and "Come visit us in Honolulu!" All kinds of nonsense. We approached the ticket counter and, I am not kidding you when I tell you this, a plane was leaving for Honolulu in fifteen minutes. Blanks didn't have enough cash but I had a chequebook and no problems. I wrote a bad cheque for two one-way tickets and I don't even want to mention the cost. We knew that we had to leave that night or we never would get to Hawaii. We said goodbye to Werther again. The airline agent at the ticket window was very confused. He suggested we wait a while for a cheaper ticket, but his practical ways meant nothing to us. He clearly did not understand the stuff of legend. Over.'

Blanks's girlfriend, Shelly, said over the CB, 'You guys are just, like, idiots! Tell me this did not happen.'

'It's true, I promise,' Hank said. 'Shelly, I've sold my soul to seven different devils in the pursuit of alcohol and women. One night I howled at the moon and said, "Take my soul, and give me something warm!" And when I die, I hope to buy some time relaxing in purgatory while the demons carry out litigation over who first damned me.'

Hank paused to catch his breath and take a large swallow of coffee. Several other drivers tried to talk on the CB at once, and so nothing coherent came through the speaker. Hank waited patiently until the squeals stopped.

'Well, anyway, Blanks and I, we ran down the terminal, tickets in hand, and barely reached the gate before take-off. On the plane we were giggling like school girls and ordering beers for everyone. That's the only time I've ever heard of anyone buying a round of beers on an aeroplane. We talked to everyone and danced in the aisles. We must have smelled awful. Come to think of it, I was surprised how many people were willing to drink on a red-eye. But then again, even snobs and tightasses love a free drink. Anyway, to make a long story longer, we were flying at last. By the time we landed, we knew everyone on the plane. We still had energy yet. What was the weather like in Honolulu, Blanks?'

'Overcast.'

'Talk about stunned! As it turned out, we had a seven-hour layover in Seattle. That was when we hit the wall. No sleep for two days and very little nourishment; we were strung out. As you know, we did more than just drink back in those days. I wasn't addicted or anything, but I did like the smell of a certain powder. To kill time we roamed around in the airport and slept on the floor, but I kept waking up every time an announcement came over the loudspeaker. We still had every intention of leaving for Hawaii in a few hours and only then did I realize what I had brought with me: a winter jacket, jeans, heavy leather boots and a sweatshirt. No shorts, no T-shirts or anything useful for the Hawaii climate. Our plan was to buy a pair of shorts and a T-shirt in the airport when we got to Hawaii. And a newspaper. We would take the newspaper to the beach and look for jobs and girls. Between us we had a total of two-hundred and twelve dollars left of actual liquid cash, plus whatever bad cheques could buy. With that money we could get clothes and maybe a sleeper apartment for a month. Since it was late December, we decided that we were going to live on the streets until

January first. We also decided our new career would be as banana pickers. Over.'

'Or pineapple.'

'Coconuts, bananas, noses, whatever,' Hank added. 'Some kind of picker. Just so we would be picking something. But I started having feelings of extreme guilt. Turns out I learned my catechism after all. I started thinking about my car, my job and the bridges I was about to burn. Not that I had much to lose: I hated my job, the Pontiac was dead (may it rest in pieces), but I couldn't stop thinking about family and the bounced cheques. Blanks was beginning to feel guilty too, but after paying so much for the tickets we simply had to go through with it. To chicken out and return home with our tails between our legs would be worse than going through with it. Blanks, you tell them what happened next. It's unbearable to say.'

'We chickened out.'

'In our winter jackets and stocking caps we stood in the terminal, heartbroken. We went to the ticketing agent and booked a one-way ticket back to Minneapolis for another obscene amount of money, another bad cheque written, and with tears in our eyes we watched the plane for Honolulu take off. It was devastating. We called Werther and told him to pick us up in Minneapolis. By the time we arrived in Immaculate everyone already knew the story, thanks to Werther's big mouth. He spilled the beans as soon as he could. Blanks and I crashed when we reached our beds – the beds in our mothers' houses. Almost sixty hours without sleep. And here I am now ploughing snow when I should be waking up to a wonderful Polynesian woman every morning. Over.'

The other drivers laughed in the solitude of their trucks and temporarily forgot about the snow meeting the windshield. Hank Murphy smiled at the conclusion of his story, but it had not been just *good clean fun*. To make the story real he would have needed to explain the withdrawal he had gone through, how he had shuddered with tremens and torn at his hair in depression, strung out in bed for the entire week. He would have had to explain in detail the desperate cravings that made his head split and his forearms feel like rats were burrowing inside him in search of the drug. But that part he kept private because it wasn't funny.

'What year did we do that?' asked Blanks. 'Did you say 1971?'

'Yeah, I think it was.'

Blanks disagreed. 'No, it was '70. I remember when we got home, the news about Ray Marak hit town.'

'Oh. Yeah, that's right. 1970 . . . yep. Yep.'

Hoping to make a joke, one of the younger drivers added, 'You mean Scarface? Over.'

The CB radio went silent for several seconds. Finally Blanks responded, 'Wow, I've never actually heard anyone say it before! Believe me, that isn't a name you want to say around Ray.'

Blanks absorbed the awkward moment by returning to the Hawaii story, tacking on a completely false ending, longer than the original story, about how on the drive home they met two hitch-hiking Australian girls who wanted to marry Hank and Blanks on the spot, which led Blanks into another story about another hitch-hiker, one who Blanks became con-vinced was Jimmy Hoffa just as soon as he had dropped the man off at a bus station in Tonnamowoc.

While Blanks talked, Hank turned his truck down the gravel road that led past the Marak farm, marking the last turn of his looping radius around Immaculate. The name 'Scarface' reminded Hank of what he knew about Ray. He considered telling that story after Blanks finished.

No one knew at first why Ray did not come home as soon as his tour of duty ended. The Army sent a letter to Ray's family regarding his expected separation date from service, but August came and went without even a phone call from Ray. In September of 1970, Mrs Marak had to contact the Red Cross to inquire about her son. Finally word came that he was missing in action. The assumption in Immaculate was that he was dead. The townspeople prayed with Mr and Mrs Marak, but the war had already lasted so long that no one remembered why it was being fought, and in time hope dis-solved. September passed. Then October and November and most of December before a ghost walked into Immaculate. It was two days before Christmas and he looked like a stray dog, bandaged up and broken down, with his face wrapped heavily in gauze, his body emaciated. The quiet man who had smiled often returned detached, sullen and nearly mute. Renee somehow picked up the pieces of Ray and glued him back together. The whole Marak family aged quickly, badly. It deformed them all.

Ray's father suffered his first heart attack on New Year's Day and died five days later. After the funeral Ray's mother cracked up and went into a nursing home, where she lived for only another month. Ray had to get out of town, right away, so he bought a motorcycle and left town with Renee, to defuse, heading south in midwinter.

No one in Immaculate mentioned Ray's face but everyone whispered about his days as a prisoner of war. Ray offered nothing to the curious. However, after a softball game one night, he told Hank a few secrets about his time outside of Immaculate. People liked to tell Hank things, probably because the whole town knew everything about him. One of Ray's stories involved a solo parachute drop into the jungle to make a helicopter landing site, armed with only a chainsaw and a pistol. Another story was about Ray's time in Chicago, after his release from the Veterans' Hospital: his uniform had drawn the wrong kind of attention from some militant protestors and they had reopened the scars on his face that had only started to heal. Then Ray abruptly stopped talking, collected his softball gear and went home.

Hank turned his truck around as he reached the county line, where the contract ended. The loop around Immaculate took Hank nearly three hours and covered the most dangerous gravel roads. Blanks followed another loop, leaving Immaculate along an icy valley and zigzagging back to town along a slippery ridge. If Hank and Blanks followed the schedule exactly, they would meet at a four-way stop where they could talk for a moment and indulge their kinder addictions: Copenhagen and coffee.

Almost as quickly as the ploughs cut through the drifts, the blowing grains of snow piled up again. As the hour neared nine o'clock, Hank and the other drivers turned the ploughs in the direction of the church, and like pinholes in black paper, headlights began to dot the roads, as church-goers journeyed through the storm against the instructions of Father Dimer.

When Hank dropped the plough blade and started back towards Immaculate, he wondered if Renee knew the war stories about Ray. Then Hank shuddered, thinking of another weighty fact he knew about Ray and Renee, something Ray himself probably did not even know yet.

15

Josh Werther didn't move from his chair except to freshen up his drink. The note sat on his lap with the words staring up at him: 'Thank you. ❤ R.'

The TV was turned on but Josh paid no attention. Storm warnings ran across the bottom of the screen continuously under a rerun of *All in the Family*. After Josh had placed the call to Renee, he had felt both ashamed and liberated. Just hearing her voice lifted his spirit, though he knew the call would anger her. He amused himself with a resolution to drink more often, so that he might phone her every day.

He mumbled, 'Ray, the great hero. The great imbecile. And she married him.'

An ugly look of derision came over his face before he took another sip. Josh's respect for Ray teetered back and forth on a daily basis, but with the wine marinating his mind he despised the man. Ray would never know all that Josh had done for him. Not only was he undeserving of his wife, he didn't even deserve his farm. Some day Renee would come to her senses.

Josh brooded in his chair until he heard a rap on his front door. His heart raced with the ridiculous thought that Renee might be standing on the other side. Before opening the door he paused to look in a mirror. He straightened his collar, touched up his hair, and took a deep breath.

Kathy stood on the stoop holding a bottle of wine. 'You haven't even changed clothes yet?'

Josh exhaled and pointed in the direction of the television. 'I've been watching the weather on TV. Not sure if we should venture out tonight. It looks bad.'

She wore a neat dress that hugged her body. She knew the fit would be thought too snug by some of the parishioners, but that was half the fun of wearing it. Her hair fell to her shoulders and her fringe was curled. She touched Josh's arm and waited for him to respond. Slowly, he moved forward and lightly touched his lips to hers.

'You've been drinking,' she declared.

'Red-handed. Purple-tongued. You caught me.' Josh held out his hands and let them fall to his sides.

Kathy held up the bottle of wine. 'Just so I don't have to scold you about drinking before church: do you mind if I join you?'

'By all means. Pour me a glass and we can drink to future workplace indecencies.'

The bottle had a twist-off cap instead of a cork: Immaculate Liquor stocked a limited wine inventory. Josh grabbed the bottle and put his arm around Kathy's waist and walked her to the kitchen. He poured two glasses of wine. They raised the glasses and Josh said, 'May our place of employment be awkward for ever more.'

Referring to the bank cleaning lady, Kathy said, 'May Sarah Reynolds forgive our indulgence.'

'May it never happen again at work,' Josh said, 'but if it does, let it be soon.'

'Amen, Goody Werther.' She set her drink down and

curled her arms around his waist. She kissed him slowly, then aggressively, until Josh set his glass down and embraced her.

'It turns me on,' said Kathy.

'What does?'

'The taste on your tongue. The liquor.'

'You're joking.'

Kathy shook her head. 'No, I like the taste of liquor on a man's breath.'

'Okay then. I'll splash myself with Irish Cream before I come to work each day.'

They picked up their glasses again and took a sip to complete the toast. Unconsciously, Josh was comparing Kathy to Renee: Kathy's button nose and devilish eyebrows reminded him of Renee, and when she pulled the glass away from her mouth, her smile reminded him of Renee. He invited her into the living room to sit on the couch.

'You really surprised me today,' Josh said. 'We've started this relationship in a backwards way, and by that I mean . . . well, you know what I mean. I feel that – and this is just an idea – maybe we should get to know each other now. For example, in case I need to get you a gift sometime, that is, from the lingerie department, what's your bra size?'

'Thirty-four C.' Kathy leaned back against the couch and smiled. 'Now do I get to ask you a question?'

'Yes, but this is not Truth or Dare.'

'Why aren't you spending Christmas Eve with your parents?'

'Uff-da,' Josh said. 'That's pretty personal.'

'And bra size isn't?'

'I thought I could start on top and work down to your

thighs. Kidding. Bra size is quantifiable, but this is more complicated. Okay, if you want to know family history, my parents and I get along just fine. Our arrangement is that I see them from time to time, but our family is not especially close. I spend Christmas Day with Mom and Dad. I was never beaten or molested by them, or if I was I've blocked it out. We're just not a real close family. Have I covered everything?'

Kathy shrugged. 'Not very interesting.'

'No, it's not. Sorry about that. Now it's my turn to ask another question. Since you bring up family, I don't know a thing about yours. Actually, that's not entirely true. I know your parents because they are my clients, but beyond finances I don't know anything really. This afternoon you made it clear that your father didn't treat your mother very good. That's a shame. But that's all I know about you. I'm not much of a gossip, unlike everyone else in Immaculate. What else should I know? Any good details?'

Kathy's face turned sour, like a sardonic teenager. 'You want to know the dirt? Is that what you're asking?'

'Of course! Doesn't everyone? Would conversation even exist in Immaculate without dirt? Talk of weather is just a warm-up to backstabbing.'

She changed the tone of her voice to sound like a princess. 'There's very little to tell about in my family. This is Immaculate – pretty and perfect. Nothing goes wrong here.' Her voice returned to normal. 'I was born in St Paul when my dad and mom were living there. Dad was working in the stockyards, but then a position in Tonnamowoc opened up and we moved back to Immaculate.'

'Your parents grew up in Immaculate?'

'Not my dad. He grew up in Tonnamowoc. He's an ass-hole. I avoid him. But my mom is my best friend. She grew up here.'

'Oh really. Who were your mother's parents?'

'Grandpa and Grandma.'

'Did they have names, or did they just go by Granny and Paps?'

'David and Cindy. Grandpa was a Freitag. Grandma was a Becker.'

And now Josh knew why Kathy reminded him of Renee. Renee's mother was a Becker. Everyone in Immaculate had heard of the famous Becker sisters. They had grown up in the forties and all nine were gorgeous enough to be talked about a generation later. Many of them had left Immaculate when men from the outside world discovered them, but Renee's mother, and apparently Kathy's mother, had stayed in the area. Josh tried to determine Kathy's relationship to Renee and figured that the women were probably second cousins – probably knew one another only casually. But now that he knew them both intimately, he saw more similarities than he had initially detected. There were the eyebrows and the smile, and now the feisty attitude and the unchecked passion.

'My turn,' Kathy said. 'How many women have you slept with?'

'Woah. That's classified.'

'How come? I mean, we've already slept together. Don't I have a right to know?'

'Yes, we have so many rights today, don't we? This is the age of entitlement. Okay, the answer is . . . four. No, it's five.'

'Liar. I hear that you are the modern Lothario.'

'Lothario?' Josh balked. 'Hardly. I'm more like a . . . Tristan . . . or better yet, a Sydney Carton kind of guy.' He wondered if his references would be appreciated by Kathy.

'Hmm, Sydney Carton.' She looked at his bookcase. 'Well, let's see. That just might be verifiable, since you drink alone. Was it port wine you were chugging today?'

Yet another similarity between Kathy and Renee – they were both readers. He suspected that all the Becker women must have been bookish.

Kathy asked, 'But would you martyr yourself for a love that you can never have?'

'I suppose I would.' Josh smiled uneasily. He looked away from Kathy and sipped his wine before changing the subject. 'I should get ready for church now. I apologize.'

'Don't apologize. I've got a whole bottle of wine to keep me company.'

Josh laughed and set his glass on the coffee table. While he showered and dressed he digested the facts put forth by Kathy.

Kathy stood and looked around the living room. She moved slowly, finding nothing of note other than that his walls did not have what most houses in Immaculate displayed with pride: a set of mounted antlers. At the bookcase she paused for some time. Thumbing through the titles, she picked up a few books and flipped through the pages. One sat alone on an empty shelf, as if it was the book Josh was currently reading. It was a small book of poems, *Sonnets from the Portuguese*. Kathy thumbed through it and noticed that certain pages were dog-eared and marked in a woman's handwriting. Kathy flipped to the title page of the book and looked for an inscription but found nothing written there. She flipped to the back and there was a lock of yellow hair and a short love note written in cursive. The inscription mimicked an opening line of a Browning poem:

> I never gave a lock of hair away
> To a man, Dearest, except this to thee.
> Love forever, R

'Oh, that's so sweet.' She pitied the old romantic letter, but wondered if 'forever' had been too long for Josh or the mysterious 'R'. Kathy put the book back on the empty shelf and continued her investigation of the living room, pausing for a moment by a picture of Josh's parents. She sat down and looked at the TV, then got up to increase the volume so that she could catch the last few minutes of *All in the Family*. She imitated both Edith and Archie, acting to an audience of no one: '*Oh Ah-chie! What is it now, Edish?*'

When she came back to the couch she noticed a piece of paper on the floor. Kathy picked it up and tossed it on the coffee table. The piece of paper flipped over and revealed another message, with the same terse signature: 'Thank you. ♥ R.' Kathy wondered how recent the inscribed book and the message were, and if this 'R' woman and Josh still dated. Kathy considered the possibility that the note had fallen from the pages of the book without her noticing.

16

Wearing his bright white Christmas vestments, Father Dimer knelt before a small statue of Mary in the sacristy. He prayed for the safety of the travellers on the roads, but doubted that many would venture out. He intended on keeping the midnight Mass short so that those who did make it could go home before the power went out. Incense burned behind him and filled his lungs. He ran over the homily he had prepared. Two books on his desk lay open. One was a book of famous sermons by Jonathan Edwards, open to a page that contained so many red pen marks that the original text was barely readable. Next to it was a book by Lucretius, *On the Nature of Things*, its pages containing only a few red underlinings.

Father Dimer closed his eyes and asked himself, 'Can I get away with a reference to Humpty Dumpty?' He looked up at the statue of Mary for advice and then answered his own question. 'Yes, I know the rule of thumb. Vague is venerable.'

John Delaney stood outside the sacristy waiting for the door to open, upon which time he would summon the altar boys for the procession and the beginning of Mass. In his exhaustive preparations, John had lit three entire boxes of candles. The altar boys were busy at the front of the church setting up a table of communion gifts, whisking chalices and towels and holy water across the altar. The boys kept one eye on John, knowing that he would raise a red handkerchief when Father Dimer was ready to begin. John's task was hardly necessary, as Father Dimer invariably began precisely on the hour. But John needed something to do and he was too old to be an altar boy, although, if asked, he gladly would have donned the little robe.

The Marak family entered the church. John stiffened when he saw Jacob. He did his best to view the family with his peripheral vision, trying to avoid a direct stare from the little devil incarnate.

Jacob's jaw dropped when he looked at the manger scene and saw where the hungry sheep now stood. He wanted to run up for a closer look, but Ray had a tight grip on his hand. With his mouth gaping, Jacob looked around the church until he spotted John.

Earlier in the day, after scolding Jacob, John had decided that the hungry sheep was singing, so in the end he placed it next to Jesus. Staring straight ahead, John sensed the evil gaze of Jacob now upon him. Unable to resist, he looked at the boy and saw his open mouth. Trembling, John snapped back to attention, as straight as an axle-rod. Still, curiosity consumed him, and he peeked over at Jacob once again, who this time looked back, dangling his tongue and pushing his nose up with his thumb.

'Now there's a droll little piggy,' John muttered, 'and don't you just know some day he'll grow up to be a damn hog.'

Jacob said loudly, 'That sheep sure does look hungry!'

'It's singing,' John shook his fist, 'you little bastard!'

Ray yanked Jacob by the arm to stifle any further outburst. The jerk startled John, too, and he returned to his position of attention, but the thought that the sheep was hungry bothered him still.

Through the thick sacristy walls, Father Dimer could hear echoes of the organ and the Christmas carols, but little else. 'O Come, All Ye Faithful' resonated in sombre minor chords. The melody barely reached him but he heard enough to know that at least the organist had made it through the storm. From his kneeling position, the priest put his elbows on the armrest and made a fist of one hand and then wrapped the other hand around it. He leaned until his nose touched his praying hands. He closed his eyes, his white eyebrows bowed inward towards his nose, and then sang quietly:

> 'O come, all ye faithful,
> Joyful and triumphant,
> O come all ye citizens to . . . Immaculate.'

Father Dimer opened his eyes and smiled at the statue of Mary. 'I couldn't resist.'

He stood up, turned to the mirror to tighten his cincture one last time and opened the door. Out of habit, he paused for a second to avoid being struck by John's arm, which shot into the air like an Indianapolis flagman's. John waved his semaphore back and forth to catch the attention of the altar boys, who could barely have missed the wild flapping if they were blind. The boys walked down a side aisle to the rear of the church where John and Father Dimer were waiting to greet them.

The priest could not believe the volume of voices and

music that poured from the pews. Looking at the size of the crowd, he felt a bulge growing in his throat. The church was full. He peeked out into the lobby and the people were queued out of the door, the cold air and snow blowing in behind them, chatting about the roads and singing.

The emergence of Father Dimer in full midnight Mass raiment made John forget Jacob and the hungry sheep. John whispered sharply, 'D'you see the crowd, Father? I let folks start filling up the basement ten minutes ago, just like you said, in case of overflow, isn't that the right thing, now there? And you told them all to stay home tonight! And then they all went and showed up here anyhow now!' John laughed and continued waving the handkerchief.

Father Dimer nervously adjusted his glasses. 'I've always suspected that no one ever listens to me.'

'Father, can't you see they all come to see you, now then there?'

Father Dimer swallowed his emotion. John had a way of validating his life with such compliments. His initial assignment to Immaculate had felt like exile, and in the early years he had wanted to leave that cold corner of the earth, but now it was that corner he cared about more than any other place. And hearing John's praise, his damp eyes twinkled in the candlelight.

One of the altar boys picked up the processional cross and planted himself at the centre of the main aisle. The ancient woman at the organ turned up the volume dial to its highest notch for the final few notes of 'O Come All Ye Faithful'. Before she began 'Hark the Herald Angels Sing', she paused to turn down her hearing aid. Then she played the keyboard with ninety-five-year-old vigour, and brought the congregation to their feet. Everyone but a few teenagers sang out loud. Father Dimer followed at the end of the opening procession, smiling and nodding at the admiring parishioners, reaching out to squeeze the cheeks of newborns, to the elation of the parents. His oesophagus visibly trembled. He wanted to hug the moment and invite everyone to stay the entire night.

When he reached the steps of the altar, he genuflected and made his way towards his chair, where he turned and sang at the top of his lungs, but his trembling throat made his voice weak and for once he did not overpower the chorus. As the second verse of 'Hark the Herald Angels Sing' was coming to a close, the organist looked up at Father Dimer to see if she should continue. Going against his plan to keep Mass short, he gave her a nod. At the end of the third verse, he could not help himself: he gave another nod. When the singing stopped, the church rang with the last note of the organ. Not a single baby cried or child complained, even Jacob Marak. Outside, however, the wind howled, and the windows rattled against the forces of the night. Father Dimer suspected that the congregation felt compensated for their journey, and yet he had to repay them personally. He felt an aura in the church, the same aura that he discovered at age twenty-five, which had convinced him to sell his Harley Davidson and enter the seminary. Whenever he felt on the verge of doubt, this feeling kept him from leaving Immaculate.

Father Dimer beamed from the altar at the people, not knowing what to say, only what to do. The people seemed to be leaning forward to hear his first words. A tension grew. Father Dimer could have commanded them like soldiers.

He said nervously, 'If it gets bad outside, I'm not going to have enough quilts for all of you.'

The audience erupted into laughter that was as loud as their singing. They grew quiet again but the tension was broken and the sound of shuffling feet soothed the air.

'I know we usually do the greeting before Communion, and if I could help myself I would wait, but I would very much like to do the greeting now. So please, everyone say hello to your neighbours, and don't be shy to reach across a few pews or go across the aisle to greet a friend if you have to. I won't be shy.'

Father Dimer made his way to the pews and plucked a baby from a mother's arms. He carried the baby with him in one arm and worked his way towards the rear of the church, shaking as many hands as possible, giving as many hugs as he could. Unlike the usual Sunday Mass, people spoke openly, even to their enemies, and grudges temporarily faded.

Ray and Renee Marak, busy shaking hands, did not notice Jacob slide underneath the pew into the row ahead of them, where he popped up like a cork and began shaking hands with everyone. Ethan laughed when he saw Jacob appear. As quickly as Jacob had popped up, he ducked down again and popped up another row ahead, and stayed in that row until he had shaken hands with everyone in that pew as well.

Ray and Renee continued to chat with friends and neighbours while the priest made his way back up the aisle towards the altar.

Ethan started to worry when he lost sight of Jacob between the moving bodies in the rows ahead. The chances of Jacob returning to his proper seat before Ray noticed were dwindling. After the afternoon incident with the bat, Ethan saw Ray's leather belt looming over this latest trick. Straining his neck, he felt a hand slapping at his shoe. Ethan looked down at Jacob's head facing up.

'Stand up!' Ethan motioned to Jacob.

'I think I'm stuck.'

'Where? What's stuck?'

'My shoestring or something. I can't reach it.'

Ethan leaned over the pew ahead to look at Jacob's feet and saw the shoestring slung over a nail on the kneeler. Rather than jump over the pew to save Jacob or direct him to unloop his shoe himself, Ethan told Jacob to kick it off. Following Ethan's orders, Jacob kicked and stood up, just as his parents returned to their pew. Had either looked closely at him, they would have seen how dishevelled his hair had become, and a fresh grease stain on his trousers, and that his shoulders slumped unevenly from the loss of his shoe. His wry smile made Ethan laugh again.

Seated in the balcony, Kathy and Josh overlooked the church and reviewed the crowd, noting the irregular attendees. They had arrived late and preferred hiding on the balcony to keep the alcohol on their breath away from the gossips perched on their informally reserved pews. Normally, only mothers with young children and those who had to leave church early sat in the balcony. Josh scanned the crowd for Renee, as he did every week; from this viewpoint he could ogle her without embarrassment. Josh felt loose and buzzed from his afternoon of brooding and drinking.

Father Dimer resumed his place on the altar and spared

no time getting through the litany and the readings. He knew that it would be selfish to keep the people for more than forty minutes. When the reading from the Gospel of Luke ended, Father Dimer went to his large white chair, as was customary while the congregation contemplated his words, but he bounced off the seat as if the chair had electricity running through it, and began the sermon, smiling the whole time. He worried that his words might not live up to the occasion, but having seen plenty of bad sermons, he knew that a redeeming one could be delivered the following week, if necessary.

He began: 'I am getting old. I've started to forget things. My imagination is growing wild. I could have sworn that I spent the afternoon playing Paul Revere, warning people about a terrible storm and how everyone should stay home for the night. Perhaps my mind has tricked me again. I am seventy-two years old. I may be starting to have delusions. Bear with me, friends.'

He paused and let the crowd get comfortable, and after a few hacking winter coughs, the real sermon began.

'I have a story that I wanted to share with you all, about driving on bad roads. It goes like this. There was a wicked road that iced over every winter, iced over quicker than all the rest, and on the icy road was a sharp turn, but no one ever put up a sign to mark the bend in the road, and without fail, every year a passing motorist, usually from out of town, went off the road. The road had no railings or barriers, and the poor folks dropped off an embankment on to a steep hillside. As the story goes, one year a couple was driving late at night when they came to the curve and went into a spin that sent them over the edge. As the car plunged the wife cried out, "God save us!" and the husband cried out, "God darn it!" He didn't say "darn", but you can imagine what he said. While the car was in the air, the wife looked at the husband and scolded him for taking the Lord's name in vain. The husband yelled out, "Well, Lord have mercy—", and miraculously the car suddenly got hung up in the branches of a large tree and their lives were saved. The couple embraced. They held tightly to each other. Then the woman said to the man, "You see, God saved us because you listened to me and you should always do so." The husband said, "I was trying to say: Lord have mercy, do you always have to get the last word in?"'

A church laugh filled the room, starting and ending quickly. Father Dimer increased the volume on the single speaker that hung from the ceiling, hoping to overcome the sound of the wind pounding against the windows.

'Tonight I want to talk about what I consider to be one meaning of Christmas. Not by any means the only reason to celebrate Christmas, but one reason to celebrate Christmas. Better yet, what I want to talk about is all of *you*, all of *us* – the "*we*" that inhabit this place tonight – the people of this parish. This place, this church, this location where we meet – this building where five roads meet. This steeple and these bricks planted in our landscape. It is an empty room most of the week. We make a journey here hoping that we will get something out of it, that we will be better off because we drove here. If we did not have that expectation, we wouldn't set out in blinding snow. We expect something to be here but can't name what it is. It's an intangible *something* that we want to leave here with. We understand, without saying it to each other, that there is something special about our coming together.'

Father Dimer lowered his glasses, pushed up his sleeve, and showed the people his wristwatch. 'As long as that togetherness doesn't go past an hour and a half, am I right?'

Another short laugh rose and fell.

'But tonight, and every time we get together, we make this room alive. What is here? We say God is here. And that's true: he is here because we want him to be. God is everywhere, but we feel him here in this space when we are together. God is here with us as much as he was with Mary and Joseph on the night Jesus was born. Luke and Matthew tell us of that cold night, how the shepherds and the flocks came in from the fields to be warm together. It was a family of strangers spending the night together because of a common need for shelter, for warmth, survival; for the feeling of God to be shared. In a way, that night was the first midnight Mass, and we try to recreate that moment. If you'll look at the nativity scene that our good man John Delaney set up, you can begin to see that we are huddled today much like the holy family was two thousand years ago. We are the extended family. In those days there was struggle, there was uncertainty, there were nights when they didn't know if they could find a way, but they stayed together and collectively had strength. Individually we can all be strong, but not all the time, even if you think you can. As you get older you start to learn that strength today is not guaranteed to be strength tomorrow. Everybody has the struggle. But when we come together, I know that our strength is greater than the sum of our parts. It grows in leaps and bounds. It grows in exponents. Three of us together are stronger than nine individuals by themselves, and four of us together are stronger than sixteen persons in solitude. On nights like tonight, when I know that some of you took a great risk to be here, and I look out at your solid faces and feel your strength, I feel stronger. That is why I often say: evil can be endured, goodness can be attained. I turn to Jesus and I am strong.'

He cleared his throat with a dry cough before moving into his anti-Edwards sermon.

'For some reason, we chose a slippery patch of earth to live on. We stand and walk in slippery places and sometimes suffer a fall. Here we are exposed to sudden changes and, in time, our foot gives out. On slippery ground, our own weight by itself can make us unstable. It is said that when that time comes, God will know when, and when the foot starts to slide, he will be there to shore your foot up, to balance the weight. God will hold you up in these slippery places, and at that very instant, he has you.

'He has an interest in seeing you through, to help you to heaven. He waits forever for you, to return you to a state of constancy, but you have to embrace life in the meantime. A martyr of truth once said, "You are wise to seek neither to escape life nor death, for life does not trouble those that embrace it. Death does not seem an evil to those embracing life." He also said, "No pleasure is a bad thing in itself, but the things which produce certain pleasures can be. It is impossible to live a pleasant life without living wisely and honourably."

'Then I say *virtue* is what we are looking for here in this church, and that's what we see in that nativity. There is no happiness in life without virtue. How wonderful is the word virtue alongside the words of Jesus, when he said, "Be not afraid, little flock." It is perhaps impossible to conceive of words that carry in them greater meaning than those. If you cry to God for help, he will pity you when you slide, show you his favor, and if you break through the ice he will tread that icy water with you.'

Hearing those words, Jacob and Ethan snapped to attention and looked at each other knowingly.

Father Dimer continued, now mixing his Catholic, Hindu and Roman philosophy freely. 'And though he knows that you can bear the weight of anything, he will make you stronger yet with his mercy; he will help you lean into that stress, and he will only sprinkle you with hardship but not freeze or ruin you. He will never hate you, but he will hold you, in his utmost hopefulness: no place shall be deemed to low for him to join you. He will walk down in the gutter with you until you walk out in triumph.

'The hardship you are exposed to is that which the world will inflict, that he might show what strength you have. God wishes to show to us both how excellent his love is and also how tolerable the wrath of others is. Sometimes men and women have a mind to show how strong they can be *against* one another instead of *with* one another, thinking they are provoked to some revenge. But God is also willing to show his reciprocal mercy, and magnify his strength against the sufferings of the world. He says, "Come to me, all you who are weary and burdened, and I will give you rest. Take my yoke upon you and *lean* with me." And the more of us who take up the yoke and lean *together*, the better the chance of getting something accomplished. But if your efforts fail, you do not need to be angry: you must learn to control your anger, because from anger comes confusion, from confusion your memory lapses, and then your understanding is lost. And from loss of understanding, sadly, you are easily ruined. When the gentle and humble flock lifts up what seemed an awful weight from you, you will be glad you did not get angry. The calm man is free from disturbance, while the angry are fully disturbed.

'I am talking about hard times. It is easy to forget his strength when you are struggling with something like money. When you are angry, then as much as ever, God will be waiting for you, and Immaculate will be waiting for you, and I will be waiting for you. At some point your strength will fade and possibly torment you – but that's why we are here tonight. You will have these hardships, but never without that handlebar of God to hang on to, and the net of community to catch you. And when you reach this state of suffering, then the rest of us hope you will withstand that test. He has said, "I will never leave you or forsake you." Then we can say with confidence, "The Lord is my helper; I will not be afraid. What can *anyone do to me?*"

'It would be dreadful to suffer this world without that assistance, but you have an extra hand. There will be no end to this. It is an open-ended invitation. When you look forward, you shall see him forever waiting for you in that moment, one more chance before you to make the right choice, and it could be yourself that saves you, but more likely it will be someone else.

'In our unity here, I feel as if we were the shepherds and

farmers who came in from the land. More than anything, we are here tonight to celebrate being together. What did we learn most of all from Jesus? He gave us a framework to build our lives and our town. We drive into a night storm without doubt, because we know in our hearts that even if we fall, Immaculate will put us and our family back together. One of us will *never* be weak when the rest can rebuild him.'

Father Dimer noticed his hand was in a fist over the lectern, and it surprised him. He flinched and his hand sprung open.

'Before I came out tonight, I wondered how full the church would be and when I looked out and saw you all I was truly overwhelmed. If Santa Claus would wait another day I would gladly keep all of you here, but I don't think the kids would appreciate that. Knowing that you came tonight through the drifting roads reminds me what adversity does to our town. Life is not so easy, after all. But then this child is born with a message, pure and simple, that can apply to every situation and challenge. It's a message that can guide you to the right decision, even when the right decision is the more difficult decision, and through this set of values we can find common ground to stand upon. Togetherness. A reason to come together, a reason to be strong. He gave us the words accompanied with action. Simple words of love, from a man that only lived thirty-three years.'

He sighed. 'Most of all, I am lucky to be in front of good people, the people of Immaculate. I am fortified by your presence. I appreciate every car that is in the parking lot tonight, because God came here inside every car.'

Father Dimer felt tired, and sighed when he took his seat to reflect on his words.

No one coughed or rustled in their seats. The audience let the words sink into them like drops falling on a dry sponge. Solemnly the Mass continued. During the silent parts of the service, when neither Father Dimer's voice nor the organ sounded, the biting wind and whipping snow could be heard rattling against the stained-glass windows and the wooden doors of the church. The pelting of the snow sounded like hail at times, but the atmosphere inside remained tranquil.

Father Dimer recited the Eucharistic from memory. Some parishioners followed, dragging their index fingers over the small type of the missal booklet, while others simply listened to the familiar chant.

As he neared the end of the prayer, Father Dimer lifted the chalice in both hands and recited the words of Jesus at the Last Supper; just as he said 'Do this in memory of me' the power went out and candlelight took over. A few children gasped but the bulk of the audience remained silent. John's excess of candles created a soft corona around the altar. The wind howled as Father Dimer invited the parishioners to begin coming forward for Communion. A single file of silent people formed in the centre aisle as the Father handed out Communion hosts. When one of the floorboards creaked, Father Dimer noticed the lack of music and glanced at the organist.

The old woman's bowed back straightened and she went to the piano and began to play the Ave Maria. Her tiny voice permeated the church, warbling between the piano and the wind, and with the vibrato of a handsaw.

Returning from Communion, Ray and Renee kneeled and held one another's hands. Josh and Kathy made their way back to the balcony in silence as the wavering old voice concluded the Ave Maria. The last footsteps thumped on the carpet and Father Dimer looked to the rear of the church and saw John Delaney grinning from scar to scar. The priest smiled at him and rose from his chair, and the crowd stood with him.

'Take care of yourselves tonight. Drive carefully. I want to ask one favour. Please, look to your left and your right. When you make it home, call each other. Also, find your closest neighbours and follow each other home so that you can verify each other's safety. I want everyone to make it home. Now if you will please bow your heads and pray for God's blessing. Have a Merry Christmas and keep Jesus in your hearts. In the name of the Father, and of the Son, and of the Holy Spirit. Amen.'

'Amen,' answered the crowd.

The organist began to sing 'Silent Night' and the congregation joined her. The procession passed the pews and Mass ended. After the first verse, people began to move towards the doors, singing along until they reached the exit.

The first man to open the church door was met with a blast of air and several inches of snow fell from over the door on to his head.

Ray and Renee stayed until the old woman stopped singing. Ray looked at the people in the pews flanking him and saw Joke's family. The sight of Joke's father, Bill, killed Ray's happiness, but he forced a smile and greeted the man.

'So Bill, who's following who?'

Bill said, 'Don't matter to me.'

'You follow me, then. I've got to go past your place anyway, and that way I won't have to slow down for you to turn.'

'You won't have to slow down for me, Ray.' Bill smiled, and Ray noticed his mouth was still crooked from drinking.

When Ray reached the door he saw a glut of snowploughs in the parking lot, all with flashing lights. Tommy Blanks and Hank Murphy had dispatched the entire fleet to converge on the church and lead the charge home.

Hank waved from the window of his truck. He yelled, 'Okay, let's go.' The diesel engines poured smoke and the trucks started to crawl down the five separate roads that met at the church. Since it was miles from Immaculate itself, the ploughmen focused on the critical roads and left the minor, gravel roads to drift.

Bill and Ray made smalltalk as they walked towards the vehicles. Car and truck tyres squealed on the ice in the parking lot, sounding like cats fighting. Ray spoke between his teeth, forcing a smile until his cheeks could take no more. He opened the door of his pickup to let Renee and the boys climb inside. The windows had a thick sheet of ice. Before closing the truck door, Ray grabbed the ice scraper.

'Boy,' Bill said, 'the weatherman wasn't kidding about tonight. This is nasty.'

Ray waited until Bill's family was inside their pickup and the door was shut. As Bill turned to open the door, Ray clamped Bill in place against his truck. Neither family could see or hear the exchanges taking place between the fathers.

Ray pinched off the blood flow in Bill's arm, and pulled him close.

Smelling the booze even in the cold wind, Ray snorted. 'You keep your whiskey too close to your work.'

Bill tried to tug his arm away, but it did not budge. 'That's none of your *fuckin'* business, Marak—'

Ray pushed the ice scraper under Bill's chin, hard enough that it closed the windpipe.

'You made it my business. You made it my business by living on my road.'

Bill gasped, 'Your road?!'

Ray pushed harder. 'And Christmas is the only reason I don't educate you right now, but you will get it before you see 1982, I promise. If I see Joke bruised again, that day will come hard on you, much harder on you than it will on Joke. I swear to God, even if I go to hell for it, I will teach you regret.'

Ray pulled back on the ice scraper to let Bill speak. Bill stared into Ray's face and gasped, 'I'll be sure to keep a rifle loaded, just for *you*, Ray.'

Another shove from the ice scraper caused Bill to gasp.

'Good. You do that,' Ray whispered. 'You might even want to sleep with it. I have been shot at a few times before, and by sober men.'

Bill's face went blank. He looked at Ray. The scars around his eye seemed to have a heartbeat. Ray let go and walked away.

'You can forget about using my combine next fall, Marak, you cocksucker.'

'That's fine, Bill, I'd rather pick the corn by hand than kiss your ass. Get that bottle out of the barn. Merry Christmas.'

Ray violently scraped his windshield, and gave Bill a final glare before getting into the truck. He slammed the door so hard that he startled Renee and the boys.

'It's almost Christmas now!' he said with a big smile. 'Time to get ready for Santa, right, boys?'

17

Kathy McKay and Josh Werther learned that there was a drawback to sitting in the balcony. They stood on the stairs while everyone in the body of the church filed out, followed by the late arrivals, who came up from the church basement. By the time Kathy and Josh made it outside, most of the cars had disappeared from the parking lot and the roads in all five directions flashed with the red blur of braking tail-lights.

Kathy shivered as the wind hit her. 'This is why, Josh. This is why I am leaving Immaculate as soon as possible.'

Josh laughed, 'I've heard that one before.'

'But I'm serious about it.'

'So was I.'

'Brrr! We should have stayed in the church. It was hotter than two mice screwing in a wool sock!'

They got in her car and she turned the key in the ignition. 'And now this.' The interior lights flickered as the crankshaft rotated slowly. 'Oh come on, little car,' Kathy pleaded. 'We've been through so much.'

'I think it's dead,' Josh said. 'We should have brought my car, huh?'

'Your car needed a jump this afternoon.'

'But now the battery is charged up.'

Kathy released the hood latch and Josh got out and searched for another car to use for a jumpstart. Father Dimer and John stood in the doorway of the church. Before Father Dimer could say anything, John had run down the church stairs and driven the priest's car over to Kathy's.

Father Dimer went inside the church. The wind slammed the front door behind him and he jumped.

'Uff-da!'

He shivered and walked into the sacristy. The shiver would not let go of his shoulders, as if someone were trying to wake him up. The cold air cut through his thick vestments as if they were pyjamas. At his desk chair he sat down and faced the wall. He shivered and bristled again, this time with an ugly expression and a loud 'Brrr!' Then he settled and looked over his shoulder to make sure no one was watching as he pulled open one of the drawers in the desk. In the drawer's false bottom was Father Dimer's secret stash. He pulled out three magazines and set them on the desk. He picked up the top magazine and sighed.

Opening the magazine to a random page, he sighed again. The picture was luscious, exquisite. He imagined himself there, laid out with a smile on his face.

Above the picture was the title of the article: 'Planning your Retirement in the Florida Keys.'

In the car, Kathy felt the cold seat against her legs and cursed her decision to wear a dress instead of trousers. Her winter jacket only went down to her knees, and her pantyhose were useless in keeping out the cold. In only a thin suit jacket, John Delaney hustled about, assisting Josh with a jumpstart. Despite his winter jacket, Josh felt the cold cut through his trousers like a bullwhip. He touched the freezing metal battery posts and instantly his fingers absorbed the cold. John insisted on connecting the battery cables but he refused.

With the jumper cables in his hands, Josh said, 'First I connect the cables to the running car, and I connect the positive post and then the negative post. Then I connect the dead car the same way: positive before negative. Am I right, John?'

'I just stick reds on reds and blacks on blacks.' John shrugged. 'I never knew there was an order to it.'

Once the cables were in place, Kathy turned the key and nothing happened. Josh adjusted the clamps and Kathy tried again but still the car failed to turn over. The third time Josh touched metal with his bare hands, his fingers became numb. On his fourth adjustment the engine turned over. Kathy floored the accelerator so that the car roared to life. Josh saw her celebrating inside the car, shaking her mittened hands over her head. She revved the engine several times.

John said goodbye and drove Father Dimer's car back to the front of the church and ran up the front steps.

Hearing the front door of the church slam shut, Father Dimer scrambled to hide his magazines and he had barely put them in the drawer when John's red face appeared in the doorway.

'What are you doin' now, Father?'

Father Dimer shrugged nervously. 'Nothing. Why?'

'No reason,' John said, 'Just wondering.'

'Nope, nothing. Not doing anything.' Father Dimer paused and then stretched his arms out. 'Nothing at all.' The drawer started to slide open and he elbowed it shut again.

They looked at each other in uncomfortable silence. John asked, 'Should I get the poker chips now, Father?'

'Absolutely.' Father Dimer exhaled and nodded.

'It's a tradition, right, Father?'

'Yes,' he lied. 'It's a secret of the priesthood. You can't tell anyone.'

'Oh, I won't.'

Any detail about the Church excited John. He turned to leave, but Father Dimer stopped him.

'Say, John?'

John stuck his head back inside the door. 'Yes, Father?'

'Bring the corkscrew, too.'

In the car Josh wrung his hands together to restore feeling. He complained about the pain for a moment but stopped when he realized the details probably weren't worth explaining to Kathy. She hunched her shoulders and drove slowly down the country road. The snow streaming over the road resembled millions of parallel white threads travelling over a black loom. Unable to make out the yellow centre line, Kathy drove down what seemed to be the middle of the road. The ploughmen had removed all the drifts but nothing could be done to improve visibility. She no longer felt the effect of the alcohol she had drunk at Josh's before church. The rear wheels slipped for only a split second, but it was enough to make her grip the wheel and nearly overcorrect the back end.

'Woah!' she laughed. 'Wow, I thought I was going to lose it.'

Puffing into his fist for warmth, Josh said, 'You're fine. Remember – never panic. Just keep the wheel pointed in the direction you want to go and you're fine.'

'All the same,' Kathy said, 'I'm going to drive twenty miles an hour the rest of the way to town.'

'Whatever feels comfortable. Fine with me.'

'I would let you drive but I don't think I can stop until we get to town. I don't want to lose momentum.'

'Oh no, you're fine.'

He resumed puffing into his hand. He encouraged her. 'I have a good down blanket at home with your name on it.'

'Oh, thank God. Oh, I'm thinking of a big blanket and a warm bed and sleeping in late. I can't wait to get out of this dress. Do you know what I want to know right now? Who is the guy that invented pantyhose? I'd love to get my hands around his neck.'

'How do you know it was a man?'

'C'mon. Why would a woman invent something like that? It had to be a man. You love to see us squirm.'

'If that weren't true, I'd take offence.'

'Ah! I'm freezing!'

'Almost there.'

'Five miles is not almost.'

The car rolled towards Immaculate. Josh watched Kathy hunched up over the wheel. He had to smile at the picture. She made him laugh. She had a spark. He stopped comparing her to Renee and simply enjoyed her company. For a moment he was happy.

Sensing his stare, she rotated her body towards him and chattered her teeth. 'What?' Her eyes darted between the road and Josh.

Josh said, 'What?'

'What are you looking at me like that for?'

'I'm just looking at you.' He sat up straight. 'And I was thinking . . . I've had a really good time with you today.'

'You better have! How often do you get to have sex at work?' She looked over at him and then added, 'Don't answer that. So are you telling me that there might be a "we" for a while? To use the words of Father Dimer, there is a "we", an "us", a "togetherness"?'

He looked out the window and paused before looking back at Kathy. 'Yes. I think that is what I'm saying. There is a "we". I feel good about this. You make me feel . . . new.'

'That's because I'm an amazing woman.'

'And modest, too,' Josh said.

Kathy laughed and looked at him.

He put his arms out in front of him, using the dashboard as a brace, and yelled, 'Kathy, look out!'

A thin poplar tree fell on to the road directly in the path of the vehicle. Kathy swerved instinctively but hit the tree, knocking it off the road. The car went into a slow spin. Kathy jerked the steering wheel back and forth but could not correct the rear end, and the car plunged over the side of the road and rolled. The roll was not violent, but rather a slow tumble, and the car came to a stop, upright and mostly intact, at a forty-five degree angle. Kathy and Josh had bounced and tossed with each roll, but only Josh had his seat belt on. Kathy never wore one.

Josh blacked out for a second when his head hit the roof of the car. When the car finally stopped moving, his eyesight slowly returned. The accident seemed unreal, like something that was happening on TV. At first he believed that he would wake up in his bed. He heard nothing – silence – for a few seconds. Then, as if the volume was slowly being turned up, a faint blowing sound grew into the grim whine of the very real storm outside. A monotonous beeping increased with the wind as he recognized the 'door ajar' sound coming from the other side of the car. He heard a groan.

Josh's head swooned, and he fought the urge to lie back and rest. He put his hands to the sides of his head to feel for blood and bruises. On his crown a lump had already formed. When he pulled his hand away from the top of his head, he rubbed between his fingers a small amount of blood. A drip fell on his shirt, and he touched his cheek to find a second cut. He looked in the vanity mirror and saw a half-inch laceration on his face. He looked at the glove compartment and noticed blood on the knob. The accident had happened so fast he hadn't felt the impact when his head had swung forward. His thoughts flitted in confused trails, but he managed to sift and filter out his confusion until he reduced his thoughts to a single, critical one.

'Kathy.'

The roof of the car had caved inward and he could not see Kathy unless he leaned over and pressed his chest against the middle console. He started to move towards her but the seat belt locked him in place. He leaned backwards and forwards but still the seat belt held him. With aggression, he lunged forward and backward several more times and then stopped.

He said, 'Okay, I need to calm down. One thing at a time.'

Slowly, he unbuckled the seat belt and slipped out of the shoulder strap. He spoke to Kathy but she did not respond, so he crawled into the back seat and positioned his body behind her. He started to grab the side lever to lean the seat back, but he worried about moving her neck. There was not enough time to think, and his head throbbed with pain. He pulled the seat lever and slowly drew the driver's seat down towards his knees. The first thing he saw made him swallow hard. She had blood on her face.

A blanket in the back seat would have worked for stopping the blood but Josh could not use it as it was the only way of keeping Kathy warm. He examined her head with his fingers, discovering a shallow, oozing gash on her forehead. Using his sleeve he wiped away the blood to see the extent of the cut, but more blood oozed from the gash and started to run down her face. Josh set his forearm against her forehead.

He spoke out loud again. 'This isn't enough pressure.'

His medical experience went no further than the injuries he'd witnessed at softball games, but he knew enough to apply pressure. He was about to tear the blanket into strips when his necktie flopped over his hand. He scrambled to remove it and rifled through the car for something bulky and absorbent. In the glove compartment he found an oily rag. It looked like a guaranteed means of infection. Throwing things out of the glove compartment to the left and right, he became increasingly frantic, until he found a roll of black electrician's tape, with which he thought he might be able to create a butterfly bandage. Inside Kathy's purse he found two tampons – sterile, wrapped, and self-described as 'super absorbent'. With his sleeve, Josh wiped as much blood from her forehead as possible and taped the tampons over the wound with the black tape, and then added more tape before lassoing her forehead with his tie and snugging a knot directly over the taped area. He took a deep breath and watched for a minute to make sure no blood was oozing out the sides. The tape, tie and tampons made for a strange headband. He decided to look her over for bruises and other bleeding. When he pressed her ribs she moaned but remained unconscious. Josh determined that no blood was showing anywhere else on Kathy's dress, but he wondered about internal bleeding and all the other things he didn't know. Swearing under his breath, he sat back in the seat to think.

Cold air seeped into the car from the broken back window. The temperature in the car dropped to the same temperature as outside, though without the wind-chill. The activity had warmed Josh's hands. Thoughts punched through his head in rapid combinations. He considered trying to remove Kathy from the car, but he didn't know precisely where they were and therefore didn't know where he would take her. At first, the idea of leaving her seemed callous, but as the alternatives dwindled he decided that it was the only sensible option.

The road above seemed miles away. Since they had been the last to leave the church and had driven home alone, the crash would have gone unseen. The car had knocked the tree off the road, and the tyre tracks would soon be drifted over.

The cold air poured into the car through the window until Josh plugged the hole with Kathy's purse and the oily rag.

'Heat,' he mumbled. What about the car heater? The idea of starting the car, having had to jumpstart it twenty minutes ago, made him laugh. But he tried the key and the car started on the first try. He laughed again and turned the heat lever to its highest setting. The air pouring from the vents gradually began to warm.

Softly the radio played 'It Came Upon a Midnight Clear', Josh turned the volume off for a moment while he leaned over Kathy to feel her breath, and then sat back in the seat again. The song ended. A disc jockey talked about the weather in St Paul, where it had reached twenty degrees below zero. Parts of the state were now at thirty-five below. Josh winced at the numbers.

Kathy looked almost peaceful.

'I may get a dose of poetic justice tonight.' Hearing his voice comforted him, so he went on. 'I'm a sucker for adventure stories, Kathy, but not actual adventure.'

He blew on his hands. 'My favourite story as a teenager was 'To Build a Fire', by Jack London. I read it in ninth grade. Maybe they don't teach it any more. It's a story about a man walking on foot in the Yukon Territory, in extremely cold weather, who ignores all the good advice of older, wiser men. The young man thinks he is invincible. When I was a kid I always thought I could survive any storm or cold. On the worst nights I used to challenge my father to walk with me to the Immaculate grocery store, thinking that it wouldn't be that hard to survive . . . just like the guy in the story . . . who, well, in the end . . . freezes to death.' He sighed. 'Crap. Well, with that preface, I am going to see if I can run through the storm and find you a better place to stay for the night. But don't worry – I won't freeze.'

Josh chuckled at his comment; he was fishing for his confidence. Touching Kathy's cheek, he said, 'This has been an amazing day, Kathy. You definitely have made it interesting. But now I've got to find some help. Stay warm.'

The time had come. He kissed her on the lips before putting the blanket over her. Once he had tucked the corners in tight around her, with great effort he pushed open the rear door of the car and stumbled out on to the steep embankment. The door slammed shut and Kathy was alone with the quiet radio and weather reports.

Attempting to get a better view of his location, Josh ran up the embankment to the road where the car had swerved. He shielded his face with his arm but the blowing snow reduced visibility to a few hundred feet. No road signs or landmarks were visible. The longer he turned in circles, the more the wind tore through his ribcage. He smiled with false confidence. 'Ah, this ain't so bad.'

He turned in a circle again, hoping to see a light somewhere, but he remembered the power failure at church. The whole grid around Immaculate had probably failed. He became terrified. His eyes yearned for a beacon. He nearly had resigned himself to waiting in the car when he saw a light appear in the sky, as if in answer to his prayer.

He yelled, 'Someone has a generator!' His teeth started to chatter and his throat hurt. The light was faint in the distance, red or green, or both, alternating, but it was a light that had not been there a moment ago. He marked the direction of the light and ran down the embankment back to the car to warm up before he set out towards it.

The car's heater poured out warm air. He shoved his fingers directly into the dashboard vents and sighed, open-mouthed and lusty, as the air teased his bones. The warmth, like a drug, seduced him. He spoke to Kathy again: 'There's a farmhouse or a barn in the distance. It must be to the west. Who am I kidding? I have no idea what direction it's in, but I'm going there anyway. If I don't come back, I hate to admit it, but that will mean I'm an ice cube. Nothing to fear in death, though, isn't that right? They'll have to dig me out like the woolly mammoth. But I'll make it, Kathy, I promise. Goodbye. Again.'

Inhaling the warm air one last time, Josh pushed open the door and, without pausing, ran in the direction of the light, but not more than fifteen steps into his run he fell in the snow. He got up and ran again, but fell after another fifteen steps. He was running through a ploughed field and its uneven surface would have been difficult to cross even in daylight. His trousers and shoes filled with snow, prompting him to run faster. Excluding a sprained ankle, Josh imagined he would reach the beacon in ten minutes or less. Pumping his arms wildly and focusing only on the light he ran recklessly through the blinding ice particles. The field had a downhill slope and the light seemed to get higher and higher as he ran, until, suddenly, it disappeared behind some invisible horizon. He yelled and swore but kept running. Blackness surrounded him but he kept on, in the direction where the light had been. His steps became more difficult as he ran uphill. Feeling the incline, he pushed himself to reach higher ground, where he would be able to see the light. Soon enough he had climbed to a crest in the field, and there it was, shining red then green.

He resumed running and fell again in the snow. His ankle nearly rolled in the fall, but he let his body go loose to avoid a sprain. As he struggled with a length of barbed wire that had snagged his trousers, he did not once take his eye off the light. Feeling ice forming on his eyelashes, he blinked and rubbed his face. When he opened his eyes, the light was gone. A strange wheeze came from his mouth as he climbed to his feet and started to run again in the direction of the lost light.

After a minute of running, the ground became almost perfectly flat. He ran faster, and just as he grew aware of what was under his feet, he became weightless for an instant.

He caught the edge of the ice with his arms and held himself up while the water sloshed up to his waist. The edge of Jacob's ice-round pinned Josh's hips in the hole. Kicking and screaming, he felt his lifeblood retreating deep into his bones. He roared and wrestled the earth for his life and clawed at the ice like an animal, frantic and desperate, until he lifted his torso high enough to roll his body up on to the ice.

Scrambling to his feet, he was soon running through branches and brush as he crossed into a new field or pasture. Recklessly, he fended off the stiff shoots and brambles, until he lurched like a bleeding deer taking its final steps. He hit the snow again and again and the cold crept into the deepest parts of his body, into his thighs and his spine. His winter jacket and frozen slacks crinkled and snapped with every step. He lunged forward, but he felt like he was floating, or that his legs did not belong to him any more. His heart pumped the last pint of warm blood, his lungs nearly burst from the cold air, but he ran and he ran and he ran, without thinking of building a fire or dying nobly.

18

'Hold that flashlight steady, Jacob.'

Ray and his sons did not relax when they arrived home from church. They changed into overalls, put on heavy boots, and went outside to start the generator. Ray had only asked Ethan to come with him but Jacob had tagged along. Ray wrenched and tugged on the generator and checked the connection to the light pole. Ethan sat on the John Deere tractor waiting for Ray's command. Unsteadily, Jacob held a flashlight so that Ray could see what he was doing.

The three of them stood outside next to the yard light, where the generator linked to the power supply. The wind forced its way through the boys' zippers. They did not break the seal of their mouths by speaking. Ray stepped back from the tractor and yelled to Ethan, 'Start it up. Keep your foot on the clutch.'

Ethan heated the glow plugs and started the tractor.

'Now put it in neutral and keep it at twenty-four hundred RPMs.'

Ethan pushed up the throttle lever and the engine became almost as loud as the wind.

'Now real slowly, pull the PTO lever.'

Very carefully, Ethan pulled the lever by his left foot and the tractor jerked. The shaft spun once and Ethan backed off the lever. He looked over his shoulder at his father.

'All the way. That's good. Good job, Ethan.'

The shaft started to spin. Ray let the generator whir for a while before he flipped the switch that sent the electricity up the light pole. The yard light lit up blue.

'Okay, Ethan, take it up to three thousand RPMs.' Ethan nudged the throttle. Still holding the flashlight, Jacob looked up and saw that the large Christmas star on the top of the silo was lit up again, its red, blue and green lights twinkling in a pattern.

'Look,' Jacob said, 'the star is on!'

'All right!' said Ray. 'That means we did good. Now let's go in the machine shop for a minute and get out of this wind.' The three of them left the tractor and shuffled single file through the wind to the tool shed's side door. Inside, the boys took off their gloves and puffed on their hands. Standing between them, Ray peered through the small glass window to make sure the generator was running smoothly.

Near the door sat an old radio. Ray turned it on to get the weather report. As long as the radio worked, he would know that the generator was functioning. Nearly every FM station was muffled by static fuzz. Ray changed the band to AM and found that the old stations were surviving the storm quite well. Twin Cities WCCO came through with clarity. 'Have a Holly Jolly Christmas' played happily under the accompaniment of the screaming winds.

'Cold, ain't it, boys?!' They nodded. Ray sighed, 'Colder than Canada.'

Jacob stopped blowing on his hands to say, 'Colder than a witch's tit.'

Ray cringed and closed his eyes. He did not want to ask, but felt compelled. 'Where did you learn that saying?'

'From Hank Murphy. I heard him say it once. What is a witch's tit?'

'Cripes,' Ray said, 'I have no idea. From now on, anything you hear Hank say, don't repeat it. Just assume that it's dirty. You don't want to go around with a filthy mouth like that guy. That guy thinks everything is funny, and it's not.'

One of Ray's triggers for smoking was the musty smell of the tool shed. He considered pulling out the pack that he had stowed behind the workbench. Renee would find out from Jacob, and he wasn't sure a single cigarette was worth the trouble. But the urge nudged him and soon the pack was in his hand. He looked around for a lighter but couldn't find one. The smell of fresh tobacco dangled under his nose.

'One of you got a lighter on you?' Ray asked. 'A book of matches?'

Ethan laughed, 'You know we don't.'

For a moment Ray expected Jacob to produce a Zippo from his pocket, but the boy didn't answer. When he got tired of poking around, Ray went to the end of the workbench and grabbed the acetylene torch, opened the acetylene and oxygen tanks and then put the striker over the torch head. When he flicked the striker a bright yellow, smoky fire jumped out of the torch. Ray held it up to his cigarette and the boys watched their father as the shadows from the flame fell across the scar on his face. Ray's right eye squinted in the smoke. The scar looked shiny and fresh in the flicker of the flame. Although they had stopped noticing the scar long ago, their father's face appeared almost diabolical. The image was tattooed into the boys' memories.

Taking a deep drag, Ray thought about what else needed to be done before he went back into the house. He thought the cows had enough warmth but he still worried. The boys listened to the radio in silence as Ray finished his cigarette. Ray looked outside at the raging storm and noticed that the star on the silo was still blinking. He decided to turn it off for the night.

Ray said, 'Nobody's going to see our star tonight.'

'What about the wise men?' Jacob asked.

Turning off a switch in a fuse box near the door of the shed, Ray said, 'A wise man wouldn't be out in this weather. That's why Hank and Blanks are.'

Ray unplugged a cord and the star on the silo disappeared. He took his time finishing the cigarette and when he finished he said, 'Okay, all is well. Let's go inside before we freeze our you-know-whats off.'

Ray walked outside and expected the boys to follow. He shielded his face from the wind with his hand. Ethan followed, but Jacob lingered for a few extra seconds to turn the star on again – for the wise men. Ethan noticed the star light up, but Ray had his head turned away and missed it. Jacob ran to catch up to the others and all the way to the house sniggered about overriding his father's decision.

When they entered the house, Ray and the boys saw Renee smiling over a pan of water on the stove. She said, 'It's boiling! And we have lights!'

'Merry Christmas, honey!' Ray kissed her on the cheek.

'I am actually excited over water boiling.' She laughed. 'I must have a simple mind.'

Church had improved Renee's mood, not least because it had distanced her from Josh Werther's phone call. In church Renee had caught a glimpse of Josh dangerously close to her second cousin, Kathy, whom Renee didn't know very well because of their age difference. She thought the age gap made their apparent dating seem a little ridiculous.

'What are you going to do with the boiling water?' asked Jacob. He reached up and grabbed the pan handle but Renee pried his fingers off before he could dump it on himself or the floor.

'Cocoa. And Jacob, remember – don't touch things on the stove. Once you get taller you can help me, but don't grab handles.'

Jacob scowled, 'I know that, Mom.'

'Good.' She turned the handle towards the wall.

Hearing Renee talk to Jacob about the stove gave Ray a headache. The same conversations happened time and again, as if he were living in an infinite loop. He recalled Jacob doing the same thing just yesterday. The forgetfulness and recklessness of the boy made Ray think that maybe Jacob was damned to be an idiot his whole life. Ray blamed himself, as he recalled with bitterness his own childhood nicknames: 'Meathead' and 'Jar'. The nicknames did not last long. Aware of his intellectual limitations, Ray always relied on his size, his God-given advantage. He wondered if Jacob would have that same asset to offset his shortcomings.

Renee mixed the cocoa and set out four mugs on the counter. The steam from the pan warmed her skin, bringing colour into her cheeks. She filled the mugs and left them to sit on the countertop for a few minutes while Ray and the boys changed into their pyjamas. It was plaid flannel and wool socks all around, except for Jacob, whose GI Joe pyjamas had 'footies' sewn right into the pants. Renee wore a shabby but thick robe over her pyjamas. With the heat turned up high and the hot stove, Renee started to sweat.

'Story time!' Jacob said as he slid across the kitchen floor in his pyjama feet.

Renee said, 'Yes, story time. But probably a shorter story time this year since it took longer to get home and you guys were outside so long.'

She tested the cocoa with her most precise thermometer – her finger – and determined that the cocoa was cool enough for young tongues. She handed a cup to each member of the family and reduced the stove's burner to low and the family went into the living room.

The Christmas tree had no presents under it yet. Ray sat on the couch and his sons sat on each side of him. In front of the couch, Renee kneeled and leaned back on her heels, taking a moment to appreciate the good things in her life. To sit silent in the moment would have pleased her, but she knew that Jacob and Ethan were eager for a story. She inhaled and nearly started to tell her grandfather's story, 'Captain Morgan and Father Drowning', but decided to try out a new tale, one taught to Renee by an elderly woman who was borrowing books for her grandchildren at the Immaculate Public Library. Most of Immaculate's myths and tales were known to everyone, but Renee had not heard the old woman's story before.

Renee spoke softly. 'All right, gentlemen, this is a story not meant to bore, one that you *probably* have not heard before, and may never again, because every time it's told, she becomes a little less bold, it becomes a little less true – so shhh! – let's just keep this between me and you. She whispers it to only one soul a year, and how lucky am I; it's my turn to share her Christmas cheer. I will tell you about Calliope and her special food, but only if you don't tell on me, for if you *do*, that will be the end of her, and her story too. For Calliope is a rabbit, you see, pretty as a perm, this hopper, called Calliope, who came to Immaculate in 1873—'

Renee was interrupted by a loud thud that jolted the living room, as if a flying object or fallen tree had struck the siding. Everyone jumped and looked at the wall.

'Is that Calliope now, Mom?' asked Jacob.

She looked at Ray for a response but he seemed settled into his chair. He wasn't worried about the thud; he wanted to hear the story.

Renee brightened and continued. Her eyelashes batted at the boys and Ethan blushed with shyness whenever Renee looked at him for too long. 'Well, Calliope now, she hopped around, she weighed *several hundred pounds*, and if she stepped on your toe—'

A scratching sound started on the living-room wall. It came from outside, in short intervals. It sounded like an ice scraper on a windshield.

Ray got up from the couch with a sigh. 'I guess I'd better go see if that's Calliope!'

'I want to see!' Jacob said.

Renee coaxed Jacob back into his seat and continued to

tell the story. Ray went to the window and looked out but could see nothing at all. Even when he put his face to the glass and shielded his eyes, the whipping snow prevented a clear view.

He said, 'Looks all right.'

'Can you please go see what it is, Ray?' Renee pleaded. Ray got up from his seat. The scratching sound waned as he left the room.

In the mudroom Ray looked at a thermometer hanging on the window. The temperature was now thirty-two degrees below zero – without the wind-chill factor. He decided not to change into his overalls. Slipping his bare feet into a pair of boots, he donned a heavy coat over his pyjamas.

As he buttoned his coat, he thought, 'Probably a branch. I should just go back in the living room and tell her it was nothing.'

But that was the extent of his protest. He grabbed a flash-light and stepped outside. The wind made it difficult for him to force the screen door shut again. Immediately he regretted his decision to wear pyjama bottoms. The wind plastered the flannel against his legs and the loose fabric whipped violently, so hard that it reminded him of jumping out of a C-130 mortar-magnet, only this wind had a cold bite that South East Asian air certainly did not. Ray swore at the weather. Even the flashlight seemed to struggle in the wind, as Ray trudged down the brick path that encircled the house. The trees nearest the house loomed over the eaves but didn't make contact, and no branches had fallen. Ray looked around the yard and something caught his eye.

'Huh. I swear that I turned that thing off,' he muttered, looking at the star on the silo. 'I must be losing it.'

He continued down the path while shining the flashlight up and down the siding until he reached the window where he could see Renee and the boys in the living room. He tapped on the window pane and saw Jacob jump off the couch and mouth, 'Calliope!' Renee looked out with concern. Ray shrugged at her and turned around to examine the trees again. The house was ringed with shrubs, all of which appeared intact. Ray turned back to the window and shrugged a second time. Instead of running back into the house, he took a moment to entertain the boys.

He yelled at the top of his lungs, 'I am Calliope! I've come to spend Christmas with you! Give me a carrot or there will be no presents!' With his hands pulled up to his chest like paws, Ray scratched at the window and made rabbit faces. The boys laughed and Renee pretended to take his picture.

Ray shut the flashlight off and backtracked towards the front door. He had gone no further than two steps when a body hurled itself backwards out of the row of bushes that surrounded the house and fell on to the path. Ray jumped back, but in an instant had the flashlight in the man's face. His eyes were frosted shut, his arms and legs almost completely immobile, and Ray feared that he was dead, but a groan escaped the puckered mouth. Ray recognized the face.

'Good night! Josh Werther – what the hell are you doing out here?'

Without hesitation, Ray dropped to his knees and lifted Josh up by the armpits. In a few seconds, he had the 180-pound man in a fireman's carry. The flashlight dropped to the ground as Ray rushed towards the front door. The wind pushed hard at him from behind. He stumbled but kept his feet beneath him. He opened the screen door with one leg and the wind nearly tore the door off its hinges. Ray reached for the inner door handle and pushed it open. Warm air retreated into the house as the bitterly cold air rushed in.

Ray shouted, 'Renee!'

The urgency in his voice caused Renee to stop her story at once. She walked swiftly through the living room and just as Ray entered the kitchen she turned on the light. She nearly fainted at what she saw: her husband holding her former lover.

Ray said with excitement, 'I just found Josh Werther frozen from his toes to his eyebrows in our bushes out front. We need to warm this boy up. What should we do?'

Speechless, Renee could not even find a word to stutter. She had read about cold injuries, but only in textbooks. But the cold injury was not the most shocking thing to Renee at the moment: how could the person in her kitchen possibly be Josh Werther? His presence stunned her. Her mind raced with possible explanations. The phone call from earlier became more mysterious. Was he suicidal? Was this him coming to her to show his love? She wanted to escape.

'Not now, Renee. No tears until we warm him up.' Still holding Josh, Ray turned on the kitchen tap. The water came out cold and Ray decided that cold water at sixty degrees was good enough to get Josh's eyes cleared of ice. He rubbed the water in Josh's face, causing him to flinch and cough.

'That's a good sign, eh?' Ray splashed a bit more water in Josh's face and wiped the snow off his cheeks. 'Don't panic, Renee. You know things like this. What's the best way to handle this? How do you thaw hamburgers quickly?'

The boys hid behind Renee's legs. Jacob shuddered and looked at Josh, recalling his own frozen state from the pond that same morning. Renee stammered, 'I, ah . . . well . . . it's not quite the same thing . . .'

Looking up at his mom, Ethan tugged on her sleeve and whispered, 'Blankets, Mom . . .'

'Yes, blankets,' Renee said, snapping out of the trance. 'Quilts. Boys, go get the quilts off your beds and bring them down here. His clothes have to come off. His clothes are frozen. We need to put him in our bed, Ray.'

Renee ran into the bedroom and ripped the sheets back. Ray followed, with the limp body slumped over his shoulder. He sat Josh on the bed and held him upright and fingered the buttons on his coat but they were completely frozen. Renee scratched at Josh's shoelaces but the shoes were caked in two inches of snow and ice.

'Christ,' Renee said, 'I can't even see the laces.'

Ray said, 'Go get a scissors.'

Renee ran to the kitchen, passing the boys as they entered the room with the quilts. She pulled open her junk drawer so fast that pens and paper flew on to the kitchen floor. She looked for the scissors frantically until she found them, then told Ethan, 'Start a pot of water on the stove. Keep the heat high.'

Without a word Ethan kneeled on the kitchen floor to open the cupboard that held the pots. He started several pots of water boiling and then he picked up the pens rolling around on the linoleum so that no one would slip on them.

A violent tearing sound came from the bedroom. Renee rushed into the room and saw Josh's coat ripped off and buttons lying on the carpet. The coat stood up on the floor, in the shape of Josh, like armour.

'Here's the scissors, Ray.'

'That's okay, I found a pliers in my coat. You use the scissors for his shirt.'

Renee watched as Ray grabbed Josh by the hair and held him steady. She wanted to ask him to be less rough. 'I got him steady, now you cut his shirt off. His whole collar is frozen stiff. Cut straight up his back and through the collar.'

Renee cut the shirt as told. Josh's torso flailed back and forth dully as Ray and Renee worked on him. Once the shirt was off, Ray leaned Josh back on to the bed and started to work on his belt and pants, but then stopped.

'It will take some force to get his shoes off,' Ray said. 'I'll get his shoes, you work on his pants.'

Without waiting for Renee's reply, Ray attacked the laces of the shoes with his pliers, stripping the ice away with downstrokes that bruised the frozen flesh on Josh's feet. Jacob stood over his father's shoulder and watched as the shoelaces broke, one by one, in the twisting pliers.

Ray said to Jacob, 'Pliers work great for everything, Jacob. Remember that. But in this case, it's just too damn slow.' From his inner coat pocket Ray produced a jackknife with a shiny clean blade recently sharpened on the grinding wheel. He stuffed his thick index finger underneath the laces of each shoe and pried up and outward. With the knife he cut through the laces in two swift motions. He then sat on the floor, and with his feet against the bed for leverage, he ripped

Josh's shoes off. After pulling the socks off, Ray took Josh's left foot in his hand and said, 'Good God, he feels like a frozen chicken breast.'

In the meantime, Renee had managed to undo the top of Josh's pants, but with his weight pressing the pants down, she could not wriggle them off him.

'Okay, switch places with me,' Ray ordered. He pulled Josh into a sitting position. Once again, he grabbed a handful of Josh's hair to steady him. Renee hopped off the bed while Ray moved around to the other side and lifted him to his feet by the armpits.

Standing directly behind Josh, Ray said, 'Jacob, Ethan, look away. Okay, Renee, drop his drawers.'

Renee looked at her husband with disbelief. 'One of us has to do it. We can switch places if you like,' Ray said and chuckled. 'I've seen one before.'

To avoid any more comments from Ray, Renee wiggled Josh's pants down to the floor.

'Do we need to take off his undies?' Ray asked, looking down at Renee. 'They're frozen, too.'

Looking at the floor, Renee said, 'Probably.'

Feeling discomfort beyond anything she could imagine, Renee removed Josh's briefs. The universes had collided. She hoped that any second she might wake up from this nightmare to a normal Christmas morning. From her knees, she glanced one time at Josh's nude body and rose to her feet as quickly as possible.

Ray lowered Josh on to the bed, adjusting his position so that his head would hit a pillow when he was laid back.

Renee lifted his feet on to the bed and they layered the quilts over him, six deep.

'Now what?' asked Ray. 'What do we do to warm him?'

Reluctant to even open her mouth, Renee said, 'He needs body heat.'

'What do you mean?'

'It means . . . someone needs to get in bed with him and be close to him. To warm him.'

Ray said, 'Fine. We all jump in bed.' He pulled the quilts back to get into the bed with Josh.

Biting her lip, Renee hated what she had to say: 'We need to have skin-on-skin.'

Ray winced, but immediately accepted the necessity: he would have to lay in bed with his banker. 'Wow,' he said, 'wouldn't this be a story for the township news?' He winked and laughed, then let his coat fall to the floor and pulled his shirt off, exposing a multitude of raised and discoloured scars on his chest and stomach. Just as quickly as his shirt came off, his pants were on the floor, and in only his briefs Ray hopped into the bed with Josh, pressing his chest and legs against the man's right side. He had been around enough dying men to know that pride had no place in times of crisis.

Ray said, 'You better not be enjoying this, Werther.'

'It's not a funny situation,' Renee said in a flat tone.

'I know it's not, so what are you waiting for?'

Renee unbuttoned her pyjamas, but moved slowly. Ray joked, 'Well come on then, don't make me be the only one. This is a frozen man here. You too, boys. Get down to your skivvies and hop in. On second thought, you two keep your pyjamas on. Just hop in as you are. He needs all the heat we can give him.'

Quickening her pace, Renee stripped to her underwear and climbed into bed with her husband and her ex-lover. She pressed herself against Josh's left flank and wrapped her legs around his leg and rubbed him with her hands. Jacob and Ethan climbed into the bed in their flannel cartoon pyjamas.

Ray said to the boys, 'Each of you take a foot and warm it up. Don't rub too hard, though.'

From under the tent of blankets, Jacob said, 'It's like camping.'

The whole family squirmed under the quilts against Josh's body.

'This is quite a Christmas, isn't it, boys?' Ray said. 'We won't forget this year, will we?'

Jacob said, 'His foot is freezing!'

'Keep warming it.'

Ray pressed his cheek against Josh's cheek, prompting Renee to do the same.

Josh's eyes opened, but neither Ray nor Renee noticed. His purple lips started to redden as he breathed in warm air. He tried to speak but his throat failed to make the right sounds. To swallow, he had to shut his eyes and concentrate. He was dazed, trapped in a glazed consciousness without any idea of where he was. Once his blood started to warm, his nose picked up on a familiar smell, a perfume, and he whispered, 'Ren.'

Ray nearly sprang out of the bed. He looked down at Josh's face and held open one of his eyelids.

'He knows it's you, Renee!' Ray was elated.

Josh stared straight up into space, whispering more clearly this time, 'Renee.'

Ray said to Josh with a big smile, 'That's enough about her now. What about me? Good to hear your voice, Werther!'

Josh turned his eyes slowly so that they fell on Ray, and then let his eyes stare straight ahead once again. The sight of Ray clarified the situation for Josh. He whispered, 'Kathy.'

Ray mocked, 'Still thinking of women, even when you're frozen like an icicle. How do you like that? I think he is going to be fine, don't you, Renee?'

'Oh no!' Renee hushed Ray. 'Oh my God, he was with Kathy at the Legion, remember? Did you see him in church?'

'I didn't see him,' said Ray.

'I think he was with Kathy.'

From underneath the covers, Jacob said, 'I saw her in the balcony. I remembered her from the Legion.'

'Was Kathy standing next to Josh?' asked Renee.

'I don't know.'

Renee gasped, 'Oh, Jesus Christ, I bet she was with him! I bet she was. Why else would he risk running in the cold? Oh, my God! Where would we even look to find her?'

Jacob climbed out of the bed so that he could take a closer look at Josh, whose eyelids lifted and fell several times. He looked at Jacob for a moment, and in delirium uttered, 'You're not my boy. Where's your brother?'

'What?' Ray laughed. 'His brother is warming your feet, Werther.'

Renee cringed and urged Josh, 'Quiet now, we need you to sleep.'

Getting out of the bed, Ray said, 'The freeze has him confused. Ethan, go see if the phone's working.'

Ethan crawled out from under the blankets, walked to the kitchen, and picked up the phone. He shook his head. The phones were dead.

19

Ethan put on his snowsuit as fast as he could. He pulled every strap and lace on his body as tight as possible in order to keep the wind out. From the doorway of the kitchen, Jacob looked on.

'Why can't I come with?'

Wishing he didn't have to answer, Ray said, 'Now is not the time, Jacob. You help your mom here. We'll be back in a flash.'

Jacob started to put his moon boots on over his pyjama feet. His eyes welled.

Ray said, 'Don't even bother putting the boots on, Jacob. You're staying here.'

Jacob pouted but got no sympathy. With his overalls, snow pants and heavy jacket on, Ray looked twice his normal size. Jacob felt intimidated by his father but could not accept his exclusion from the grand expedition.

'Careful, Jacob; if that lip hangs any lower you might step on it.'

Ray checked over Ethan's clothing and stuffed two flashlights into his son's coat pockets. Ray and Ethan put on heavy facemasks, tightened the strings of their hoods and donned huge snowmobile mittens that went up to the elbow. The only flesh visible was their eyelids.

Still lying in the bed in her underwear, Renee yelled from

the bedroom, 'His footsteps will be covered by now, Ray. It's too risky to go out there.'

Ray's voice was muffled by the facemask. 'We are dressed like bears. And I don't plan on telling Kathy's family we didn't bother looking for her because it wasn't convenient at the time. You keep trying to call the police to let them know there was an accident. The cops will contact Hank Murphy to have his ploughmen on the lookout. Keep tapping on Josh – maybe he'll wake up. We'll be back in no time. Ethan: grab those two leather jackets and bring them with you.'

Renee started to rebut but withheld the thought. His mind was made up, and she knew he was right to go and search for Kathy.

Jacob stuck his tongue out at Ethan, who smiled underneath his facemask. This was the reward for being good. Jacob stood on his tiptoes to look out the window, but the shadowy figures of his father and brother had already melted into the storm.

Ethan stayed two steps behind Ray at all times. The wind broke on Ray's chest and Ethan stayed in his father's slipstream. When they reached the tool shed Ray ushered Ethan inside. The faint smell of cigarette smoke still lingered in the cold, musty air. They moved through the shed towards a rear door that connected to another shed, where the Polaris snowmobile was parked. Ray wondered if the engine would even start in the cold weather. When it was new, the Polaris was top-of-the-line. That was in 1972. Now it had just enough power to pull the kids around on the hood of an old Volkswagen Beetle that Ray had found in a junkyard.

Ray began to yank the starter cord. To Ethan, it looked

like Ray was beating and torturing the old machine. The engine sputtered, rolled, and fell silent with each pull. Ethan watched in amazement as Ray tugged off twenty or thirty consecutive pulls without stopping for a breath. The starter cord on the snowmobile had become a test of manhood between Ethan and Jacob; neither of the boys could pull it even halfway without the recoil reeling them back in.

The engine turned over a few extra revolutions on each pull, as if it wanted to start. Ray smiled through his face-mask, but Ethan did not notice. Blue smoke began to spew from the exhaust pipe. Finally, the spark took and Ray revved the throttle until the shed filled with smoke and the rich smell of gas and oil. Ray said, 'That's a good smell tonight.' He motioned for Ethan to hold the throttle while he worked on opening the shed door – no small task, because a large snowdrift had formed against it. Even with several great heaves, Ray only managed to move the door a few inches. He backed off and instead grabbed a thick steel rod, which he planted at the base of the door and pried outward. When he removed the steel rod from its fulcrum the door swung down and in, and the movement allowed enough space for Ray to slide the door open along its track. When the door opened Ethan drove the snowmobile out of the blue haze and into the torrents of flying snow. Ray pulled the door shut and pointed at the silos nearby, prompting Ethan to drive in that direction while Ray ran alongside. Ray ran between the two silos and returned with the Volkswagen hood and a long rope. He tied the rope through the hood in several places and to each side of the snowmobile. The chariot was ready.

Ray took control of the snowmobile, pushing Ethan back

in the seat. Relief came over the boy as he wrapped his arms around his father. The snowmobile lunged off in the direction of the barn, where Ray ordered Ethan to jump off and gather two tarps from the milkhouse. Ray stacked the tarps between his legs. As soon as he felt Ethan's arms firmly gripping his sides again Ray opened the throttle wide and they were off looking for footprints.

'You look over my left shoulder,' yelled Ray, 'and I'll look right. I figure Josh must have came from this direction since he ran into this side of the house.'

They drove slowly at first, just able to make out Josh's last footsteps. Ray turned around periodically to check the Volkswagen hood as it glided softly over the snow. His eyesight was not that good and he had to rely on Ethan's perfect vision.

'You can see a trail almost,' the boy said. 'He must have been dragging his feet towards the end. The snow is not so deep there, you see it?'

Ethan's arm pointed through one of Ray's armpits. Ray grunted in agreement, trusting Ethan's guidance more than his own. They started to pick up speed but some of the terrain rode roughly. Had he been by himself, Ray might have driven recklessly, but not with Ethan along. The excitement of the search made Ray forget the cold, while Ethan became wired with excitement and fear as he sensed the scene of the accident getting closer.

The path led them to the pond and Ethan looked for the ice hole. When he saw it, he was aghast to see how close Josh's footsteps came to the edge, but he said nothing about it to his father. The footsteps kept going but became harder to see in the snow.

They entered a field. Ray gradually increased the speed until a large tree appeared in front of him. He barely swerved in time to avoid a collision. The Volkswagen hood bounced off the tree and straightened out again behind the snowmobile. Ray knew the tree well from working in the fields. The near miss helped him to determine their location and suddenly he knew exactly which road Josh had started out from. The footsteps didn't matter any more. Ray steered in the direction of a county road and marvelled at how far Josh had run wearing only a small winter coat and church shoes.

Ray and Ethan dipped into the shallow valley of a small stream, long since frozen over for the winter. With a bit of a struggle the snowmobile sputtered up the other side of the hill. Both Ray and Ethan shouted out when they spotted two specks of light ahead of them. The specks grew into headlights and the adrenaline flowed in the boy and his father as they began to fear what they might find inside the car.

Ethan was surprised when his father drove right past the car, up the steep embankment, and on to the road. Ray wanted to avoid getting stuck. He stopped the snowmobile and dismounted, keeping his hand on the throttle until Ethan took over.

'Keep the engine running,' Ray said. 'I'll be right back.' Then he grabbed a tarp and both leather jackets, and disappeared over the side of the road.

What Ethan noticed immediately was loneliness, even with his father no more than a hundred feet away. The swirling snow made Ethan aware of his vulnerability. When he heard his teeth chattering he revved the engine, as if the sound could banish the chill growing in his core.

Ray shone his flashlight through the rear window. He noticed the roof had caved in on the driver side. To his surprise, he heard the slow hum of the engine. The exhaust pipe lay partially buried in the snow and Ray wondered how much exhaust was circling back inside the car. He pried at the front door handle but it did not budge. In the driver's seat he could see the shape of Kathy, but the ice and frost on the window hid her face. Ray moved to the rear door. It opened easily and he climbed inside. He looked over the seat at Kathy. The cobbled bandage on Kathy's forehead made Ray pause. Apart from the streaks of blood drying on her face, Kathy appeared to be only sleeping. Ray put his cheek over her mouth and felt a puff of breath.

He turned his head to face Kathy's ear and said, 'I hate to move you from where it's warm, girl, but you can't stay here all night.'

He went to work on transferring Kathy into the back seat of the car as quickly and smoothly as possible. He laid the tarp on the back seat and slowly pulled Kathy up and over the lowered front seat. She grimaced from the pain in her ribs but Ray continued. When he had pulled her fully into the back seat, he started to wrap her in the tarp and the leather jackets. Ray traded his own jacket for one of the smaller leather jackets Ethan had brought and put it on Kathy. It had thick insulation and was warm from his body heat. He moved quickly, feeling guilty for being in the warm car while Ethan sat up on the road in the wind.

With firm tugs Ray wrapped a coat around her legs,

followed by a tarp, and then he cinched her legs together with rope. Ray tied her up so well that she looked like as if she was rolled up in a carpet. He made a mummy of her, leaving only her face exposed to the elements. He made every attempt to be gentle, but several times she let out a groan when he made contact with her bruised ribs and abdomen. As soon as the last knot was tied, Ray reached behind him and opened the car door, then scooped Kathy in his arms. He trudged up the embankment. Under the din of the howling wind Ray could hear the snowmobile engine purring. When he made it to the road he saw his good son sitting patiently on the snowmobile. Ray knew the boy must be freezing. He also knew that Ethan would not admit it.

'Cold enough yet?'

'Not really,' Ethan answered.

Ray used the loose ends of the towing rope to secure Kathy to the Volkswagen hood.

He yelled to Ethan, 'I would ride back there with her but I'm too heavy. I want you to lay right beside her, shoulder to shoulder. You will keep her from sliding around, do you understand?'

Ethan nodded. He kept the engine idling at a medium speed while his father spoke.

'Okay, then,' Ray continued. 'I'm going to switch places with you.'

Ethan ran back to the sled and shimmied underneath the ropes until he lay next to Kathy. He wondered if she could hear anything. Just in case, he introduced himself and explained the plan to her.

Ray gunned the engine a few times, but he accidentally let

off the gas and the engine died. The wind made a hellish sound. Ray swore and began yanking the starter cord like a wild man. Ethan stared up at the sky, listening to the short bursts and purrs of the engine as the crankshaft tried to roll over. Feeling the cold enter his toes, Ethan muttered, 'C'mon, Dad, get it started.'

A flicker of doubt came into Ray, but he kept pulling the cord. He considered moving everyone into the crashed car for warmth. The options were few if the snowmobile engine did not start. He tried again, and finally the welcome sound of a running motor struck out against the night.

'There she goes, Ethan! This old nag is good for about one more ride!'

This time Ray did not let off the gas at all. He began to drive straight ahead, down the county road.

Looking back, Ray noticed that the sled was following unevenly. He feared that the hood might flip. When they were playing, the boys loved it when the hood flipped, but this ride allowed for no errors. Ray considered driving down into the embankment and following their tracks over the hills and through the fields, but that meant taking Kathy over a bumpy surface. He knew that going through the fields would be faster.

'Let's go get warm,' Ray said. He steered the front skis of the snowmobile towards the embankment then hit the brakes when he saw the incline. The abrupt stop nearly made the sled collide with the rear of the snowmobile. A few inches short, the hood slid to a halt.

Ray changed his mind and yelled back to Ethan, 'We are

going to take the roads home, Ethan. Should be a smooth ride. Hold on tight, bud.'

Ethan chattered, 'I'm already holding on tight.'

Ray opened up the throttle. They had got to the scene of the accident as the crow flies, but they went home the long way: they had four miles to travel. To Ethan the trip felt like he was travelling on water, with each snowdrift on the road feeling like a wave. As Ray made the turn from the county road to a connecting road where no ploughs had yet passed, the waves became bigger and bigger.

20

At the window, Jacob pined about the hardships of age discrimination. He watched the snowmobile lights move farther away from the yard until suddenly they seemed to disappear altogether, like a snuffed match. The anger on his face was obvious as he stewed over his exclusion from what looked to be the greatest adventure of his young life. The events of the day – falling into the ice; the argument with John about the nativity scene at church; the bat incident – weighed on him. And none of it was his fault. His father hated him, his brother considered him an annoyance and his mother only tolerated him because she had to. He could never do anything right, any time, for anybody, anywhere. The thought of Christmas barely concerned him any more. For as long as he could stand it, he looked out of window, waiting for the return of the snowmobile, but his patience waned, and he ran off to sulk in his bedroom.

Renee felt Josh's fingertips getting warmer in her hands. She moved several times underneath the quilts to reposition herself against him, from one side to the other, until she started to sweat under the pile of quilts laced with hot water bottles.

She kept her ear near Josh's lips to check his breathing. After his initial utterance, Josh's eyes had closed again and he had fallen silent. By the time Ethan and Ray left, Renee was beginning to wonder if Josh would survive the hour.

Tears began to well in her eyes as she looked down at him. Gently, she pressed her hand against his chest to feel his heart beating. Between her fingers were chest hairs that hadn't existed the last time she had touched him. She curled her leg over his abdomen, bending her knee to rub Josh's thighs. She looked at his face and his resting lips. The room was silent. She moved her hand through his matted hair then let her palm rest on his cheek. His vulnerability made him seem young again. She thought of the night when they had danced in Tonnamowoc. She had longed many times, over the years, for the days when love was simple, when everything seemed figured and factored – when Ray was gone. As bad as she felt considering it, if things had worked out as planned, Ray would have stayed gone. Her misgivings about the past never truly faded, nor would they, as long as she stayed planted in Immaculate. Josh's face was part of Renee's tapestry, and as she touched his forehead she remembered her young life.

She remembered the fields in which they had laid together that summer, when they stayed out late in the night, with a blanket and a battery-powered radio, sitting on the tailgate of her father's truck, or bedded down in the tall alfalfa. After working all day – he at the bank and she on the farm – they would rendezvous in secret, on a dirt road between the farms of the Killarney and Steiger families, and they began loving again right where they left off the night before. They were nineteen, one year out of high school. The cliques of school friends had mostly disbanded and the rumour mill was no longer so active. Renee's friends wondered where she went every night but never found out about Josh. Renee and Josh did not speak of the relationship to anyone, almost as if they both expected it to end with the summer, when Josh would go back to school in Duluth and Renee was due to return to Minneapolis.

They were both aware of Ray looming somewhere in the distance, though his name rarely came up. When Ray's letters stopped coming from Vietnam, Renee stopped writing to him, and as the summer heated up, she and Josh became feverish. On hot nights they barely slept, finding endless hours of conversation teeming inside them, discovering each other's bodies every few hours, making music in the field out of sighs and laughter. Josh turned out to be a sensitive, educated man with ideas that Renee found interesting.

She smiled as she remembered the last day of that summer, the night before Josh returned to the university in Duluth. She closed her eyes and inhaled, recalling the smell of the lavender cologne she had bought for him. He was lean with a flat stomach and she remembered watching his navel move between her thighs. By the last night, Josh was an expert. It was as if he had mapped her entire body and detailed every sensitive inch. He also learned the complexities of her moods, the idiosyncrasies of her body, how to time the rise and fall, and tease out sundry nuances of pleasure that she might otherwise never have known. He learned the right spots and the right times; the right time to tickle, the right time to grab, to pinch – to go further. He learned to talk dirty with decorum. And Renee was grateful for his diligence.

On that last humid night, Josh took his time to show her the fullness of his summer education, and what they did in the field could never be done again. They made love until she became overstimulated. She felt almost combustible in her hot heart. They performed every act under the curtain of night, and when finished they lay openly on the blanket, in the alfalfa field under the sky, knowing that a threshold had been crossed, that the moment was the last of its kind.

With Renee leaning against his chest, Josh stroked her stomach and stared at the stars. She did the same. She wanted to postpone the end of summer. They stayed awake all night.

In the early hours, Renee sighed, 'Orion. He's back.'

'What about Orion?' Josh asked.

'When Orion shows up on the horizon, it means the end of summer. And whenever he appears, I can't look up at the sky without seeing him. All winter, he is the first thing I see.' She added, 'I wish he would stay away.'

'It's better to look at the whole sky all at once, and not focus on the constellations.'

'I don't know how to do that. Orion is a hunter. He hunts me.'

'No, you hunt for Orion. Try to relax and forget the shapes. Try closing your eyes for a few seconds, and then open up and take in the whole sky. Think of nothing. Be amazed.'

'I don't know . . .'

'Imagine you were the first person to ever look up at the stars.'

Renee did as Josh suggested. She closed her eyes and felt her surroundings. The warm air licked at her long hair and passed underneath the curve of her back. Josh's hand caressed her forearm. His other hand circled her navel and then wandered up and down from her breasts to her thighs. She smelled Josh and soft lavender and summer . . .

She opened her eyes and looked up, ignoring her education, and drank it in. A meditative peace entered her as she allowed her muscles to relax. The stripe in the middle, the Milky Way, shined clearly in the rich unknown universe.

'You are the first person to ever see the universe,' Josh said. 'What do you see?'

Renee held her breath and thought of her mother. She said to Josh, 'I see the past drawn into the centre of the sky, towards the Milky Way. The lights are falling into the middle, gathering like pilgrims, but God is not there; it's just people without their baggage. It's the tiny spark inside us that keeps burning when we die and lives up there, in a safe place, where no earth, wind, fire or water can get to it.'

Neither of them said anything for a moment. Then Josh said, 'Wow. I've always just imagined the universe to be the inverse of a woman's orgasm.'

Renee rolled over on Josh. 'Oh, I think I like that better.'

'I love you, Renee.' He touched her back with one hand. 'When I'm with you, I'm where I want to be for ever.'

She curled into him and stopped talking.

The summer came to an end with a promise between them of a future together, but without any of the details filled in. He returned to college, but she stayed at home with her father. They saw each other on weekends, until Christmas. But in December it ended.

In her marital bed, Renee leaned over Josh with compassion as she finished wandering through the happy memories. Tears shined in her eyes. Thinking that Josh was asleep, she caressed his cheek and said, 'Don't die on me, Josh Werther. We've been through too much for that.'

A tear rolled down her nose and fell on to his cheek. Without opening his eyes, Josh spoke.

'How did I end up here . . . with you, Ren?'

Renee's heart jumped; the old feeling came back to her. The silence of the room and the situation allowed it to enter. She leaned back and said, 'You're okay?'

Josh turned his head towards her. 'I'm not dreaming?'

'No, Josh.'

'Then I'm in heaven.'

'No. It's still Immaculate.'

'That's hell.'

'That's enough of that talk.' Renee smiled. 'You nearly froze running through the storm. I don't know what you were thinking. That's how you got to the Marak hotel.'

The word Marak woke Josh a little more. 'I didn't know whose house it was, Renee. It must be . . . by design.'

'I am only here to warm you up, Josh.'

'And I am warmer now, and you are still here.'

'You're right,' Renee said. 'I should get out of bed now.'

She made a move to get up from the bed, but Josh pulled her back. He pulled her face to his and kissed her lips, trying to make it a kiss like their first, in the parking lot of the Hop-Haus.

Renee let herself be kissed, and when she tried to back away she could not. The first kiss led to a second and a third. She pushed her hands against his chest and moved her legs over the top of him, pushing and pulling at the same time against him, against herself; she wanted to stay and to leave. He pressed his chilled body upward against hers. Finally she broke free from the embrace and extricated herself from Josh and the bed.

Standing, she said, 'I get the feeling this is all a stage. Like freezing yourself to death was a way to get in the door. Like your little phone call tonight.'

Josh shook his head and coughed. 'That's not true, not at all. What I wanted to tell you on the phone tonight was something very important.'

'It's too late, Josh. Don't bother.'

'No it isn't.' He sat up in the bed. 'It's never too late.'

'You know what I would have said anyway. You'll have to wait another ten years, and after that, another ten. You have to get over *us*, Josh.'

Josh breathed heavy and his body shivered. 'Fate makes decisions for us, Renee. How else could you explain the fact that I ran blindly through the storm and ended up here tonight?'

'Oh,' she said, throwing up her hands, 'so now the great agnostic is taking on fate! What a reversal you've undergone, or did you find your religion in the woods tonight? I don't believe you ran *blindly*, Josh. In case you've forgotten, Immaculate isn't that big of a place. It's not as if you were wandering roads you had never travelled before, or you happened upon this place wandering through the woods dropping breadcrumbs like Hansel and Gretel. Not to mention that you sounded drunk on the phone earlier. It's long overdue for you to get over it, Josh. You had your chance to ask when Ray was dead, and you weren't ready for it. End of story.'

Renee looked down at herself and recalled that she was in her underwear. She pushed her hands through her hair and said to an absent audience, 'Oh Jesus, why am I talking about ancient history at a time like this?' She spoke more directly to Josh, 'Was Kathy with you in the car?'

'Yes.'

'Is she alive?'

'She's injured. On her head and body. That's why I ran.'

'Then we had better prepare for her. You can help, now that you are awake.' She looked at him lying nude in the bed. 'Or should I say aroused?'

'That's my girl. Still sassy.'

Renee pulled on her pyjama bottoms. 'And that's you, Josh – still a skirt-chaser. How old is Kathy anyway – nineteen?'

Energy surged into Josh. He got out of bed and approached Renee. 'I wouldn't have spent a decade dating other women if you hadn't ditched me.' A rush of blood went to his head. He staggered, put a hand out to find the edge of the bed and sat down before he passed out. In his excitement he had forgotten the pain of the cold leaving his body. The blood in his limbs still needed hours of warmth.

'I left you?' Renee said with disbelief, ignoring her outfit again. 'I left you?' She gritted her teeth. 'I think the frost must have got into your head. Within a week of seeing each other you were already banging Claire Walker – and I know that you slept with her, Josh. I found out.'

'That's a lie! I never touched anyone until it was obvious

you didn't want love in your life. You wanted your loveless commitment – to him!'

'What the hell would you know about commitment? What do you know about love? Put some clothes on – you're disgusting.' She bent over and dug through one of Ray's drawers to find some clothes for Josh.

She threw a T-shirt and a pair of jeans over her shoulder. Josh approached Renee from behind. He dodged the airborne pair of jeans. Confidently, he walked up to her with an audacious swagger. Grabbing her arm, he spun her round to face him and started to kiss her neck. She looked vacuously at the light fixture as he embraced her.

'I know more about love and commitment than you do, Renee,' he murmured.

'Well, you can stop making payments on our behalf. Do you think we'll starve? Ray, of all men, doesn't need charity from you, of all *boys*.'

'As Ray's banker,' Josh said, 'oh yes, he does.' Then he whispered in Renee's ear, 'But I'm not talking about that. I'm talking about the things that I have done for you that you don't even know. I have loved you, every day, every hour.'

'You had the chance, but as soon as Ray came home, you ran. You were scared of him, weren't you? So much for your word – but oh, of course, you hadn't slept with enough women yet, and you know what, Josh? You never will. And because of that, you're not the kind of man to fight for.'

Josh lightly kissed her neck's sensitive places. 'I have waited for a moment like this for so long, Renee. I never dreamed it would happen this way, but I've been dying, waiting in vain for you. I know that we can be together, Renee, somehow. We'll have *our* family, as it should be.' He slipped his arm around her back and then slid his hand down until his hand entered beneath the waistband of her loose pyjama bottoms. His fingers pressed softly against her panties, and he said, 'I want you to be with me.'

'Don't.' Although she hated him, she wanted to kiss him again. She put her hands up in defence at first, but then let herself fall into him and let her hands slide down his back, down his body. In the dresser mirror Josh watched himself undoing Renee's bra with one hand as he reached his hand inside the front of Renee's panties with his other. She exhaled desire but her expression was pained. She did not protest. She leaned back on the dresser. Together they moved like they were floating on waves. The pleasure washed away her wifehood, flustered her reality. And the embrace ended abruptly.

The front door slammed shut in the wind and the sound of boots on linoleum was accompanied by Ray's voice thundering through the house. 'Make room on the bed for Kathy!'

Josh lunged backward from Renee and scurried under the covers again. Renee kicked her bra out of sight around the corner of the dresser and pulled her pyjama top on. Fortunately Josh had not removed her pyjama bottoms so she only had to adjust them. Her cheeks were pink when Ray entered the bedroom holding Kathy McKay.

Ray laid the mummy on the bed next to Josh. Using his knife he cut the ropes while Ethan removed the jackets from Kathy and collected the ropes.

'She's bruised up pretty good,' said Ray. 'But she could be worse.'

'Should I get the medical book, Mom?' Ethan asked, shivering while he spoke.

Josh lay flat on the bed. He was exhausted but at the same time mentally rejuvenated by Renee. Her touch empowered him, but the voice of Ray Marak had the opposite effect.

'Mom?' Ethan tugged on her sleeve. 'Mom? Should I, Mom?'

Absentmindedly, Renee nodded. She felt corrupted, standing in the bedroom next to her husband who had just risked life and limb to bring Kathy in. The chemicals in her body warred. Ray always returned with bad timing. She wished, for a moment, that he had not returned this time. She wished he had ridden out in the snow like the hero that he was, and just kept on riding.

21

Renee focused on Kathy. She decided she should sleep. The family decided against driving to the Tonnamowoc hospital until the storm stopped. The best Renee could do was monitor her breathing and pulse throughout the night, both of which seemed strong and rhythmic.

Josh underwent various warming treatments once Ray came home. The Marak family force-fed lukewarm water to him while he sat in a warm bathtub. Once, he nearly vomited, but Ray ordered him to swallow it all down. After the bath the boys rubbed his toes and fingers while he sat on a chair in front of the oven. Renee warmed blankets in the dryer and rotated them every ten minutes. Before long, everyone in the house, including Josh, had sweat running down their backs.

The family gathered in the living room, with Josh as the guest of honour, looking diminutive in Ray's clothes.

The Christmas lights flickered in the dim living room. The smell of cocoa filled the air. Ray stood by with the kettle ready to refill Josh's mug.

'Drink more. More. Keep drinking. You need to fill every corner of your toes with cocoa.' Ray beamed at him.

Nodding and smiling, Josh slowly sipped from the mug. He said, 'My fingers and toes are really starting to hurt.'

'Best pain you'll ever feel,' Ray said. 'As frozen as I found you, I'm surprised your toes don't need to be amputated. You felt like a frozen Butterball turkey.'

Other than Ray's enthusiasm, the room was quiet. Renee could only muster a plastic smile and a few nods from time to time. Ethan sat on the couch drinking his cocoa in tiny sips. Even Jacob said nothing because he resented being left out of the great snowmobile ride.

Ray said, 'I just have to ask you one thing, Josh Werther.'

Josh's muscles clenched, thinking that perhaps Ray knew more than he showed. Renee looked at the floor, expecting the worst.

'What exactly in the hell were you thinking, running off in the storm like that? You must have run two miles!'

Relief came over Josh. 'I don't think I was thinking at the time.'

'I mean, we couldn't believe our eyes, could we, Ethan?'

Ethan shook his head.

'The footsteps,' Ray said. 'Faint as they were in the snow, they just kept going on and on. I thought for sure you would be dead by the time we got back here. But look at you now; you look better than you have in years, Werther!'

Josh laughed and shrugged.

'I think we should have a drink. This calls for a drink. No question about it.'

Renee said, 'Oh, I don't know if we need to do that. What time is it—'

'Yes, we most certainly will have to drink something tonight!' Ray said. He took inventory of his blessings. 'Tonight we will have a drink, hell yes we will. Kathy is bruised, but will be fine, and we found out tonight that Josh

Werther is an Eskimo. Look at him – he's looking better every minute. I think we are lucky, and I am thankful for the Lord watching over us on Christmas Eve. Ethan and I almost got stuck out there, but we made it back, too. We all made it back! The power is working in the house. It's too good not to have a drink. I have just the thing for this.' Ray clapped his hands and rubbed them together. 'I'll be right back.'

When Ray strutted out of the room, Renee and Josh exchanged glances, and Josh had the audacity to wink. She looked away and picked at the arm of her chair.

Ray returned holding five glasses and a decanter shaped like Elvis. The decanter was filled with premium brandy.

'If you are still feeling cold after drinking this, you'll always be frigid. Renee's dad gave this to us a while ago. See there, the seal is still intact.' He held up his left hand and vowed, 'I promise you won't go blind if you drink it.'

Ray poured the brandy into the glasses and then set Elvis down on the coffee table. He even poured a small shot for Jacob and Ethan, figuring that such a rare occasion merited a small dose for everyone.

Jacob ignored his glass at first, but when no one was looking, he drank the liquor down immediately. His face turned sour and he buried his head in the cushion of his chair, so that no one could see his grimace.

A short attempt at conversation quickly backfired on Josh. Noticing Jacob's head in the couch and feeling the need to say something, he joked, 'Is that an ostrich with his head in the cushion?'

Before anyone could reply, Jacob jerked his head out of

the cushion, looked up and repeated what Josh had said in delirium.

'You're not my dad. Where's *your* brother?' Then Jacob ducked his head back into the cushion, leaving Josh stunned and Renee petrified.

Ray said, 'Be nice, Jacob!' and briefly pondered the words he had heard twice in the last hour, but finding nothing in it he turned to Ethan, Josh and Renee to propose a toast. The four of them clinked their glasses together. The adults tossed the brandy down their throats, but Ethan sniffed at the outer rim of the glass and decided that if it tasted anything like it smelled, then brandy was not for him. He set the glass on the coffee table next to Elvis.

Ray's eyes seemed to twinkle under the multicoloured Christmas lights. He turned to the record player in the room and put on George Strait's *Unwound* album. The music played loudly through a mono speaker until Renee, worried about disturbing Kathy, made Ray turn the volume down. After a profuse apology, Ray turned the music down and did a little dance towards Renee and made her dance with him for a moment so that he could twirl her around. He lightly poked at Jacob, who pulled his head out of the cushions and stuck his tongue out at Ray. Ethan stayed seated on the couch but enjoyed seeing his dad happy. Josh tapped his foot rigidly and when Ray finally let go of Renee she sat down right away with a blank expression.

'I don't see any reason,' said Ray, 'why we can't have one more drink.' He poured three refills for the adults and stuffed the glasses into each open hand, but he was the only one having fun. The glasses clinked together a second time.

'Wow,' said Josh, 'that is stiff. Uff-da.' He sat back and crossed his legs.

Ray smiled. 'Ninety proof. Uff-da is right. Another?'

'I think two is enough,' Renee said. 'I knew having one would lead to many.'

'Well, I do have a drinking problem,' Ray joked. 'I have two hands and one mouth.' He laughed, and then collected the glasses. In the kitchen, he turned on the lights and went to the sink. The sound of small footsteps followed him into the kitchen. Standing at the sink, Ray looked into the window over the sink and saw what he thought was Josh Werther's reflection. He turned around to speak to Josh, but standing in front of him was his son, Ethan.

'You forgot a glass, Dad.'

Hearing the voice and seeing Ethan's face nearly toppled Ray backwards on to the countertop. In disbelief he looked at his son's face, trying to collect his thoughts. He tried to look away and shake the image, but when he looked back at Ethan he noticed that Ethan had the same face as Josh Werther.

From where he stood, Ray could see Josh in the living room. He stopped Ethan from leaving.

'Hold on. What's that on the side of your face?'

Ethan said, 'I don't know.'

Ray grabbed Ethan's entire mandible in his large hand and turned the boy's head to one side to look at his profile. Gazing from Ethan to Josh, Ray looked at the features on each of their faces, and the similarities were striking as he matched eye for eye on Ethan and Josh. Suddenly, Josh's delirious utterance in the bedroom and Jacob's reiteration came to the tip of Ray's tongue. He felt blood rising to the top of his head. With sharp eyes, he looked hard at Josh Werther, tracing the outline of the nose and forehead a second time. Ethan felt the hand on his head tightening into a cruel grip.

'Ouch, Dad.'

'Oh, sorry, Ethan. Just the shadows on your face, I guess.' He let go of Ethan's jaw abruptly. 'Jacob – come in here for a minute.'

Ethan went back into the living room rubbing his chin.

Jacob whined on the couch and did not move. Ray loudly repeated his order. Slowly Jacob dawdled into the kitchen but when he saw his father's face he wanted to run in the other direction. Ray grabbed him by the chin and looked hard at the boy's face. He went over Jacob's features several times. Unsatisfied, he picked up Jacob by his pyjamas and the scruff of his neck, like a kitten, almost, and held the boy in front of the darkened window to compare his own face to Jacob's.

Ray set Jacob down on the kitchen floor and peered long into the boy's face while the strange words – you're not my boy; where's your brother? – started to fill his thoughts virally.

Feeling the stare last too long, Jacob asked, 'What did I do wrong now?'

'Just get out of here.'

Jacob looked up with big eyes of disappointment. He whined, 'What did I do now? How come—'

'I said get the hell out of here.'

For Jacob, that was the last straw. If they wanted him to get out then that's what he'd do. Into the bathroom he went.

Ray turned back to the sink and stared out of the window. He tried to calm himself, but the indelible reflection of Ethan and Josh now stared back at him. In the background he heard Josh talking to Renee. Josh Werther, the man he had just encouraged his wife to strip down and hop into bed with, brought on Ray's next thought, one that added new wood to the pile of evidence. Ray thought he saw a shadow streak past the kitchen window, but he ignored it as his thoughts started to divide inside him like cells. He went back into the living room and sat down. He stared at the floor as if in a catatonic stupor, constantly mulling Josh's bedside words to Jacob, Ethan's face and Renee's hidden birth control pills.

The change in Ray's mood altered the mood of the entire room. No one spoke for a long time. They sat quietly for forty minutes, listening to George Strait, as if in meditation. Sensing the atmosphere, Ethan went upstairs to bed. A nervous energy permeated the air, one of paranoia and disdain. Though they were tired, none of the adults slept.

22

The scream came from upstairs.

'Jacob!'

Renee ran up and down the stairs.

'Jacob!'

Renee cried out, 'Oh my God!' as if Jacob was dead, and she came downstairs so fast that she nearly tumbled, and then she ran outside into the storm wearing only her pyjamas. Ray jumped up and rushed out after her. Neither of them had shoes on. Ray caught her by the arm.

'What's going on? You mean he's not in the house?'

'I looked everywhere. He must have gone outside. But where? How? Let me go, Ray. Jacob!'

Ray jerked her by the arm. 'No! Get your head on! Go back inside and put some warm clothes on.'

Josh ran outside and overheard the last few words. Now all three adults stood in the fierce wind improperly dressed and freezing. Renee and Ray looked at Josh. They said nothing but now he felt terribly out of place on the farm.

Ray took Renee back into the house. Josh followed. Renee screamed, and with that outburst veered dangerously close to nervous breakdown. The night had gathered too many aspects of her past and present into one place. She looked up at Ray's face while he carried her, and his eyes were wet with hurt. She had a bizarre moment of serenity in her terror, suddenly understanding why Ray had become quiet in the living room, why he'd called the boys into the kitchen one at a time.

'You know.' Her voice was no longer steady. 'You know now, don't you, Ray?'

Ray looked down at her once, and then set his eyes straight ahead again. 'I don't want to know, Renee.'

'I can explain it all to you. I can.'

'It's not necessary.' Ray continued to stare straight ahead.

She wanted to explain, but first Jacob had to be found. For a moment Renee worried about Josh's safety now that Ray knew the truth. She had seen it in Ray's face. She let out a short, crazed laugh.

They dressed and went outside again to search for Jacob. They yelled against the wind but their voices were overpowered. The storm owned the night. They went in three different directions. Josh searched as frantically as Ray, and Ethan joined them to search all of Jacob's known hiding spaces and summer forts. The four of them looked in every shed and behind every hay and straw bale. They turned over the whole farm.

But Jacob was not lost. In their search, the adults passed by the boy many times. Jacob had crawled out of the bathroom window and shut it behind him, with only his jacket and a small flashlight. He pointed the flashlight at the surprised animals and climbed right over them. Tippy, with his mouth open wide, seemed to laugh at Jacob's arrival. Jacob huddled with Tippy and the twelve cats. The wind outside knocked down the desperate calls of the searchers. Jacob aired his complaints to the animals. With all the bodies churning out heat, the kennel became so hot that one of the cats ventured outside to cool off, but feeling the wind-blast squeezed back inside immediately. Not once did the commotion and terror of the adults interrupt Jacob's discussion with the animals. Other than his own complaints, the wind was the only noise he heard. He settled on a plan: he would run away from home when the wind stopped blowing; and then he fell asleep with his head propped against a confused cat.

23

After two hours in the cold, three of the four searchers returned to the house, dripping in sweat under their gear, but with cold lingering in their extremities. They were fatigued and dehydrated and none of them had found footprints or any signs of Jacob.

Ethan lay down on the living-room couch and immediately dozed off.

Renee climbed the stairs and threw herself on Jacob's bed. She rolled and twisted the sheets in her fingers, but lacked the energy to wail. Her mouth opened in torment, her nose ran and she wept.

Josh stumbled into the kitchen and sat down at the table. He pulled his gloves off with his teeth and looked at his hands. Several of his fingernails had separated from their beds as a result of his wild scratching at the pond-ice during his journey from the car. He blew on his fingertips.

One searcher remained. Ray's voice rasped as he kept calling. He turned over every piece of equipment and even climbed the silo all the way to the star, where the wind nearly blew him to his death. He climbed the tree house and every other structure, using a ladder that wavered in the wind and nearly tossed him. Behind the farm, he went into the woods with a flashlight, and then far into the pasture near the frozen feed bunkers. The wind lashed Ray's unprotected lips until the skin flaked off. Some locations he combed four times. When he finally ran out of places to look, Ray ducked into the milkhouse to think.

Ray should not have let his mind wander. He knew that Jacob was his only son. The boy's loss would make Ray the odd man out. Josh Werther must have set out to accomplish this, to reclaim Renee and Ethan. He stood in the milkhouse, looking out at his farm.

His own wife had lied to him for ten years. His marriage was a sham, his religion was a sham. His banker and his wife had had sex together and lived it up while Ray was getting tortured. A metallic tingle ran down his arms, his intestines writhed under his skin. From his body rage desired to be born. He looked out of the window and thought about betrayal. The sinews in his neck squirmed, his hands opened and closed into fists. The nerves in his forearms tightened as he chewed on his soul and let his muscles harden under his clothing. He gripped the edge of the stainless steel sink and nearly ripped it from its bolts. The whole massive body started to flex. He chomped short kill-bites that made his temples and jaw muscles rise and fall. His diaphragm heaved and stretched against the wrath pushing from inside. Standing at the window, he gazed out and saw nothing but red.

A buried notion erupted, one that he had buried the day he learned that Renee was pregnant with Ethan. Home five weeks from Vietnam and she was pregnant. It had happened too fast. Even at the time, he knew that Ethan had been born too fast. The night Renee told him, he had smiled and hugged her, only briefly wondering how and when. Home at last, he only wanted simplicity, happiness; he only wanted Renee, whom he had dreamed of during so many nights of loneliness; he only wanted to hold on to what he had been holding on to – the one truth left that made any sense. Wearing scars that had not had time to heal, hugging his pregnant wife, he had looked over her shoulder with doubt in his eyes.

When Ethan was born, Renee had claimed he was premature, but the baby weighed over seven pounds. Ray remembered arresting his doubt, locking it and burying it. To let mistrust take root would devour his newfound stability, and he was content to believe that either he or God himself impregnated Renee Masterson, because that's what he believed – because that's what he believed.

It was a lie.

Ray squirmed to escape his skin. The thought wouldn't stay buried. That original doubt was the maggot of a great lie, and it flew out in full bloom.

The past requested an accounting. He thought of Hanoi, and then his parents, and his father's heart that burst not once, but twice. He thought of his mother on the rack of insanity, funerals and burned bridges between himself and his siblings, all now long departed from Immaculate. On top of these losses were heaped a thousand smaller defeats, from the schoolyard to the feed store, from mockery that he had nodded and smiled at, to every argument at home. The weight of defeat piled up on him from three decades of losing, and Ray did not know how to unload any of it. His heart became too hot.

Silently, he started to cry, clamping his eyelids tight to keep the tears from squeezing out. His cheekbones lifted, his mouth opened briefly and his face contorted in pain like a melting candle, until he bowed his head on to his chest.

After his mother's funeral, Ray had purchased a battered AMC Indian, and without saying anything, Renee, three months pregnant with Ethan, hopped on the back, and they went south.

They drove away from Immaculate, riding through cold air, freezing all the way to Kansas City. Making no conversation, they kept riding. They rarely pulled into truck stops or gas stations, and made little more than eye-contact with one another all the way to El Paso. Renee leaned her head against Ray's jacket while they raced south. He leaned back to feel her against him. The poetry was long gone from Ray. Those words he wrote to her during the war were his last soft notions.

He had one idea about where they would ride: to Fort Bliss, to visit his best friend from basic training, Shawn Gable, an Arizona ranchhand turned artillery man. Ray assumed he was back from the war by now. His last letter to Ray ended had with, 'Meet me back in El Paso where we can drink it all away.'

But his friend wasn't in El Paso. A civil affairs officer, freshly anointed as a lieutenant, told Ray what happened. Shawn Gable was in Arlington now, clutching a Purple Heart and a Silver Star in his casket.

Ray had laughed out loud. The officer was even more stunned when Renee started to laugh along with Ray.

'You laugh at a man that died?' he asked, incredulous. 'A hero who died fighting for his country, with valour?'

'Valour?' Ray stopped laughing. 'Did you say valour? I'll

show you valour.' He ripped the officer out of his chair, slapped him around the office, and then tore the gold lieutenant bars from his shirt collar. He made the officer plead for mercy.

'How's it feel to know valour? How does it feel to be a fucking hero?' He let the officer fall and punched a hole through the wall, just above the man's head. Then he turned to Renee and shrugged. 'Everyone is dead, Renee. Everyone.'

'This world, Ray,' she shook her head. 'This world.'

He put a hand over his eyebrows to control his emotion. 'What now, Ray?' asked Renee.

In the barn Ray thought hard about what Renee had told him next. He spoke out loud at the brick wall. 'That's right, Renee. You said to me, "What now, Ray? Virginia? Home?" And I said, "No more headstones. No more cemeteries. Let's go west," and you said, "Go west? Maybe we should go home."'

He paused and flexed his neck to stifle his nausea. 'You wanted to get home to see him, didn't you?'

That strange exchange of words in El Paso echoed in his mind. Renee had nudged him and convinced him to start driving home. He'd compromised by taking the long way. After El Paso, they drove under the setting sun and began to speak again. The AMC motorcycle sputtered into New Mexico, into the heat. They parked in the desert and picnicked, sharing the cruellest brand of humour between them: hopelessness. There on the white sands of Alamogordo they threw rocks at the sun, shouted into the empty space of the south-west and ran up to the tops of the dunes. Renee threw a rock that struck Ray in the back. The impact surprised him, and he turned around to see her standing with her fists clenched, as if ready to fight him. She threw another rock at him, which he ducked.

'Did you just throw a rock at me?'

Renee picked up another rock. She nodded.

'Why?'

'To see if you're a ghost.' She threw the next rock.

Ray picked up a pebble to return the favour. She pointed at her belly: 'You can't throw at me!'

He smiled and went to her and picked her up in his arms. 'I'll never throw at you.'

In New Mexico, the baby became real to them. The baby was something yet to hope for, something worth the effort of picking up the pieces and starting again. It was only the thought of new life that kept Ray from driving over the edge of the Grand Canyon. Suddenly, with his beautiful, pregnant wife in his arms, Ray understood a bit of his religion. The centre had held for him because he had Renee, a strong woman, waiting for him in Immaculate. Other veterans had not been so lucky, those who had come home to an empty house and a hollow life. What others lacked, Ray had. He realized then that only by Renee, the baby and the grace of God could he avoid becoming one of those haunted shells of men. Family and God would be his buffer, and Ethan became the wellspring of Ray's restoration.

From that moment his ability to live as a man was gathered from the boy. It was in flesh, not spirit, that he found the deepest root of religion. It was in the attachment to life that staved off the ugly anger that he felt grooming itself inside him. In the war, not only his sensitivity had died, but his innocence too, and in its place brooded a sleeping rage that he hoped to permanently quell. The fury that girdled his chest and banded his arms could be oppressed, but only by the proof of life that he beheld in his wife and unborn son. And all the doting on Renee, the fawning over the kicks in her belly, the praying at night for a healthy child, the great lengths taken to give comfort to her, the rushing to the hospital with tears in his eyes, and the first sight of the precious gift of Ethan and Renee in the hospital room – all that time and emotion was nothing now, a meaningless event. He had played surrogate to Josh Werther.

He remembered the rock striking him in the back; it might as well have been a knife. He remembered how she had stood defiantly after the throw, alone in the white sands. She wanted Werther, then; she likely wanted Werther now. Werther, the dodger, the man who never felt the draft but instead stayed home to party, protest and impregnate women. What was Werther? He was the owner of Ray's only successful achievement: fatherhood.

Something awoke within him. On one of the holiest of Christian nights, Ray Marak's body was possessed. Poison spilled into Ray's veins and engorged him with rage. The indecencies of people, all the people he had ever known, wrenched in his stomach until he felt sick. A catalogue of faces paraded in front of his eyes. There was Joke's father; Jerry the feed swindler; the creamery baron; the doctor; the bartender. They barked at Ray like a pack of craven dogs. He started to sweat hard in the cold milkhouse. More faces emerged, in shades of green and black: faces from a platoon picture in El Paso; faces black with dried blood; faces of men and children with cheeks filleted and skulls holed; faces of charred smoke; faces of American and Vietnamese butchers disguised in patriot camouflage. And then there was the face of one Vietnamese man at Hoa Lo that taught Ray the true meaning of broken. There in Maison Centrale, wearing the faded pink prison garb meant to shame, Ray wasted away, squabbled with his fellow captives over wet mouldy bread, and shivered in the rain. He spent his nights shuddering, listening to the others retching and sobbing, and bided his time in terror between his visits to the blue room where a smiling nameless officer nodded at his henchmen to carry out the unspeakable.

Ray's flesh hardened like sheet metal. He saw the face of Josh Werther making love to his lying wife Renee and that was the end. The night would get bloody for someone. He wanted to destroy something. He kicked open the door of the milkhouse and marched out. The wind surged against him, as if trying to hold him back.

The lights went out just as Ray entered the mudroom. His fury slowed enough for him to speak. He practically frothed at the mouth but spoke with enough volume to disguise the tremors.

'Shit, I'll have to go back outside,' Ray said, slapping his gloves on his thigh. 'Goddamn generator must have puked out again.'

Sitting at the kitchen table, Josh said, 'I'll help.'

'Don't you think you oughtta stay inside? You almost died once already tonight.'

Josh insisted.

In Jacob's room, Renee heard Ray's voice rumbling through the walls of the house. She recognized the quiver and it made her afraid. The sound had come from Ray on only one other occasion, when the harvest had not dried properly and the corn had ended up rotting in the bins. In the darkness, she listened attentively. Everything was falling to pieces.

'Nobody else goes outside tonight,' Ray declared.

Still dressed in his outerwear, Ray stood in the mudroom in the dark. When he heard Josh approaching, he flipped on a flashlight and pointed the beam at Josh's face. Guided by the light, Josh came into the mudroom, and quietly dressed to go outside with Ray.

Renee bit her fingernails, wondering what came next. She sat up and yelled, 'I love you!'

But the door slammed shut as she spoke. Neither of the men could have heard it. From Jacob's window, Renee watched the two dark shapes trudging across the yard towards the tool shed, before disappearing in the blowing snow. She considered rushing out to tell Ray everything, but her knees locked up and she did not move; her body felt paralysed.

Ray led Josh towards the tractor that powered the generator. Ray pulled a lever on the tractor to disengage the power take-off, and then got down on his hands and knees in the snow. He crawled around for a while underneath the equipment, flipping from his belly to his back, until he discovered a pin lying in the snow. One end of it was mangled. Ray slid out from underneath the generator and showed the pin to Josh.

Leaning over Ray, Josh asked, 'What happened?'

'Shear pin got sheared.'

'Oh. Could be worse, huh?' Josh bit his tongue.

Without bothering to answer, Ray got up off the ground and went inside the tool shed. Josh followed close behind. Inside, Ray violently dug his fingers through drawers of bolts and pins. Finally he found a pin of the correct width, but it was an inch too long and needed to be cut with a hacksaw.

Ray's sharp movements made Josh flinch.

'How can I help, Ray?'

Examining the new pin against the broken pin, Ray said, 'This one should do 'er. We'll need to cut a little off the top. Can you do me a favour and put this pin in that vice over there?'

'Sure thing.' Josh moved towards the cast-iron vice and started turning the handle clockwise to close the heavy sides on to the pin, hindered by his thick gloves and the pain in his fingers. He had only a few turns left to clamp the pin in place when he felt a hand seize his left wrist.

'Sorry, Ray, my hands are slow—'

Before he could finish, his hand had been forced down into the vice. In one quick movement, using two fingers, Ray spun the vice handle around, sandwiching Josh's hand inside along with the pin. Ray made one full turn of the handle to lock the hand in place and Josh screamed as he felt his hand flattening out and his fingers being crushed against the pin and the iron.

He jerked his arm and used his free hand to slap at Ray's back, saying, 'Ray, what the hell are you doing?'

Casually, Ray removed the vice handle and tossed it on to the workbench out of Josh's reach. The handle made a loud clang against the other tools on the bench. In the dark, Ray fished out his pack of cigarettes and pulled one out using only his mouth. He reached for the acetylene torch and the striker and lit the torch. The smoky yellow flame burned bright in the dark tool shed, and each man could read the other's eyes and one pair said fear and the other said control. Raising the torch to his face, Ray lit his cigarette. Josh pulled on his hand hysterically.

Ray said nothing.

'This ain't right, Ray.'

A laugh and a puff of smoke came from Ray. He smiled at Josh behind the flame.

'I'd love to hear a good joke. Know any good ones about Ray Marak?'

'Nobody tells jokes about you, Ray. Jesus Christ, everybody in town admires you – they fucking love you. Don't be stupid!'

Ray's face stiffened as he scratched his forehead with the thumb of the hand that held the torch. He appeared to emit smoke and fire from both hands as he moved the torch and the cigarette around.

'Well, that's a great comfort, Josh, coming from the father of my son.'

Josh stammered, 'I don't know what you're talking about—'

In two steps Ray was across the room and the torch was

next to Josh's eye. The acetylene flame licked at his quivering cheek. Ray kept it back just enough to keep Josh's flesh from boiling but the black smoke dirtied Josh's face and forehead.

'This is the coolest flame that comes out of this torch, Werther. I haven't even touched the oxygen yet.'

Josh's Adam's apple rose up and down as he followed the bouncing yellow flame and the heat started to sear his neck. Ray looked psychotic, all smiles and scars.

'I'll tell you, just please—'

'Shh.'

Ray held the flame closer and let the tongue give a long lick to the flexed neck. Then he removed the torch and twisted the oxygen nozzle and the flame hissed and tightened into a blue spear, shooting out six inches from the head of the torch. Josh clenched his teeth and shook. In a swift step and shove, Ray pushed his hip into Josh and pinned him against the bench. Ray moved the torch closer to Josh's neck, but at the same time opened the oxygen nozzle further. Just as Josh thought the flame would meet his skin Ray added oxygen, shortening the cone of the flame as it approached Josh's neck. The hissing became louder and hotter as more oxygen mixed. Josh quivered but could not move. Ray moved the flame within an inch of the skin and the torch went out with a loud snap.

'Pop!'

Ray mimicked the sound of the torch in Josh's ear, and then laughed as Josh whimpered.

'Too much fuel suffocates the flame, Werther. Is that what happened?'

Without the torch, the tool shed was dark again. Only the beams of the flashlights lying on the workbench and the cherry of Ray's cigarette let Josh know where his torturer stood. Ray handed a hacksaw to Josh.

'What is this?' Josh asked.

'Take an inch off that pin so I can get the power back on inside the house. So your son doesn't freeze to death tonight.'

Breathing heavily, Josh accepted the hacksaw and did as Ray asked. Having his dominant left hand locked in the vice made sawing with his right hand difficult. Ray picked up a flashlight and pointed it at Josh's face. Josh squinted and squirmed while he sawed and the pin pressed against his crushed hand. Ray was humming softly and seemed almost serene, while Josh panted like an animal in a trap.

The last few cuts made Josh grunt. The top inch of the pin fell off and Josh dropped the hacksaw to the floor at the same time. Ray approached with something in his hand, keeping the flashlight trained on Josh's eyes. Josh heard metal clinking. He looked down. Ray had put the handle back in the vice, but again he moved too quickly for Josh to react. Ray had loosened the vice and plucked the pin out of the crushed hand, then tightened the vice again before Josh could react. But this time Ray left the vice handle in place. Walking to the door, his lips still curled around his cigarette, Ray said: 'Relax.'

The door swung shut, and Josh loomed over his smashed hand, wondering what 'relax' meant. Josh decided to loosen the vice a three-quarter turn, enough for him to appear trapped, but able to pull his hand out if he needed to.

On the cold ground outside, Ray inched under the generator and replaced the pin. He acted calm while puffing on his cigarette. Once the pin was in place he stood up and dusted the snow off his pants before engaging the power take-off on the tractor. As soon as the shaft started to spin, the windows of the house glowed and the star on the silo lit up.

Ray went back into the tool shed. When he flipped the light switch he witnessed Josh touching the vice handle, and Josh's eyes brightened like a discovered opossum. Ray laughed. 'Now you look confused. Are you trying to tell me that you didn't undo the vice yet? Remember: it's righty-tighty, lefty-loosy. I bet you loosened it up though, dint-ya, Josh?'

Panic jumped in Josh's chest. Ray said, 'You remember that pain earlier, that pain that I said was the best pain you'll ever feel. Remember?'

Josh's heart raced with terror and his chest visibly heaved under his shirt.

'I'm inclined to give you the other end of that scale, but I don't know if I should, because I'd like to get some sleep tonight yet. But first things first: I'm going to let you finish your story.'

Ray picked up a large socket wrench and leaned against the bench. Ray held one end of the tool and turned it slowly. The clicking sound filled the room.

Ray said, 'Well, you were saying?'

'I wasn't saying anything.' Josh's voice cracked.

'But you could say something, so why don't you, Josh.'

'What do you want me to say? That you don't deserve her?'

Ray nodded. 'Maybe not. I never did, did I? She was out

of my league. I held her back. I can't give her the life she wants. Let's see, what else is there? I'm an ignorant man. I haven't been to the library in fifteen years. My list of flaws is long.' Ray paused to scratch his face. 'But I know one thing about Josh Werther. He's a self-serving snake that would bang his sister if she said yes.'

'Cut the act, Ray . . .'

'Cut the *shit*, Werther!' Ray slammed the socket wrench against the wall, rattling every tool in the shed, knocking several shelves down and causing wrenches to bounce off their hooks and clatter on the bench. Josh expected to be hit, but Ray sat down on a stool and turned his back to him. As if suddenly calmed, Ray fiddled with the radio dial and stopped at an AM station playing 'I'll Be Home for Christmas'.

'Ah, a classic. I'll be home for Christmas. Mom, Dad, I'll be home.' Ray laughed. 'If only in my dreams, Mom, I'll be conscious and roll out of this VA. I'll be home for funerals. Pregnant? Bless her heart.'

With one hand on the radio knob, Ray used his other hand to flip a switch underneath the workbench. Josh did not see the movement. The switch was for an arc welder. The radio played loud enough to drown out the electrical hum, though Josh wouldn't have recognized the sound anyway. While Ray had his back turned, Josh tugged on his hand and grimaced. With both hands free, he looked up and down the workbench for a weapon. The steel handle of the vice was too small to knock Ray down. Time passed too quickly for Josh to make a good decision. He started to panic, until he looked up at the wall and saw the pipe wrench. Carefully, he lifted the wrench off its wall hook and held it in both hands like an axe, squaring his body up with Ray's back. It was three steps to Ray, one swing, and then freedom. To attack Ray Marak would have seemed insane an hour earlier, but now to bide his time and hope for Ray's goodwill seemed like suicide.

Gripping the pipe wrench between his hands, with five smashed fingers and ten aching fingertips, Josh made his charge. With the wrench high over his head, he aimed at Ray's shoulder and collarbone.

At the height of Josh's backswing, Ray nonchalantly turned around on the stool, making sure to keep his feet up off the ground. In Ray's hand was a clamp with a welding rod, and he planted the white rod into Josh's abdomen, just beneath his ribs.

A spark flickered. Josh grounded the arc. The electricity passed into Josh and blew his feet out from under him and he fell to the ground in a horizontal flop. The pipe wrench fell alongside him and struck the ground at the same time, and together they made a thud and a clank. The infusion of energy into Josh forced him back to his feet. He felt acutely aware of the world around him. Almost euphoric, he put his arms out for balance but was too stunned to say or do anything.

Ray cheered, 'Bravo! I've never seen a banker bounce!' Then Ray touched the tip of the welding rod to Josh a second time, and Josh crumpled to the floor with a wilting groan.

Ray laughed. 'Foreclosure! Only two shocks for a banker. Any good electrician can take up to five shocks like that in a single day.'

He lifted Josh to his feet, and threw the limp body over

his shoulder and then kicked the shed door open and carried Josh towards the milkhouse, the barn and the shredder. Had Ray looked down in the snow, he would have seen a fresh set of small footprints directly beneath his boots.

24

Hank Murphy and Tommy Blanks met at the intersection where their routes crossed. They passed the tobacco back and forth between trucks until it bulged in their lower lips. Hank noticed the temperature starting to rise and the wind dying off. With so much ploughing still to do, Hank and Blanks kept their discussion short and left each other with their customary greeting – a raised middle finger.

The ploughing crew crawled through the night without incident or accident. Hank counted his blessings every time all of his drivers checked in.

Blanks started to drone over the CB about his favourite meals. Hank could not believe how many hours the subject of food held the drivers' interest. Many of the others, anticipating a Christmas meal when they finished ploughing, added their two cents. Hank considered a new topic for the all-night radio show. Many of his stories seemed redundant. He almost felt cheap, patching them together into such extravagant lies, but he couldn't bear to be bored or know that people around him were bored. For the time being, however, the topic of Christmas hams and turkeys seemed to satisfy everyone.

In Jacob's room, Renee gazed out with a bloodshot stare. She picked up the phone and set it back down. The phones could be down all day, or several days. Tears pooled in her eyes as she thought about her life, and felt liable to all of them – Ray, Josh, Ethan and Jacob – as if she had failed them all somehow. She put her head in her hands and looked up to heaven, and then looked at the statue of Mary in the yard and tried to understand what it all meant. She could see Mary's outstretched hands and the hint of a smile.

The blustering wind continued to rock the trees outside, but the storm's force had passed its zenith. Renee caught a glimpse of a shape in the darkness and closed her eyes. The salty tearstreams on her windburnt cheeks ran to the corners of her mouth. She opened her eyes again to look out the window, this time through the prism of her tears. She wiped her face with her sleeve. The shape, the black mass in the darkness, moved once again, across the yard, slowly plodding, marching in the storm. She wiped her eyes again. The movement stirred hope in her, only she could not discern the owner of the shape. It appeared alone at first, but on closer inspection she noticed something dragging in the snow. She pressed her nose against the window pane and shielded her eyes with her hands to get a better view.

She scrambled to her feet and ran to the stairs, but rounding the corner she caught her pyjama bottoms on the railing. The cloth at her waistline twisted on a loose screw, and the more she pulled, the tighter the cloth twisted. She tried to free herself without destroying the railing, until it infuriated her, this tether, and nearly drove her to strip off the pyjamas and leave them there. For half a minute she picked at the mess of thread, cursing and breathing hard, with her dextrous fingers plucking at the damned threads nervously, and finally with a yell she lunged backward, freeing herself, tearing the screw out of the wall and letting the railing fall to the stairs. She tumbled into the wall, rapped her head, and dropped hard on to the steps. Without pausing, she flung herself down the stairs. She felt a chill on her neck when she realized that the shape she had seen could mean one of two things: hope or murder.

Hearing Renee on the stairwell, Ethan rubbed his eyes awake and peeked out of his room. The aura of growing madness in the house kept him quiet. When he saw his mother descend the steps, he tailed her, hiding around corners and in rooms as he followed. He paused in his parents' room for a moment, where he noticed Kathy was sitting up on the bed, rubbing an eye with one hand and holding her sore neck with the other. He said nothing to her and slipped out again quietly.

After Renee tore out of the house, Ethan pulled on his boots and chased her, not knowing what called her outside at this odd hour unless it was Jacob.

Whatever lukewarm hope stirred inside Renee flummoxed against the cold despondence in her stomach. If the shape in the darkness, dragging some object, did not belong to Jacob, then it belonged to Ray. Perhaps the time had already passed when she might still explain this life to these two men. In pyjamas and slippers, she rushed into the waning storm. She caught a glimpse of the milkhouse door slamming shut and assumed the nameless shape and its burden had stepped inside. Her voice rasped against the wind. She tried to yell again, her throat flexed, but her mouth emitted only a frantic whisper.

Renee entered the milkhouse but found it empty. A humming sound from the barn beckoned her forward. She continued through the empty parlour and pushed open a rear door to the barn, freezing for an instant in the dingy light of the barn, amid the sound of a roaring bale-shredder. There, in the alleyway, with both sides of the aisle lined with terrified cow-eyes, she saw Ray bent over Josh's inert body.

The shredding machine blared beside Ray. The noise did not wake Josh. Ray grabbed a handful of Josh's hair and picked him up by the head. Josh's mouth hung open.

Renee found her voice and screamed, 'Ray!!'

She started to run towards him but several startled cattle stood up and blocked her path. She kicked and slapped at their legs and backs. The cows moved slowly, with jerky steps and unsure movements, affected by the noise, the storm, the hour and the strange acts of humans.

Her eyes pleaded as she approached Ray. He wore a sacrificial and trancelike gaze. His face looked like split hardwood, his eye sockets like drilled holes containing countersunk silver bullets. Under any other circumstance, Renee would have turned around and left the building, but she rushed forward and slid on her knees into a position of supplication, right through the cow manure, and seized Ray's knees with both arms and looked up at him.

Ray stood with both Renee and Josh at his feet, like conquered foes, and he let go of Josh's hair and Josh withered down to the concrete floor. Ray's face did not relent or show pity when he looked down at his wife, as faith and mercy evacuated his mind. In the tool shed, the good man abandoned him, was chased out by a ruthless fiend with a cruel appetite. Ray seized Renee's hands, separated them from his knees and threw her aside.

On the floor, her blonde hair mingled with the barn's filth. She lay still, sobbing for an instant, and managed to look at Josh's face. His eyes did not open, but he opened and closed his mouth one time before his face settled into a peaceful expression, which terrified Renee even further.

Rising to her knees, she reattached herself to Ray and cried out, 'Ray, I thought you were dead! I thought I'd lost you.' She pounded his thighs with both hands. 'Don't you know that it's not our fault?'

Her words evaporated off Ray. The sound of the shredder raged against her coarsening voice.

'Josh was here. I didn't try to fall in love with him. I should have told you but I couldn't. When you came home, you were so damaged, Ray – you were so close to the end – how could I hurt you more when I knew how much it meant for you to come home and live a normal life? I didn't mean for it to happen, nor did Josh. I knew one day you would find out, I just didn't know when, and not tonight. Jesus Christ, not tonight, Ray.' She tugged on his leather belt with both hands. 'I knew this day would come, and it has haunted me since you came home, and now it all happened at once. There was no way to plan for a storm and a car accident. And now our son is missing.' She wiped her face with her forearm, smearing the mess into a streak of mud.

'My *only* son,' Ray said, 'and mine . . . the idiot. Like father, like son. I should have known *years* ago. The one that can't do anything right . . .'

'He can, Ray. He's a smart boy. He's just not the same as

Ethan. Do you want Jacob to be like Ethan? Or do you just want them to be like you? Jacob will have all the chances that you didn't. We'll let him grow up and he won't have to go to war. And he won't have to be tortured for some Goddamn place he's never heard of, Ray. We won't let anyone do that to him.'

'Don't bury your head in another fucking lie! If he's outside, by now he's frozen to death!'

'He's not gone, Ray. He's just lost right now, Ray.'

He shook his head. 'Don't lie to my face.' He picked up one knee and pushed her away, but she bounced right back again.

'Ray! I love you, Ray!'

'What did I just tell you?'

'I have always loved you, I am telling you now!'

'Bullshit!'

She looked around, hoping to find another way of reasoning with him. She looked up at his face and said, 'Where is your advice now, Ray? Why pray, Ray, if you neglect it when you need it most?' She shook her head back and forth, swinging her hair.

Ethan, meanwhile, clung to a wooden beam and watched his parents. Despite his urge to rush forward and stop them, he wanted to hear the secrets of his life, to make sense of his existence.

Ray looked down at Renee. Intolerable memories surged within him, and his mind dragged him to a graveyard of the past. He shook his head to free his mind, but he could not undo the boiling in his heart. The shredder continued to rattle and whine, sounding less safe by the minute. Ray spoke sharply to Renee. 'Why?'

Renee echoed, 'Why?'

'For ten *years* . . .'

'Because, Ray! Because of everything.' She struggled to find an answer. 'Imagine, Ray, for once, imagine me here while you were away. My mother *dead*; my father a *wreck*. And my parents took longer to crack up than yours, Ray. How different was I from you? I would have lost my mind, too, were it not for Josh Werther. Call him whatever you like. You don't want to hear it, but I would have married Josh. We were all set to move away from Immaculate. But I waited for you – even after you were *dead*! If that means nothing to you, then let this sink in: how do you think it felt to go with your mother and father to speak with the mortician about *your* funeral? Your parents wouldn't hear of it, so the mortician came to talk to me in private about the size of your casket. Everyone thought you had died. Josh helped me get through it and I loved him for it. I was drowning, bobbing on my last breaths. The dream of going to college had ended. I had to go home and milk cows because Dad couldn't hack it. Do you think that's what I dreamed my life would be? All I had left was a fading high school sweetheart, who was probably dead, and if not dead, then ruined, a total mess like the others, like Jimmy Mathers and Walt Flask.'

Locked in his thoughts, Ray said, 'I suggested "Ray Jr", and you said no . . .'

'Oh, Ray. The best name for Ethan would have been Raymond Joshua Marak, is that what you want to hear? I knew this day would come, Ray! Imagine now, if Ethan was named

Ray and how that would make you feel. And there's something else you don't know. Something that I know and Josh
knows, but you don't know.'

Ray said, 'I have no doubt. Nothing about what you've
done with him will surprise me.'

'Your loans, Ray.'

'What about 'em?' He seized Josh's hair in his fist.

'He makes payments, Ray. The bank has almost come out
three times to repossess the cattle, but they haven't, and do
you know why? Because Josh Werther has made payments
for us, without you knowing about it, so you could keep this
place and your pride. He watches over us, and is putting
money away for Ethan to go to college. He's a good man,
Ray. He has kept you out of bankruptcy, and he has done so
even after I urged him not to. I told him not to. I told him to
let the chips fall. You have to understand, Ray, Josh is not
trying to harm you or take Ethan or be Ethan's father.'

'But he is the father!'

'Then let your pride rage, Ray, and let it burn you down.
It will burn us all: you and me and Josh and Ethan and Jacob.
I decided long ago to live with my decisions, and it's not our
fault, Ray, the way things work out. And Jacob and Ethan
are wonderful boys to have. Tell me you don't love Ethan as
much as Jacob!'

Ray shouted, 'More!'

'Then you are not the father I thought you were! You've
been Ethan's father for ten years, and now would you spill
Josh's blood to go to prison, so you could be alone with your
pride?'

Ray's face rebounded to its normal shape. However, the

change did not comfort Renee. She pulled herself up by his belt and reached one hand to seize his shirt collar, as if she were climbing him. 'Ray, you always say, you say that if you can just hold on a little longer that the next day will come. In the morning it will be better. That's your rule, Ray. The night is almost over. There is just a little night left. We can hold on. I can hold on. Jesus Christ, Ray, I'm begging you. I am on my knees to beg you, and not out of love for Josh, but out of love for you and the boys!' Renee sobbed on his belt, and wrapped an arm around his hips while still holding his shirt collar with her other hand. She held him close and looked straight up at his face.

He opened his eyes and let a few tears fall.

Renee pushed up his chin with her hand, to grab his eyes with her own.

Through the blur, he looked at her and then past her, to the corner of the shed where he saw the old motorcycle, the AMC Indian. It had sat and rusted there ever since he and Renee came back from the only road trip they ever took.

The sight allowed the trance of anger to possess him again, to rob him of all balance. He could not let go of Josh's hair while his pride wanted redemption. What remained unresolved was the loss of Jacob.

The shredder whined and started to rattle. The bolt that had fallen out during morning chores had not been replaced. Jerking Josh by the hair, Ray pulled him to his knees and then dipped his shoulder under Josh's arm to lift him.

In her pyjamas, Renee clung to one of Ray's legs, and she was dragged along through the dirt and manure. She pleaded, but he moved towards the shredder with finality. Lifting Josh into the air, he prepared to drop him into the whirling blades. As he neared the machine he started to cry harder, but his mind could not stop his body.

He thought he heard his name being called but ignored it.

The machine roared, and Renee screamed. Again, Ray heard the faint sound of his name being yelled, but it was not a woman's voice. The voice shouted 'Ray!' repeatedly.

The machine began to shake itself apart, the strain fracturing the remaining bolts.

Ray lifted Josh's body higher to dump him into the machine, head first, but was suddenly knocked to the ground.

Josh and Ray scattered. Ray landed in the manure and looked up, expecting to see Renee as the force behind it.

But Renee was still on the ground beside Josh. Looking towards the shredder, Ray was stunned to see Hank Murphy, breathing heavily and wearing a rare, serious expression.

The machine wobbled and the metal box began to bounce. Hank approached the shredder and tried to locate the switch to turn it off but the irregular bounce and clatter prevented him from getting close enough. Then a high-pitched shriek of metal rang through the barn, as the protective metal box tipped over, exposing the whirling blades. The metal box hung by a single remaining bolt, but the frame of the machine started to bend. Hank retreated and advanced several times as the machine lunged at him. He extended his left arm and reached over the blades to turn off the switch. But before he could kill the engine, an explosion ripped through the barn. The whirling blades ejected at deadly speeds and landed with two frightening thuds, and when the echo faded the barn was silent.

The immediate silence in the barn made Hank question if he was still alive. He ran his hands up and down his chest and his neck. He touched his face, his legs. He lifted his hands up his sides, into the armpits, and on his left side he felt where the blade had sliced through his coat. Lifting his arm, he looked at the tear in the fabric and for the second time in his life, he almost considered praying. Instead, he marvelled at his good luck.

Looking past Hank, Ray saw Jacob in the doorway, alive and well. When Renee saw him, she made a gloriously awful sound of joy mixed with pain. She and Ray sprang to their feet as Jacob ran to them. He reached them before they could straighten themselves, and when they embraced the boy they dropped back to their knees. Josh, on the floor next to them, opened his eyes, unaware of his surroundings.

Hank held out his hands. 'Did I . . . come at a bad time?'

No one answered, so he dropped his hands to his sides and slowly put them into his pockets.

Hank watched the family and became slightly emotional himself. He felt compelled to explain how he came to Marak's barn.

'I nearly ran him over. Crazy kid. He was walking down the centre of the road, pulling a toboggan with a dog tied down on it.' Hank laughed, but his voice faded. 'And the dog didn't look too happy . . .' His words trailed off. He went on talking, explaining to the wide-eyed cows what had happened. 'And Jacob told me he was running away, but I told him, "Hey, kid, I wrote the book on running away, and it doesn't work that well." Running away never goes according to plan. So I scooped him up and brought him in and . . . when I got into the yard I turned off my truck engine. I saw fresh footprints going to the barn. I looked at my watch and figured you were probably doing chores by now, Ray. Then I heard the machine back here, and I just walked in and . . .'

Still, no one responded.

'And I didn't really see much of anything.' He scratched his head and looked around, taking mental notes.

Hank had never witnessed such a family secret, but he realized that the story of the Marak household, the night of sheer madness, would never be known unless he told it.

He waited for the family to separate, but they held on to each other and sobbed. Ethan emerged from his hiding spot and came to join the hug. Ray pulled him into his wide arms. Then Ray grabbed Josh Werther by the arm and lifted him into the embrace. Regaining consciousness for the second time that night, Josh knew that he had missed something important, and that everything had changed. His life, already inextricable from the Marak family, now was openly so. For the first time ever, Josh hugged his son.

Jacob, tired of being hugged, reminded them about Kathy.

'Just wait a minute, Jacob,' Renee said. Over the children, the three adults leaned their heads together, and Ray kept his arms as tightly around Josh as he did Renee.

Hank walked to the barn door and looked back at the family circle. He caught a glimpse of Tanya, the cow, standing in the final stall chewing her dull cud. She turned her head at Hank like a surly waitress. He looked closely at the black and white pattern on her side and thought perhaps it looked something like an image of Christ. Maybe Christ with Down's Syndrome, but nevertheless, Blanks would be interested. Hank pushed open the barn door and put a cigarette in his mouth. He raised his eyebrows and shook his head before climbing into his truck cab. The engine grunted, the plough blade lowered on to the driveway and he cleared a path to the road.

Picking up the CB radio, Hank pushed the button to tell the other drivers what he'd seen. But he changed his mind and released the button. 'No, this one I'll keep. For now, anyway.' To the mirror he added, 'Maybe some day, you know. Who knows?' He stopped and scowled at his reflection. 'Why . . . why am I talking to you?'

At the end of the driveway, he turned to the right. It was a clear day, and he could see far. In the sea of white he saw silos like lighthouses, each farm an island with its own history, where for every tragedy there was an equal and opposite comedy.

Hank couldn't stay quiet or wax poetic for long. He picked up the CB again and pushed the button. 'Is the discussion about turkeys and cranberries finally over with?'

Blanks replied, 'Ten minutes ago. Where were you?'

The cigarette on his lips bounced with the words. Hank said, 'I've often wondered about something. Many times I lay awake in bed, staring at the ceiling, pondering one thing: why couldn't I have been born rich, instead of so damn good looking and lucky? If anyone knows why, please, throw me a bone. And by the way: Blanks, Ray Marak has a cow you might be interested in. Now, have I told anyone the joke about the bar pianist?'

*

Hank's snowplough slowly started down the road as sunlight poured over the rim of the earth and spilled on to the farm. In the sky, the ghost of summer, the winter Minnesota sun, rose with Christmas and revealed the newly whited world around the house and barn. The day was calm. The statue of Mary in the yard, the gracious advocate of Immaculate, mourned under a heavy veil of new snow, with her face slightly canted to one side and her arms extended outward. Her robes of white and blue flowed into a snow bank and her mysterious hint of a smile was intact. The hoof- and foot-prints in the snow were filled, the evidence of the night disappeared, the cowpies were frozen, the soil was sealed beneath waiting for the spring thaw and the planting of seeds, and it was as it ever shall be, world without end, Immaculate.

ACKNOWLEDGEMENTS

I need to give credit to some people who helped to build this story. First of all, my gratitude to all of the writers and editors, Portlanders mostly, who were brave enough to give one of the drafts a read. Specifically, thanks to Ralph Wright, who was the first person to see it, and Khalid Adad (times two), Gloria Harrison, Grier Phillips, Patrick Koohafkan and Sylvia Kaye. Many thanks to Macmillan and Will Atkins. Thanks to my own family, and most importantly, thank you to my wife and best friend, Denise. I should also thank my friends (particularly for the 'Hank and Blanks' Hawaii story).

Peter Anthony
Zurich, 2007